ISiS

Beach Read

Reality is fragile as glass

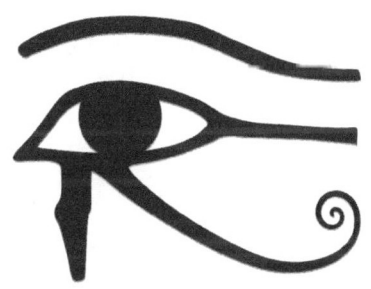

sandra gore

ISBN 978-0-9853445-4-2

Published by Tajine Publishing, Las Vegas NV
This book is available in eVersion.

Author website: www.SLGore.com

AUTHOR'S NOTE
This book is a work of fiction. Names, characters, places and
incidents are the product of the author's imagination or are
used fictitiously, and any resemblance to actual persons, living
or dead, or events is entirely coincidental.

"The perfect book to lose yourself. It moves. Isis is a new kind of adventure story - I've never read anything quite like it."
Mark – Brooklyn NY

"Sailing down the Nile. Sandstorms. Temples and markets. I was there. Sandra took me to Ancient Egypt - and Las Vegas."
Suzanne – Boston MA

What a page turner! I couldn't put it down. Passionate, smart, and filled with thrilling action! Thank you!"
Carol – Shell Beach CA

"Adventure! Mystery! Egyptian culture and history! Beach Read is the zippy version of The Red Mirror - I like them both."
Leslie – Ann Arbor MI

"Sandra has created her own genre—romantic, historical and edgy. The twists and turns and the surprise appearances kept me guessing and wanting to know more."
Charise – Denver CO

"Sandra's a painter. She paints a story with words..."
Hillie – Amsterdam NL

"The Wynn – Whew! Gimme a cigarette!"
Joan – Fresno CA

"Isis is a real page turner. A great adventure story for anyone – not just women."
Eric – Montreal QUE

"I loved the Egypt details. Just enough to give atmosphere. It's great to learn while having such a good time."
Elaine – Easton PA

"Isis was flat amazing. Towns along the Nile, jewelry, weaponry... Sandra makes ancient Egypt come alive."
Curt – Las Vegas NV

"Four lovers to die for. I want one of those guys!"
Jerilee – Kansas City MO

"Isis is 50 shades of color! Adventure, Ancient Egypt, Las Vegas, hot men. A great, fun, edgy read."
Ann – Los Osos CA

I dedicate this flight of fancy to Egypt lovers everywhere.

Thank you to my three muses, Jesper, Carol and David,
for traveling the Isis journey with me every step of the way.

And to the Writers Bench.

TABLE OF CONTENTS

MAP OF EGYPT 500 BC

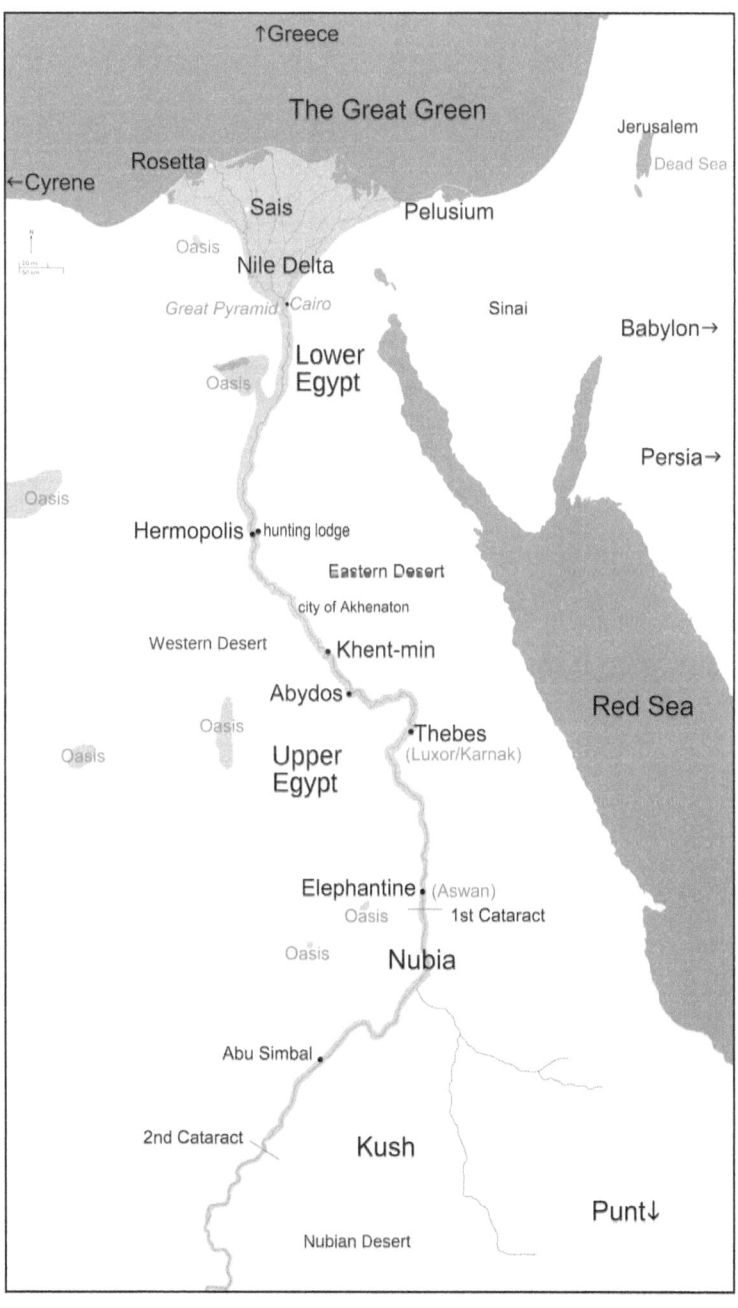

↑Greece

The Great Green

Jerusalem

Dead Sea

←Cyrene

Rosetta

Sais

Pelusium

Oasis

Nile Delta

Great Pyramid •Cairo

Sinai

Babylon→

Lower
Egypt

Oasis

Persia→

Oasis

Hermopolis ••hunting lodge

Eastern Desert

city of Akhenaton

Western Desert

•Khent-min

Abydos•

Oasis

Red Sea

Oasis

Upper
Egypt

•Thebes
(Luxor/Karnak)

Elephantine• (Aswan)

Oasis

1st Cataract

Oasis

Nubia

Abu Simbal •

2nd Cataract

Kush

Punt↓

Nubian Desert

THE RED MIRROR

CHAPTER 1 OBSESSION

Sheets entangled in my legs, pillows tossed all around, I woke up in a sweat in my wide, empty bed. The technicolor images still played in the cinema of my mind when I opened my eyes to the bright sunshine streaming across the carpet. The Red Mirror. I'd dreamed of it again.

Please understand that a love affair with an object isn't unusual for me. But most of the time the attraction is a one-night stand, forgotten as soon as out of sight. Now and then I'm seized hard and buy right away. My condo is full of treasures that grabbed me and wouldn't let go.

But the old mirror was special. It had become an obsession—hypnotic and irresistible. I couldn't get it out of my mind. Haunting my dreams, plaguing my days, it drew me back like a wild mating call to the jungle.

I didn't see it the first time I walked past the cluttered stall. It was only on the way back from my wanderings deep in the maze of the antique mall that I noticed the red aura in the shadows.

I stopped—doubting my eyes—and then stepped into the stall. Almost breast high, slightly taller than wide, the mirror leaned backward against a Chinese screen aflame with yellow chrysanthemums and orange-crested song birds. I stepped around fragile vases and toppled statues until I stood just in front of the old glass in its dirty painted frame.

Inhale. Exhale. Inhale. Exhale. The mirror breathed.

Every hair follicle on my body screamed. The touch of wool on my skin was painful; having clothes on was painful. I wanted to take everything off.

"Barb! Over here. Come look. Do you see anything...weird?"

"See what? What's there to see?"

"The mirror, Barb, the red mirror."

"Some old Mexican thing." She dismissed it without another look. "Let's have lunch."

We got the last table in the Market Tea Room. A white vase full of cornflowers stood on a tablecloth splashed with yellow daisies. Colorful country prints in painted frames covered the lemon walls.

Sunshine poured in the window pane, warming my back, shimmering on Barb's straw-straight, wheat-colored hair. Her latest cut was chin-length with long bangs that covered her eyebrows. She wasn't wearing her contacts today. Hot pink rectangles framed her blue eyes.

"Let's order the high tea," I said expectantly, although I already knew Barb's answer.

"No sweets for me. I've put on two pounds."

"The minestrone," she told the waiter. "No bread."

I secretly craved a fresh scone with Devonshire cream and raspberry jam.

Our tea arrived in a white porcelain pot with a green cozy. Barb's china cup had big red roses; violets sprinkled mine. Both sets were edged with gold.

"How was your date?" she asked without much interest.

She poured the tea, holding her angular arms close to her sides, never spilling a drop. Barb never spilled anything.

"I don't think I'm going see him again."

"Another one who's not perfect?"

"Be fair, Barb. He was a bore. Everyone in Vegas is trying to sell you something."

"There must be *some* good men around. They can't all be useless."

I took a sip of Earl Grey and braced myself. When Barb got that tight little mouth and her blue eyes went steely, I knew I was in for a lecture. But I was saved by her cell.

"I've got to take this call. It's the answer to our offer on the Summerland house."

The oak chair scraped on the wood floor when she stood to step outside.

Tendrils of steam rose in the sunbeams. My mind went back to the mirror. Even surrounded by chattering ladies, I saw the mirror so clearly that it might have been leaning against the window frame right next to my chair.

Inhale. Exhale. Inhale. Exhale. It still breathed when Barb came back.

She didn't waste a minute before starting in.

"Just how long are you going to wait for Mr. Right to carry you off on his white horse?"

God, she could be tedious. But she meant well. And she'd earned the right to talk to me like this; she listened to my complaints on a daily basis.

"You hate your job—and you should. Yes, Ed is a jerk," she nagged. "Most bosses are. Stop feeling sorry for yourself. Do something about it. There's more to life than a party."

I sighed. Barb was right about one thing. I did feel a little sorry for myself.

"I should go somewhere…have some adventure…you know… meet some new men."

"Where would you go?"

"Some place exotic…far away…nothing like here."

I didn't buy the mirror that day or even the next, but I dreamed of it every night. Finally, I lied to my boss with a stupid excuse and sped to the mall. Of course, the mirror hadn't sold. It waited patiently for me, knowing I would come.

The red frame pulsed; the glass shimmered. Phantom fingers caressed my shoulders and trailed across my throat. Moist, insistent tongues teased.

I longed to stand naked in front of it, inviting whatever spirits dwelled there to explore. I would spread wide my limbs and invite all who had ever gazed into this mirror to enter into me.

"Hey, ya wanna make an offer? I can call the owner."

The voice belonged to a fresh freckled face above a tight T-shirt stretched by broad shoulders. He managed to maintain eye contact while checking me out from boot to bust.

"I'll be right back."

I waited. The minutes ticked away on a Grandfather clock. My feet hurt in my high-heeled boots, and my lower back begged for a rest. I sank to a green velvet hassock and refused even to look at the mirror.

It was in the hands of the Universe now. If the price was right, then the mirror was right. It was a simple strategy that absolved me from responsibility. Reacting to the moment rather than planning ahead had become somewhat of a life path. I call it 'going with the flow.'

The bulky rectangle wouldn't fit in the trunk or through the doors of my little white BMW convertible. I started the engine and held my finger on the release button while the top eased into its hiding place and exposed the leather seats.

Together Freckles and I slid the mirror behind the driver's seat, bottom on the floorboard and head sticking up like a passenger.

The sun was just setting in a cloudless Vegas sky. I zipped up my leather jacket, jammed a blue M3 cap on my head, and gave Freckles a quick peck on the cheek.

"Do you need any help unloading?" he offered hopefully.

The kid was cute, but younger than I like. A guy his age should be satisfied with a smile from a woman like me.

I buzzed through rush hour traffic, glancing constantly in the rearview mirror at the other mirror riding in the backseat. I congratulated myself. I was in tune with the Universe.

I pushed a couple of iffy yellow lights—okay, maybe one was red—in my hurry to get home. Somewhere along Eastern Avenue between Tropicana and Flamingo, the dirty old thing from the rejects of an estate sale was christened 'The Red Mirror.'

The vibration of the engine reverberated through the leather seat. The traffic light turned red. My fingers slid between my legs. I breathed out a deep sigh and leaned my head back, closing my eyes.

The roar of a motor pulled me back, and when I looked up, it was at a blue pickup truck with 'Jack the Plumber' painted in yellow letters on the door. Two men leered down at me.

A face out of Deliverance pressed his nose against the passenger window. Jack—it must have been Jack—leaned as far as he could to the right and still stay in the driver's seat.

I gripped the steering wheel with two hands, stared straight ahead and willed the light to change. *Whoa girl! Slow down. What is wrong with you?*

My lane went green, and Jack and his buddy were stuck waiting for a left turn. I sped ahead. It must be the mirror. It was the mirror's fault. Blame the Red Mirror for everything.

I managed to get the mirror out of the car and lug it to the elevator on my own. The doors slid open to reveal an empty shopping cart. More good karma. With the glass side up, I heaved it onto the top of the cart, pushed the button for the 3rd floor and rolled the Red Mirror out the elevator down to my blue-tiled entrance with the Laughing Buddha.

Aisha was just inside the door, purring like a well-tuned engine. Ever hopeful and ready, she rubbed up against my heels, circling with back arched and tail lifted high. Her black fur gleamed in the low light from the red shade of the lamp on the bar.

I leaned the mirror against a white wall, poured a glass of Merlot, lit three fat candles on the glass coffee table, and dropped my leather pants to the zebra carpet. Aisha tried to jump into my lap when I settled into my grey leather armchair next to the fireplace. But I had other ideas.

"You can start to glow now, Red. You can start to make *me* glow."

Nothing happened. No red glow, no seductive promises, no phantom caress. I felt no warmth; I felt nothing except doubt. I hate doubt. I never know what to do with it.

Please don't let this be another daydream.

I could hear Barb. *You bought that old mirror because it turned you on?*

Yes, Barb, the mirror first baited me and then enticed me, but when the seduction was complete, it went cold. Having made me an addict, the mirror refused to give me a fix.

Robbed. I felt robbed.

Aisha snuggled into her favorite spot; her purr vibrated against my groin. I took another sip of Merlot and studied the mirror. That's when I saw the flash. And then another. There was silver trying to shine from under that black layer of crud.

Aisha tumbled to the carpet when I jumped up to find a clean cotton cloth and grab a bottle of olive oil from the kitchen.

Sixteen silver struts, barely visible, braced the four sides of the lacquered frame. I could just make out a star pattern in each corner. Settling cross-legged on the white marble floor, I began to massage one of the silver struts slowly and gently with my index finger, applying just the right pressure through the oil-soaked cloth. Aisha purred on my bare thigh.

I barely noticed the first change. Just a bit of light-headedness. An odd woody, smoky scent, heavy and sweet, made me a little dizzy. Then it was suddenly very hot. I closed my eyes; my thoughts melted like butter in the sun.

Drugged and dreamy, I drifted outside of time in a velvet sea. It was dark, not pitch-dark, but shadowy. Gone were my familiar things—the black lacquer table, cherry red sofa and the Pink Lady oil painting that covered one wall. I sensed vague shapes moving in the shadows; tongues of fire licked the walls. Aisha no longer vibrated against me.

The green eyes startled me when I turned back to my reflection. They should've been my eyes, but these were too bold—so bold—and heavily outlined in black. The woman in the mirror was exotic, foreign-looking, yet her face was familiar, like someone I knew from a dream.

She stared straight into my soul; I couldn't look away.

I was aware of my body—more aware than I ever remember—but the room around me was simply gone. Was I still sitting Indian-style on the cool tiles of my living room floor? I felt nothing through my panties, nothing at all.

"Who are you?" I whispered. The words swam to my ears as through deep water. "Can you…see me?"

Apparently sound couldn't cross the glass because she gave no sign of having heard me. Instead her hand came up and adjusted a stray lock of jet black hair. She lifted her chin and angled her head slightly, looking straight at me with those emerald green eyes.

Something in that moment, in the way she tilted her face and in her satisfied look, gave it away. She wasn't looking at me at all but admiring her own reflection. I saw her, but she didn't see me—a strategic advantage.

I touched myself. Everything was there. I had come this far without harm. The Universe opened a door to something magical—an *adventure*. I had only to step through the Red Mirror.

CHAPTER 2   RIVER GOD

I don't know how it happened; I can't explain the mechanics. But the chorus of a thousand songbirds shattered the silence, and I opened my eyes to another world. The air was rich with the earthy scent of loam and sweet flowers. The bare whisper of a breeze kissed my skin.

I reclined in a long gown of white linen pleats on a lush carpet of grass among date palms, tall stone columns and flowering trees. Birds sang from every branch. Brown sparrows, yellow finches, blue warblers—I'd never seen so many birds. Hundreds of straw nests filled every crack and crevice in the ornate capitals of what could only be Egyptian columns.

Not far away, at the end of the grassy lawn, flowed a wide river where the last traces of mist melted in the rising sun. Distant cliffs on the far bank brightened to gold. The sky was blue without a cloud.

I stretched out my legs and wiggled my toes. My muscles were well-toned, my thighs firm. I felt very fit. I must walk a lot. I liked the new me.

My fingernails and toenails were stained rust-red. Tiny geometric designs trailed across the tops of narrow feet, and a crisscross pattern encircled my ankles. At first I thought the designs were tattoos, but when I realized they were painted, I recognized henna from photos in an old National Geographic.

From the look of my soft hands and pampered alabaster skin, I led a privileged life. A ring with golden horns around a grape-sized lapis lazuli stone gleamed from the middle finger of my right hand. Two heavy gold bands coiled around thin upper arms. They felt like they had always been there, molded to my flesh. A wide gold collar around the base of my throat fastened with a short length of chain falling down my back, under my hair.

Only it wasn't my hair. It was a wig. And it was heavy. My head itched under the shoulder-length mass. I pulled it off; the fresh breeze caressed my bare scalp. I was a little timid to touch this new body, but dared to scratch my smooth, shaved head very gently. Emboldened, I ran my fingertips around a wide mouth with full lips and then felt a familiar cleft in my chin. My neck seemed as long as a swan's.

I was me, but not me, all at the same time. I should have been afraid, but I wasn't in the least. In fact, I felt more relaxed than I could ever remember. The sweet air, the birdsong, the rustle of palm leaves in the warm breeze lulled me—even the flow of the river had a narcotic effect.

The curves of my belly and thighs in the sheer cloth that concealed nothing were impossibly slim. My pubic hair was gone; a mound the same dark rose color as my nipples showed through the linen. No underwear at all.

I breathed slowly, drinking in the perfumed air. Yes, I liked the new me.

"Isis!"

I had a name, the name of a goddess. I also had a man. At least I saw one coming right at me—a River God of bronzed flesh and snowy linen.

A stiff white kilt wrapped around his hips and ended just above the knees. He had the strong ankles, long calves and taut thighs of a runner. His chest, bare except for a wide, beaded collar, glowed like burnished stone; broad shoulders tapered to a narrow waist. With his triangular torso and headdress of blue-and-white stripes, he was an ancient painting come alive. Oh yes, definitely a god.

I wondered if he also was without underwear.

When I took his hand, and he pulled me to my feet, his exotic scent went straight to my head. We stood very close, almost nothing between us.

I stopped myself just before I reached out to run my fingers down his flat belly and under the snowy kilt. I was never this bold on the other side of the mirror.

I wanted to touch him, to fondle him, to make him quake with desire.

Thick black *kohl* outlined his eyes. His face was almost, but not quite, too angular. The skin stretched over well-defined cheekbones and determined jaw. There was nothing about him I would call lush, except for his mouth. Both hard and sensuous at the same time, his perfect lips had been chiseled by a master sculptor.

I wanted to feel those lips on my neck. I wanted him to explore. Could he not feel the waves of my desire crashing on his shore?

My fingertips as light as the wings of a butterfly stroked the smooth muscle of his chest. Slowly I traced down his biceps and along his forearms to the wide gold bracelets at his wrists. The tiny hairs on his skin rose at my touch.

Ever so slowly, a man savoring each touch, he guided my fingers from his wrist, over his forearm, past his biceps, along his shoulder, across his throat and finally, to his chiseled mouth; his eyes never left mine. He teased me with a half-smile full of promises. When he put my fingers between his lips, I touched his wet tongue.

"Not now, Isis. Not here," he breathed in my ear.

He stroked once across the hollow of my throat. His breath was hot and moist on my neck.

"I shall come to you later and drink of your nectar," he whispered. "You will fly to the stars with my tongue on your lotus."

Then he stepped back, his arms at his sides in the erect, rigid posture of a military man.

"Come. You will be late for the Temple."

Temple? What temple? Late for what? Who would be there? *Would they be able to tell?*

I looked at River God. If he saw anything different about Isis, he didn't show it. His seductive half smile held no hint of suspicion.

We walked side by side, not touching, down a stone path just wide enough for two. It ran perfectly straight through a garden aflame with flowers and shaded by date palms, sycamores and rows of almond and fig. A square field of red poppies swayed in the light wind.

I was grateful he didn't look for conversation. Whatever language he spoke, I understood every word, but what would happen when I tried to speak?

We passed under trellises laden with grapevines. Fountains gurgled like springs into rectangular pools covered with green lotus pads; tall white blooms trembled on slender stalks. There were birds everywhere, hundreds of them, of all colors and sizes, each with their own song.

The tiny bells in the wig tinkled at every step. The graceful pleats of the gown flowed against my thighs, caressing my hips and the small rise of my belly. I took long strides in fine-tooled leather sandals, pointed at the tips. Light on my feet, at ease with my body, every muscle well-toned, I could be a dancer.

The path ended in a wide avenue with a phalanx of stone sphinxes marching down each side. In the distance, I heard the clanging of metal against stone—repetitive, rhythmic, without pause. The sounds of construction.

A sea of foot traffic flowed in both directions, but no one hurried. Many eyes turned toward me; a group of men in long white skirts bowed their shaved heads.

River God stopped at an obelisk with a gold-tipped point.

"Your Nubian waits."

A giant with oiled ebony skin stood as erect as a statue. His biceps were like ripe melons; thick thighs bulged. Striated scars from some age-old tribal ceremony covered his cheeks. His onyx eyes were careful not to look directly at me.

"I shall come to you in the heat of the afternoon," River God whispered as we parted. "When the others are sleeping."

Others? My throat closed. I felt dizzy and slightly sick at my stomach. Heat rose off the pavement in shimmering waves. The sun overhead was white-hot.

I watched River God move through the bronze bodies in snowy linen until his blue-and-white striped headdress disappeared in the crowd, and I was left with Goliath.

We didn't go far on the wide, paved boulevard before turning to a massive pillared temple. Great red and yellow flags on wooden poles set high up on the walls snapped in the hot wind.

Passing through a gate built for giants, we entered a forest of columns carved at the top with the heads of a cow-eared goddess.

Goliath stopped at the granite lintel painted with outstretched wings, and I crossed alone from day into shadow.

CHAPTER 3 THE TEMPLE

Soft filtered light streamed through square openings at the roofline; the narrow sunbeams pierced clouds of frankincense and deep shadows. The only sound was the soft murmur of chanting.

A garland of olive leaves mixed with cornflowers and lotus petals was draped around my neck by a young girl with skin as flawless as fine ivory. My eyes stung; the floral scent softened the tang of burning aromatic woods.

The chamber was another forest of elaborate, painted columns topped by cow-eared goddesses. Wild-colored murals, bright geometric patterns and neon hieroglyphs covered every surface. Giants with mystical crowns or the heads of animals performed strange rituals in splendid reds, yellows, and blues.

I resisted leaning my head back to take in the ornate high ceiling, absorbing as much as possible without being obvious. But I couldn't stop my eyes from traveling everywhere at once.

The next chamber was smaller with even more incense and no sunlight at all. Hundreds of alabaster lamps glowed.

Women as graceful as sea nymphs moved about in long white gowns like mine; the glide of their sandals was silent on the stone. No one else wore a flower garland.

A hush stilled the room when I entered and all heads bowed low toward me. Instantly aware of every cell in my body, I vibrated from deep within.

The priestesses approached me one after another, each with offerings of blue lotus and baskets filled with figs, dates and pomegranates. When my arms could hold no more, two older women with elaborate headdresses murmured an incantation and took everything from my arms. One was tall, but stooped; the other's cheeks were pitted with pox scars. Their eyes were all-seeing.

I stood very still and never spoke. I didn't feel danger; every touch was reverent. Warm fingers loosened the ties of my gown and I stood naked, the folds of fine linen around my ankles. The two Ancient Ones painted symbols on my arms and then my bare thighs. My heart raced; my mouth was dry, but not my secret valley. My nipples tightened.

They paid no attention to the changes in my body, but continued to draw designs with a kind of black ink. Each symbol had its own incantation.

They replaced my necklace and garland with a heavy, beaded collar that finished in a counterpoise down my back. The old women chanted as they circled me, repeating the word *menit* over and over. Without knowing how, I knew they sang about the necklace. No one else uttered a sound.

When the chanting stopped, the chamber was silent as a tomb.

The first sound of the finger cymbals was like a distant tinkle of tiny bells. The jingling grew louder but never brassy. Golden rain tickled my ears.

A woman with the yellow-green eyes of cat drifted toward me. She carried a tall headdress with twin ostrich feathers and two golden horns holding a shiny, gold disk; white feathers fluttered at each step as she approached.

The room of priestesses chanted in unison as four hands balanced the solar disk headdress on my wig.

Anet-hra-k Hathor! (Hail to Thee, Hathor!)
Auksh satet-v en Amenta (O daughter of Heaven)
un uat er Isenkhebe Nefrusobek (open a way to Isenkhebe Nefrusobek)
Anet-hra-k Hathor! (Hail to Thee, Hathor!)

I imagined myself as a figure in one of the vividly painted murals, but how would I walk?

Finally, the Ancient Ones anointed my shoulders, breasts and belly with musk and led me by both hands toward two tall doors covered with gilt.

When the doors opened, I walked through alone.

Watching me from the shadows were two men. I could just make out the whites of their eyes. I felt their heat and smelled their scented sweat.

My oiled naked body gleamed in the low light. There was a heavy new perfume here, a narcotic smoke that blurred my vision and made the air rush in my ears. The chamber was electric. My head pounded, and I felt light-headed and dizzy.

The sanctum shimmered in gold around an alabaster statue of a seated goddess with a solar disk headdress and a large ankh in her right hand resting on her thigh. A dozen alabaster lamps at her feet cast a soft, flickering light.

Without any conscious direction on my part, my hand moved to a silver shaker gleaming in a wooden case on a black marble pedestal. A graceful silver loop held three delicate rods pierced with dozens of small metallic disks. The gleaming silver handle formed into twin heads of Hathor, the cow-eared goddess sitting on the altar throne.

A sensual tinkling sound broke the silence when I lifted the sacred *sistrum* from its ebony box inlaid with ivory. The men stirred when they heard the low music. It was so still in the chamber, I could hear them inhale and exhale, together as one person.

Every action was as natural to me as breathing. I held the necklace out from my throat toward the statue, shaking the *sistrum* in a slow, even rhythm that grew more and more feverish. When I opened my lips to sing, the words flowed like magic from me without effort.

"*O Hathor,*
O Divine Cow and giver of milk,
O Goddess of Fertility,
O Goddess of wine, music and dance,
O Goddess of Love.

We adore you.
We ask your blessings for this Son of the Pharaoh,
this First Prince of Egypt."

The two moved next to me, one on each side. The taller one took the *sistrum* from my hand and returned it carefully to its wooden case. The shorter of the two lifted my headdress and set it on the altar at Hathor's feet. The royal insignia hung from a thick gold chain around his neck.

I stood stock still while they each stroked my body, four hands caressing my breasts, my buttocks, the insides of my loins. The heavy scent of musk filled my shallow breath.

Together they led me to a low divan and laid me down on my back. The two started at my feet and began to suck one toe after another, in perfect unison. Then their wet mouths moved to my ankles, and then trailed up my calves to the inside of my loins, where they lingered like preening cats.

Edging closer and closer to the moist valley of desire, they took their time, teasing me, enjoying the straining of my hips and my low cries when they came near, then moved away. Tremors moved through me. I flushed with heat.

But just before their tongues found my sacred lotus, the two joined hands, rolled back onto their heels, one on my left, one on my right, and chanted in unison.

"O beauteous one, O great one,
O great magician, O splendid lady.
The Pharaoh reveres you; give that his Son may live!
Behold him, Hathor, flaming one,
His manhood is straight,
The Son of Pharaoh reveres you, O Gold of Gods,
Give of your milk that he live!"

With that they came to me again, each suckling my breasts, hands kneading like babes at their mother's teats. I lay on the divan, electric shocks rolling through me, moans reverberating in my throat and chest.

The royal one mounted me while the other licked my open lips with his broad tongue. He did not kiss me.

Rocking slowly, his chest rising each time his hips moved forward, the son of the Pharaoh thrust again and again. The pendant insignia swung back and forth on the heavy chain. He didn't look into my face but only at the other man.

Then he stopped and lay his manhood on my stomach just as a flood of white milk spewed. The other quickly bent and lapped it up with his tongue. Then they leaned forward and kissed each other, the royal one taking back the semen with an open mouth.

They chanted once more.

"His gift has been given,
He defiles not his gift.
Clean is his offering,
It has come from the Prince of Egypt,
He has cleansed what he offers to Her."

It was over.

The two knelt before the statue of the goddess Hathor and placed a leather pouch each on the altar. Not looking back, they opened the heavy golden doors and disappeared.

I lay panting and stunned on the low sofa. I didn't think I could stand.

What kind of a priestess was I, anyway?

The doors opened, and the Ancient Ones, now wearing simple wigs with twinkling gold chains, entered. They came straight for me in the dark. They moved silently across the basalt floor, one carrying an alabaster bowl, the other a roll of snow-white linen.

They cleaned me everywhere with jasmine-scented water. With the hands of a mother on child, they washed the symbols and all trace of fluids away. I relaxed into the soft fur of the divan and let them cool my fire.

"The Goddess is pleased," the old women with scarred cheeks

assured me. "The Pharaoh will be pleased. The spell of Set the Destroyer on the First Son of Egypt, the son-of-Horus, has been broken. The Golden One has given the Crown Prince back his manhood."

"Not very likely," I muttered under my breath. It was best to keep my doubts to myself.

CHAPTER 4 SIT-HATHOR

Fussing with my body, muttering incantations, the Ancient Ones never ceased praising the healing power of the Goddess as manifested through me. Not much healing had gone on that I could see, but what did I care about the Pharaoh or his son? I'd done my job as high priestess. What happened in the Temple, stayed in the Temple.

When they'd finished soothing me with warm oils, I hurried from the ritual chamber and through the forest of columns to find Goliath.

I was thinking only of River God's promise of a flight to the stars, when a short, fat priest with a large amethyst dangling from his right earlobe stepped from nowhere into my path. A soft leopard skin draped his fleshy shoulder.

There was something odd about him that I couldn't quite place; I sensed no sexual energy at all.

"Greetings and Good Health, Isenkhebe Nefrusobek," the priest squeaked. "Sit-hathor, The Highest-of-High, Golden of the Golden One, High Priestess of the Two Lands commands Isenkhebe's presence."

He addressed me by my formal name in the high-pitched voice of a eunuch. I stifled an impulse to laugh; it was obvious that Isis felt nothing but disdain for him.

The set of the old priest's shoulders and the steady look in his eyes told me there was no room for discussion. River God would have to wait. I reluctantly followed the fat priest back into the inner temple and down a dark passageway lit by tall torches in deep alcoves.

High double doors with golden lionhead knobs swung open into a blaze of lanterns. A wild chorus of high-pitched male voices stopped in mid-note. It was so quiet I could hear the lamps consume oil.

"*Enter,*" the old eunuch commanded without speaking. "*Sit-hathor awaits her daughter.*"

His swinging amethyst earring splintered the light.

I had heard him clearly, yet no words passed his lips. He spoke directly to my mind. Could he also read my thoughts? If he had suspicions about Isis, he gave no sign. His eyes were as fathomless as a well in the desert.

He backed out of the chamber, closing the doors as he exited, leaving me with a roomful of staring eyes.

"Approach, Isenkhebe my child, that we may feast on your beauty."

A striking woman in her middle age called out to me in a voice of liquid gold. The legs of her gilded chair were carved into the four limbs of a lion with paws and claws at the feet; the arms of the chair ended in lionheads.

Sit-hathor held out her right hand, and I climbed three short steps and sank to my knees, kissing the giant lapis lazuli ring with golden horns identical to mine. Like me, she wore hers on the right middle finger. Her nails were long and stained dark-red with henna.

"Too much time has passed, my daughter. Our duties are many; the hours are few."

Her lips curved into a small smile without showing any teeth. Heavy lines of *kohl* framed her black eyes; blue mica sparkled from her lids, up to her eyebrows and out to her temples. Her chin-length wig of thick waves shimmered in a golden mesh.

She placed her hand on my bowed head. The affection flowed from her heart through her palm into my tingling crown. This woman loved me. But I felt another energy, too. An intense current flowed through me, spreading quickly right down to my womb. Her energy buzzed around my body, igniting my cells. I vibrated once again to my core.

"I have a mission for you, Isis," she whispered. "The time is full, the need great, and you are ready."

Mission? My head jerked in surprise, but her hand kept me from pulling back. I felt the pressure of each fingertip, even through the wig. Her energy flowed stronger.

Then Sit-hathor took her hand away and the current stopped as abruptly as a plug yanked from a socket.

"You are the flesh of my body and a piece of my *Ka*," she crooned. "You shall not neglect to serve your Goddess."

"My mother, my mistress," I murmured. "It is said that the work of the Goddess Hathor is what acts upon women. I pray that the task you set before me is in alignment with Her path for me."

I'd never seen anyone change so quickly. It was clear that Sit-hathor was not a woman whose demands were questioned. Her lush lips hardened, and her eyes narrowed. I thought she might strike me down with a look.

"Would you doubt the will of Hathor, Queen of Gods?" she asked in an icy tone. "She has spoken as clearly to me as I now speak to you."

The buzzing in the chamber was loud as a beehive. This was not going well. I made sure my next words were ones that would please.

"My mistress, giver of my life, the fault in every kind of character comes from not listening. My ears are full open to receive your words. My heart is full open to fulfill your wishes."

Sit-hathor morphed again; she warmed instantly, smiling ever so slightly. The tension in the room eased with a collective sigh.

Leaning forward, her face just inches from mine, she pressed a gold charm into my hand. Tiny glyphs saying 'one-who-has-entered-the-heart' formed a single large glyph for 'heart.'

"By this amulet, your father will recognize you as his daughter."

I must have looked shocked at her words, because she put her long fingers under my chin, drawing me even closer to her face.

"Yes, you have a father," she hissed. Her black eyes flashed a warning that she would brook no opposition. "The time has come for you to meet him."

She settled back in her chair and although her shoulders relaxed somewhat, her spine was still as straight as a spear.

"Prepare for a river voyage. Put your trust in the eunuch Qeb-ha."

No! Not that fat little freak with only half his manhood.

"Allow the whisperings of the Goddess to enter your heart, my daughter." Sit-hathor's tone softened; she was almost kind. "Even a fool acts wisely if he follows his heart."

"There is no protector save the Gods," I intoned.

Then she signalled that I should rise and the interview was over. But before I stepped down, her inky eyes held mine for a long moment.

"Know well, Isenkhebe Nefrusobek, that there is nothing left but the doing."

I had forgotten that it was day. The sun was a white disk in the washed-out sky when I left the dark temple through the courtyard with columns crowned by carved heads of Hathor with cow ears. I blinked and shielded my eyes from the harsh light.

The fat old priest Qeb-ha appeared suddenly out of the shadows.

"Do not resist," he said clearly. Only his lips didn't move. *"Isenkhebe Nefrusobek is the chosen one. It is the will of the Goddess."*

He startled me, coming from nowhere and speaking with no words.

"We sail at dawn," he said in his repugnant squeaky voice, but at least he spoke out loud.

Tomorrow I sailed with a castrated old priest who could read my thoughts. Who knows how deep he could probe?

I brushed past him in a panic to get away, to get to River God. I had to make the most of my time before dawn.

I would caress River God's smooth, unquestionably male body. I would stroke down his chest and across his belly to settle on his undamaged manhood and watch him swell with desire.

Goliath the Magnificent waited where I had left him under

the lintel adorned with green-and-orange outstretched wings. My eyes traveled from the white triangle of his headdress to the white triangle of his loincloth, noting his massive chest along the way. I found myself dreaming of the dark places I could taste.

If River God had come and gone, I would command the Nubian to service me. Yes, Goliath would do just fine.

CHAPTER 5   THE BATH

Chaos greeted me at the small villa set in a lavish garden behind white walls. I could hear the high voices, all talking at once, before I came in the door. More than a dozen chests, large and small, were scattered on the mosaic floors. A bird-like woman surrounded by an electric field screeched orders at everyone. Egyptians were not always so calm, after all.

She stopped only to tell me that Maia was packing my jewels and potions.

There seemed no chance now for a stolen afternoon with River God. Even Goliath was out of the question, certainly not here and now.

When I entered my bedchamber, a delicate young girl prostrated herself, stretching her thin arms along the floor and touching her forehead to a rich mosaic of marsh birds. Her black wig had tiny braids twisted with white and blue linen cords.

"Rise up," I commanded.

Then I whispered in the hushed tone of a conspirator, "Did he come?"

She blushed and lowered her eyes. Thick lines of *kohl* extended out toward her temples, and blue mica sparkled on her eyelids.

"Yes, Isenkhebe Nefrusobek, he came after the second meal."

Maia avoided looking at me. It was more than obvious that she didn't approve.

"He did not speak to me, mistress. He entered this sacred chamber through the forbidden door but left when he saw the preparations for our holy journey."

My guess was that River God would be back. He wouldn't let me leave without a visit to my bed. His touch in the garden told me that. The packing couldn't go on forever. I still had tonight.

I would always do my duty to the Goddess, but I had my own needs. The plans of a god are one thing; the thoughts of men are another.

I settled on a mound of pillows and sent for roast duck and unwatered wine. I was enjoying the new me.

Maia brought me a black purring cat.

"Will Pehtes travel with us?" she asked.

"Of course. Who else shall I caress on the long nights?"

Pehtes settled in my lap, between my thighs, just like Aisha.

"Is that not right, Pehtes? I fear you will be stroked on this voyage far more often than me."

The Sun God Re finally traveled to his nightly battle in the Underworld that ended at dawn when he would rise victorious once again. Curtains of the finest linen embroidered with blue ankhs billowed around the low bed. The scent of gardenia and jasmine drifted on the warm breeze.

Maia lighted alabaster lamps with scented oil in preparation for my evening bath. A sheer canopy of pink gauze tented the portico of the rose marble pool. White lotus blossoms floated on the glassy water. Small colored-glass bottles of perfumed oils stood on the edge.

I slipped into liquid velvet and closed my eyes. The water was the same temperature as my body and the evening air. We were one. A nightingale, the only sound in the stillness of the new night, sang just outside my bedchamber in the darkening garden.

He was silent. I sensed his presence rather than heard him. My first sight was bare feet and sturdy ankles. My eyes traveled up straight runner's legs past the engorged penis, head glistening in the lamplight, into the face of River God.

O Hathor! You are indeed the Highest-of-High.

He was in the water before I could move, straddling me, pushing me back into the unyielding stone of the pool wall. I didn't complain.

I tried to reach him with my fingertips, with my tongue, but he teased me and held my hands, not letting me touch him.

He eased down into the water on top of me, my neck on the edge of the pool, his hardness pushing against the softness of my belly. I stretched to reach his sculptured lips with mine. Gentle and tender now, he breathed into my ear.

"Isis, do not move, or my seed will issue. I want it to last."

Releasing my hands, he pulled me full into the pool. I floated on my back, white lotus blossoms with dazzling yellow centers swirling in eddies around us. My nipples rose from the water; the aureoles of my breasts were dark circles just at the surface. On his knees beside me, his erection pierced the clear water.

He started with my closed eyes, then my open lips, not touching me, but blowing warm puffs of air like a gentle wind across my flesh. His breath was sweet with a trace of myrrh. He blew softly in my ear, down the side of my neck, and across my throat.

The water was warm on my back, and the air warm on my face. His breath was warmer stillon my breasts. He lingered, blowing round and round, never touhing.

I felt his hand slide between my thighs. I was content to do nothing, to exert nothing, to have no will of my own. He stroked my swollen bud in small circular movements, with almost no pressure. I drifted in sheer pleasure among sweet-scented blossoms

His hands cupped my buttocks, and he raised me to his lips, his tongue swirling my throbbing lotus.

The orgasm cascaded through my womb, the muscles of my vagina rolling in contraction after contraction. A long, pitched cry escaped my throat.

River God's mouth was on mine in an instant.

"Sh-h-h, Isis. The household is awake and nearby."

Too late for that. By now, every eye looked to my rooms. Every ear strained to hear more.

He stood up in the pool with the water coming to mid-thigh. He had gone tense and his erection slack. I could feel every taut nerve in his body. River God knew he tasted forbidden fruit.

My hands in his, he drew me slowly to my feet. We stood inches apart, water streaming off, our skin glowing in the yellow light of the flickering lamps, the air sweet with their perfumed oil. My breasts rose and fell with each breath.

"They will stay away. I have given orders to be alone."

He stared hard at me for a moment, an animal alert to danger. His eyes were so dark, I couldn't see the pupils. Then the hint of a smile shone through his caution, and he was mine again.

His lips were full and dry and covered mine with ease, his tongue slow, exploring, taking his time. He sucked gently on my own tongue and drew me to him with his muscled arms, my breasts pressing into his hard chest. I arched my back to bring my hips closer to his pelvis. His erection was back.

I found myself outside of the pool, gliding backward, two bodies moving as one as he guided us to the bed with billowing sails. The curtains brushed our bare flesh, but didn't cling; our skin had dried in the desert night air.

We sank together onto the cushions of a bed designed more for pleasure than sleep. Smelling the mating scent, Pehtes purred round my ears.

I lay spread on soft linen, my shaved head resting among cool silk pillows and warm cat fur. River God's mouth was on mine again in a deep lingering kiss probing with his tongue. His touch was more sensual than sexual. He savored me as one does a fine wine, something precious you loathe to finish.

I had a sudden thought.

"Sail with me tomorrow. With you in my bed by night, I can face anything by day."

Startled, River God stopped his caress and stared at me, his eyes wide in disbelief.

"I cannot do that. I am bound to my duty as you are to yours." His voice was incredulous.

I might have asked him to fly.

"You could appeal to the Governor," I insisted.

Alarms rang in my head, but I didn't have the sense to stop.

"I am the daughter of Sit-hathor. I am in need of protection. Who better to protect me than you?"

He changed in that moment. I felt him begin to pull away. When he spoke, his tone was already distant. There was a note of patience that one uses with a child.

"Isis, sweet and dangerous Isis, you know that our destinies were foretold when we came from the womb."

Time slowed. I could almost see the thoughts turning in his head. The nightingale sang sweetly, unaware that the world had changed. The air, utterly still, was abuzz with the hum of insects. The cries of night creatures carried from the Nile.

I felt him slipping away. I traced my fingers lightly along his forearm. The hairs rose, and I had hope.

"I feel alone. I do not want to go on this voyage alone. I fear it. I fear everything about it."

I pleaded with him, but in my heart, I knew he wouldn't go. This journey was for me only—and Qeb-ha. It was as Sit-hathor had said. *All that is left is the doing.*

He stroked my face, then along the bone at the base of my throat out to my shoulder. I was like a cat before him. Pehtes tried to crawl into my armpit; I wanted to follow her there.

"I desire you more than any woman I have ever known or seen, Isis."

His voice was gentle and very low, barely above a whisper. His eyes had a new steely resolve that frightened me.

"But I must place myself away from you. The Gods have set us on separate paths. Mine is to serve the Pharaoh, yours the Goddess."

He paused to watch his fingers trace the mound of my breast. How could he touch me while saying goodbye?

"The great glory of a wise man is to control himself in his manner of life," he said.

I hated those words. I wanted to put my hands over my ears

to keep them from entering. It was my fault. I was too needy. I had gone too far.

He bent and kissed my lips with lingering tenderness. A chisel split my heart in two as cleanly as a piece of granite. The pain pierced my soul.

"The Fate and Fortune that come, Isis, it is the Gods that send them."

I had been taught a thousand ways to make a man desire me. Now there was nothing I could say or do to make him stay. He was gone as quickly and silently as he had come. I had a terrible feeling that I would never see him again.

CHAPTER 6 ENCOUNTER

The bells kept ringing and ringing, louder and louder. Would they never stop?

I felt Pehtes purring against me, but when I looked, it wasn't Pehtes. It was Aisha.

I was back. The cold marble tiles of my living room were hard and my back hurt. How long had I been lying here? Had it been hours—or days?

What was that incessant ringing? It stopped, and then started again. I found my cell on the coffee table next to my keys and checked the caller ID before answering. It was Barb.

"Where have you been? Didn't you get my messages?"

"Barb, I have to tell you something…something big."

"Save it. This is more important. I need you to get over here to the Stirling Club right away."

Stirling Club? When I last saw her, it was lunch and seemed like only a few minutes ago.

"What time is it?"

I didn't dare ask what day.

"It's Happy Hour. I'm here with clients—two *very* good-looking men buying drinks and making intelligent—let me repeat— *intelligent* conversation."

"Barb…I bought the Red Mirror."

"What red mirror?"

"The one I showed you. The day we had lunch.

"God, I hope you got a deal."

I heard live music in the background. Then Barb said something about a glass of Chardonnay to someone.

"Barb, listen. It has some kind of power."

"Power? What are you talking about? How can a mirror have

power?"

She paused just a moment.

"What *kind* of power?"

"That's what I wanted to tell you. I got...well...turned on... looking at it."

My plan was to lead up to River God, but Barb wasn't focused at all.

"Looking at what?" she snapped.

"The *mirror*, Barb, the Red Mirror."

"You got turned on by a mirror?" Then she whispered, "Have you been smoking something?"

"I had this kind of...dream. Only it wasn't a dream. At least...I don't think it was. I was myself...but not myself...and...and I was in Egypt. You know...when there were Pharaohs and stuff."

It sounded ridiculous, even to me, when I said it out loud.

"Forget the Pharaohs," Barb snorted. "I'm here with two gorgeous men. They're buying drinks and making intelligent conversation. I repeat, *intelligent* conversation. You can tell me about this Egypt dream later."

"But Barb—"

"Here's your choice." Her voice took on the sharp bossy tone that signals she's run out of patience. "You can stay home with your mirror and go on some kind of fantasy trip. Or you can put on your stilettos and get over here where a real-life man is waiting for you."

"But—"

"And *please* don't tell me that you have to think about this."

"Okay. Okay. I'll be there in half an hour."

"You won't regret it. These guys are quality goods. Who knows? Maybe he's Mr. Right."

Barb had won. I hadn't put up much of a fight.

I saw Barb at the same time she saw me. Tall and thin like a model with platinum hair, she's easy to spot in a crowd. She smiled and waved discreetly. Perched on a high leather bar chair, she faced two tall men standing with their backs to me. I already liked the cut of their suits and the square of their shoulders. Money and confidence. I saw it from across the room.

"Hi, Barb! I made it." I kissed her on the cheek before turning around.

My knees went weak. Barb grabbed my arm and kept me on my feet. Standing just in front of me, dressed in a charcoal silk suit with a blue paisley tie, was River God.

Well, River God with green eyes. Green instead of dark; green like mine.

I had the sense to realize I was staring at him with a gaping mouth and snapped my teeth together. If he recognized me, he didn't show it, but half-smiled in his amused way, just like the morning I first saw him on the banks of the Nile.

Tailored to fit perfectly over his broad shoulders, his suit narrowed at the waist. It took no effort at all to visualize the triangular torso underneath.

His sensuous lips and sharp angled-face had been carved by the same master sculptor. He had thick black hair now, styled in an expensive salon cut.

He was shorter. No, he was the same. I was wearing three-inch heels and my eyes were on level with his luscious mouth.

I stared at him. The other three stared at me.

"You look exactly like someone I used to know," I said lamely. I couldn't think of anything else.

"You look like you could use a drink." His voice was incredibly, impossibly, the same.

He turned away to talk to the bartender and then looked right back at me. I got the impression he was searching for something in my eyes.

Barb introduced him as Rasheed. His blond friend was Lars.

We settled in one of the small rooms just off the lounge, semi-private, with walls covered in traditional oil paintings in gilt frames.

An ochre velvet sofa was against the wall. Plush velvet armchairs, one on each end, formed a U around a low mahogany table.

Barb planted herself on the sofa, motioning for Nordic-looking Lars to sit in the chair beside her. It was obvious how the pairing would go.

I sank into the down-filled cushions at the other end of the sofa and crossed my black-silky legs. My skirt rode up to mid-thigh. The red patent of my heels shone in the yellow light.

Rasheed relaxed into the chair next to me, close but not too close. He radiated an energy that was both animal and sensual. Just sitting next to him rendered me helpless and without a will of my own. I sensed that he knew it. But he kept very cool with that slightly amused, seductive smile curving his lips.

Rasheed didn't try to make conversation, but looked around, observing. I decided to be silent and mysterious—like Isis. I glanced slyly at the muscles of his thighs stretching his silk trousers.

A drummer and guitarist joined the pianist. The lounge was filling up. The noise level rose several decibels, and it was too loud really to talk. But by this time of the evening, most people had other things on their mind.

Sipping my Plymouth martini, toying with the olive on a plastic stick, I studied him from under lowered lashes. It was not my imagination. Rasheed looked exactly like River God—except for the suit and hair—and the green eyes. But more than that, he *felt* like him. It was the way he moved and his voice—and the way his eyes probed for secrets.

I thought he'd forgotten me. Then he suddenly turned and caught me staring at him. The corners of his lips curved up again ever so slightly, and he leaned into me, the silk fabric of his suit tightening across his shoulders. He didn't try to hide the bulge in his pants.

His look was magnetic. I couldn't have torn my eyes away if I wanted to. I smelled his cologne, very faint but exotic.

"I know." He traced his middle finger lightly over my knee. A shock ran straight up the inside of my thigh. "I really feel you, too."

When he offered his hand to help me stand to dance, I was transported at once to the bank of the Nile in the early morning sun. His movements were fluid; I followed without effort. I don't think I've ever seen a man so masculine move with such grace.

He breathed in my scent, and I thanked Carolina Herrera for my perfume—sweet, animal, ethereal.

There were a dozen couples on the dance floor, each lost in their own universe. Rasheed guided us among the other galaxies, never brushing a star.

Strangers in the Night. We didn't feel like strangers at all. Rasheed lifted my hair with his fingers and put his lips to the spot where the line of my neck curves into my shoulder. The magic spot that opens all doors. The brush of his hot breath lasted only a second but burned on forever.

Lars and Barb danced too. They looked like they were getting along just fine. Lars laughed a lot; he was low-key, ready for fun, the type who just enjoys being alive.

"I'm starving," he declared. "What's your favorite restaurant?"

"Eiffel Tower," I said immediately, and then immediately regretted it. It's very pricey.

"You need reservations," I stumbled. "We probably couldn't get a table."

"I don't think it'll be a problem." Rasheed said it like a man who rarely encounters problems.

Standing by the tasting room were two men, both over six feet, well-built and well-dressed in tailored suits. They fell in behind us, following closely down the wide marble staircase and out the leaded glass doors.

A valet came up immediately. Rasheed nodded, and the taller of the two handed the valet the claim ticket. My internal warning light flashed red. I hadn't agreed to go anywhere with four men.

Rasheed leaned close, touching my elbow. I felt his breath in my ear.

"Marcos and Gamel go everywhere I go. They are always with me. There is no danger. But I need to keep it that way."

Go everywhere he goes? Are we talking about *bodyguards*?

"I have my own car." My voice was edgy, the pitch a little too high.

I looked at Barb for reassurance. She looked embarrassed, but not nervous.

"Gamel can bring your car. He's an excellent driver." Rasheed was calm, his voice reasonable.

Gamel looked at me briefly and then away. His hair was shiny black and brushed back from his brow. The silk of his suit stretched across the bulk of his powerful shoulders. I imagined I saw the outline of a gun at his armpit.

Rasheed's eyes told me, *This is going to be fine.*

I opened my bag and handed him the stub. A limo pulled up and the other man—did Rasheed call him Marcos?—took the driver's seat. Gamel opened the passenger door, and everyone looked at me.

The tension eased when I got into the limo. Barb followed and was immediately apologetic.

"Jeeze, Barb," I hissed. "Bodyguards? Yes, you might have mentioned that."

Lars climbed in and rummaged in the bar.

"What about some champagne? Isn't that what you do in a limo in Vegas?" He popped the cork and looked for flutes.

"*Skål!*"

Rasheed put his hand on my hand resting at the top of my thigh, next to the gateway to pleasure. His heat seared through flesh and fabric. I envisioned a brand on my skin in the shape of his palm.

"You don't have to worry about anything happening that you don't want." He spoke low, only for me to hear.

I looked directly into his eyes and then at his lips only inches from mine. At that moment, there was only one thing I wanted. Too bad Barb and Lars were in the way.

Rasheed was right about reservations being no problem. I saw a bill discretely change hands, and we sped up the private elevator. The *maitre d'* ushered us to a prime table against tall windows overlooking the Strip.

Bright lights and hi-def signs blazed. The Paris balloon was a huge lighted ball against the black sky. The fountain show at the Bellagio across Las Vegas Boulevard started with the first tentative sprays, and then exploded in a lavish ballet of white lights and sparkling water jets orchestrated with music. Each segment ended in thundering crescendos soaring high into the air.

"Great choice!" Lars was enthusiastic. "If the food is half as good as the view, I'm in heaven."

Course after delicious course arrived, each paired with the best wines served by the *sommelier*. Waiters in tuxedos buzzed around the table. The fountains played every fifteen minutes.

Lars told stories about skiing in Norway. Barb chattered about real estate. Rasheed said practically nothing. His knee pressed against mine; sometimes I felt his hand burning on my thigh. I felt electric just sitting next to him. He looked directly at me from time to time; the corners of his mouth curled up in his half-smile that made me feel he knew a secret I didn't know.

The *piece de resistance* was the baked chocolate soufflé with warm vanilla sauce. Courvoisier filled crystal snifters. Waiters served dark espresso with lemon peel in tiny porcelain *demitasse* cups. Lumps of raw sugar nestled in a sterling silver bowl on the white damask tablecloth.

I didn't want to think about the bill. It would cover a month's rent and all my utilities and still have some left over. The check never came to the table. Rasheed had apparently arranged that with the *maitre d'* too.

Barb and Lars laughed all the way down the elevator. Rasheed was quiet but kept close to me. Neither of us spoke. I was aware of nothing but the heat of his body. When he put his hand on the small of my back, my flesh blistered.

Our entourage passed through the throng in the Paris Casino and made for valet parking, Gamel in the lead. The blood pumped in my ears; I had sampled a lot of wine. Between the furnace of Rasheed's body and the drink, I was light-headed.

Rasheed took hold of my arm and said to the others, "Please excuse us for a moment."

He guided me around a corner and backed me up to the wall. His body pressed against mine, and I felt him grow hard. I could almost feel him throbbing.

"Listen to me. Don't say a word." His voice was low and urgent. "I want you to come with me to my hotel. I don't want you to say no."

I felt a twinge of fear. He looked just like him, but could I trust Rasheed to *be* like River God? What would he do if I refused? Until five minutes ago, I would have gone anywhere with him. Heat radiated from his body; I burned as if next to a furnace. The power of his muscles pulsed in his silk suit.

The suddenly he relaxed; his whole body relaxed. The angles in his face were less sharp. He was River God of the bath.

He put his hands on each side of my face, fingers in my hair, and kissed me. His tongue found mine. He was gentle and full of longing.

"I desire you more than any woman I've ever known or seen."

His words riveted me; they were word-for-word the same as 2500 years ago—or was it only five hours? I couldn't make sense out of this; it made no sense. But he had said those exact words to me before, and then walked away. I wasn't going to let that happen again.

"Okay," I whispered and nodded my head. "Okay."

CHAPTER 7   THE WYNN

Rasheed had a suite at the Wynn, in the tower with private entrance and check-in. We rode the elevator in silence to the top floor. Ceiling-to-floor windows looked out on Trump Tower and the blazing lights of Vegas Valley. Quiet words were exchanged with Gamel and Marcos, and they disappeared.

His arms went around my waist, pulling me back into him.

"They will stay away. I've given orders to be alone," he breathed in my ear.

Hadn't I said the same words to him in my pink marble pool with white lotus blossoms?

He lifted my hair with one hand and held me tight with the other, kissing each vertebra down the back of my neck and between my shoulder blades.

I still had on my heels; my pelvis tilted into his. I felt him grow hard as stone against my hips. His hand moved down from my waist, across my belly, to rest on my mound and push hard on the tip of my womb. His palm cupping me burned hot through the knit of my dress.

I moaned low in my throat. Desire overwhelmed me. I wanted him to stroke me like a cat. I would roll onto my back and give him my belly, my legs spread wide.

His hand traveled down the front of my thigh to the knee and then up to the back of my buttocks. He still kissed the nape of my neck and my shoulders. He let my hair fall, and his hand found my breast. When he touched my nipple through my bra and dress, I cried out.

We stood like that for an eternity, my back to his front, his hands caressing me all over. We swayed back and forth, something primordial coursing through our veins.

He turned me in his arms and kissed me long and deep. I pressed my thighs against his with all my strength. I felt him huge on my belly, an iron post, and put my hand down to fondle him through his pants. It was his time to moan.

Low lights burned in the room; a mirror covered an entire wall, reflecting our silhouettes against the Vegas night sky. I glimpsed a lush king bed through an open double doorway.

He eased the zipper of my dress, the slider inching slowly past each tooth. I unbuckled his belt and unzipped his pants. He slid my dress off my shoulders, and it dropped to my ankles, bundling on top of the shiny red heels. I slipped his trousers down past his hard thighs, and they fell to his polished loafers.

We looked into each other's eyes. We didn't say a word. We didn't even kiss. We wanted no distraction from the unveiling.

I helped him out of his jacket. I loosened his tie and lifted it over his head. His starched shirt was snowy white in the red and black room. I undid every tiny button and unfastened slowly the gold cuff links at his wrists. When the shirt came off, I had my first sight of his bronzed chest and flat belly. No doubt about it, this was River God.

My fingers tugged at the elastic band of his trunks, pulling them down to his knees. Heart pounding and blood rushing all around inside my head, I went to my knees. I could fell his body shaking, every muscle tense and rock hard.

"Do not move," he whispered with his hands on my face, lifting me to my feet, "or I will come. I want more time. I want it to last."

More words from the past. I could no longer distinguish between dreams.

His hands slid around me, undid my bra and eased the straps off my shoulders. He was slow, deliberate, not in a hurry. My breasts were swollen white mounds with blushing halos. He took one in each hand. A sound caught in his throat. His eyes filled with a new light.

I arched my back, begging him silently to take me into his

mouth. I knew that one touch of his moist tongue and I would explode.

Instead, he slid one hand under my panties and between my thighs. He brought back his hand and spread my own wet on my breast.

The first rolling wave of an orgasm washed through my womb. I moaned and moaned louder with each successive surge, swaying on my feet, tumbling in a satin sea. I would have lost my way, if he had not held me fast.

Without hurry, he eased my panties down past the slim garters to join my crumpled dress. I lowered my head to his chest. I didn't know a body so limp could still stand. He held me stable, dragging my clothes away with his foot as I shifted balance from one leg to the other.

I stood naked in black silk stockings, black and red garters, and my red patent shoes.

He kicked his own clothes away and faced me, hands on my hips, pulling me forward, sliding his iron rod between my clasped legs.

Moving in perfect unison, he walked me backward toward the open doorway. We glided as one person to the lush bed. He lowered me, his eyes fixed unblinking on mine.

Like dancers in a waltz, our eyes locked in a spinning room.

He kissed my forehead, then each eyelid, the tip of my nose and then full on the mouth, his lips smothering mine, sucking languidly, his tongue penetrating and unhurried. Lingering long over each kiss, he still took his time.

I was wild to feel him inside me, to fill me, to pound me. But I surrendered on the rich covers of the bed and let him do with me what he willed. He knew every sensitive spot to touch and exactly how much pressure to bear. He knew my secret places and claimed them as his own.

His finger hooked under the elastic of my left garter and slipped it slowly down my leg and over my foot. He rolled the stocking carefully over my knee, along my calf, over my ankle, and past my toes. One kiss on the arch of my foot, and just as slowly, he removed the right garter and then the stocking, ending with his lips on each toe. He kissed the shallow red marks left by each garter, first high on the left thigh, then on the right.

When I first felt his tongue in my secret valley, I relaxed—home again after lifetimes of being lost.

He teased while shocks jolted my body. An electric current pulsed through the soft under-bottom of my buttocks. When he sensed my need unbearable, he pulled himself up the length of my body, and I felt the tip of him at my gate.

I wrapped my arms around his broad back, and at last, he was full inside me. We both exhaled deep at the same moment, a long sigh echoing across eternity.

At first he didn't move. We breathed in and out, together. My vagina pulsed, on fire, swallowing him whole.

Then like a starved beast, he began to devour me. Lust and desire replaced tenderness. Animal sounds escaped from our throats.

A wave crested, and a rapid succession of endless contractions of pure ecstasy rolled through me. His body convulsed, froze, and then shuddered. He collapsed on top of me. I could feel his heart pounding in his chest next to mine.

We slept. I slept. The sky was barely light when he woke me. Rasheed was dressed in a starched white shirt, dark blue suit, and a navy tie with tiny white polka dots. His eyes were shiny bright, glittery like emeralds. I looked up at him in surprise.

He sat on the bed next to me and traced my features with his fingertip as if he were memorizing each one.

"I have to go now."

"But—" I started to interrupt him.

He placed his finger on my lips.

"Sh-h-h-h. Listen to me. There are things I can't tell you. Things you mustn't know. It's better this way."

I stared at him in disbelief. He wanted secrets after last night?

We'd been one body, no division, nothing separating us.

"When will I see you again? I don't know anything about you. I don't have your cell number—or your email." I was in a panic. For a microsecond, I even thought of Facebook.

"I know how to find you." He smiled his secret half-smile, not with the usual amusement, but sweet with longing.

He could walk away though; he had the strength for that. He leaned down and kissed me with such tenderness my heart cracked, again with the same chisel. The pain this time was also the same.

"We have known each other before, Isis, and we will know each other again."

"No-o-o-o!" I cried out.

But he was gone.

Barb called just as I got home to a hungry cat. I put food in Aisha's bowl and turned on the kettle while Barb shouted in my ear.

"Why haven't you called me? I've been worried sick!" She paused, but not long enough for me to answer.

"Are you okay? TALK to me!"

"I'm fine."

"You don't sound fine. What the bloody hell happened last night? I can't believe you went off with that Rasheed guy."

She paused again.

"He didn't hurt you, did he?"

Did breaking my heart count? But I knew what Barb meant.

"No, he didn't…hurt me. He wouldn't do that."

"How do you know? *Mr. Mystery Man with his bodyguards.* He scares me. I'm sorry I got you mixed up with him."

"I'm not."

Silence.

"Are you home?" Then she whispered, "Are you with *him?*"

"He's gone, Barb. Gone."

"Unlikely," she snorted. "Lars told me Rasheed's Coptic. That's some kind of Middle-Easterner; you know how obsessive they can get."

"Trust me. He's not obsessed. He walked right out the door. And don't be sorry about last night. Calling me was exactly the right thing to do. I'm not sure you had any…choice. I'm not sure any of us had any choice."

"Choice? What are you talking about?"

Then she remembered our phone conversation before the Stirling Club.

"You never told me about the mirror. What was that Egypt stuff about?"

"I'll tell you later, Barb. I need to go."

There was no way I could go to work. I called in sick, turned off my cell and sat at my laptop, sipping Assam tea with milk from an old X-Files mug. Aisha crawled into my lap.

'Copt-Wikipedia,' came up in the Google search. I skimmed the religious part explaining that Copts are modern day Egyptian Christians, and then read, "Copts are direct descendants of the Ancient Egyptians."

I looked over at the Red Mirror. I had no idea how any of this was possible, but I was not crazy—or dreaming. I never felt more sober or awake in my life.

Next I googled 'Hathor.' A photo of the goddess in the temple popped up. If it wasn't the same statue, it was close enough. I tried to remember if I'd seen it before, to explain how it appeared in my dream. But I didn't really believe I had dreamed about Egypt.

Rasheed had called me "Isis." I heard him clearly. There was no doubt in my mind. Rasheed was River God, and he knew it, too.

Vegas bookies wouldn't give odds on the chances of our meeting at the Stirling Club. The Universe put River God and I together for a reason, and I didn't intend to leave our path to fate—or the gods. I had the Red Mirror. I was going back.

I curled up in my gray leather chair with Aisha and stared at the mirror, replaying each sight and smell, each change in the room. How did it begin? The cleaning! The transition started with the cleaning, or rather the rubbing. Rubbing was the key. The comparison to Aladdin's lamp was obvious; this was some genie I'd summoned.

I put out extra food for Aisha and filled her box and a plastic dishpan with clean litter. I made sure the lid was up on the toilets. The bottle of oil and the cloth were still beside the mirror.

Metal strips gleamed all around the frame. I rejected trying another strut; I needed to return exactly where I had left. I'm not much of a scientist, but remember from high school chemistry that you have to limit your variables.

Sitting cross-legged on the floor, just like yesterday, except dressed now in sweats, I picked up the cloth. Aisha snuggled against one thigh. She was already familiar with this routine. She liked it; she knew it meant I would stay put for a while. At least, that's how it would seem to her.

CHAPTER 8   THE NILE

It was utterly still except for a hum in my ears. I drifted with no birdsong, no sound of hammer on stone, no rustle of wind through palms. The hum was not constant, but more a repeating subtle rise and crest, a kind of "swoosh," somewhat like the sea trapped in a conch, but without any hint of a roar.

Golden sunshine filtered through saffron drapes. Not even the faintest breath of breeze relieved the heaviness in the air. A light layer of perspiration swelled on my skin.

I sat straight up. Not in my gardens, not in my chambers, not at the Temple, I wasn't anywhere I recognized. The river! The swooshing sound was the current of the Nile as it swirled under and all around me. I had come back, but after we sailed from Thebes. How would I find River God now?

I could easily see through the sheer drapes onto the deck and beyond. Below lay a dozen or more men sleeping under awnings hung for shelter from the fire of the sun. The banks of the Nile were distant bands of green against tall dunes bleached white in the glare.

The boat was long and narrow. My pavilion divided the barge in two with just room for a man to pass on the sides. Both the bow and stern of the ship were carved into bundled papyrus reeds.

Long wooden oars with blades at the ends leaned against the low railings. Only the steersman at the massive pole-like rudder was awake. A blue-and-green winged cobra covered a square sail, lifeless now in the afternoon doldrums.

Bodies stirred in the corner nearby. Young women lay on mats, very close to each other. I counted four from my household, plus me, all in this small cabin filled with chests. The voyage was going to be even longer than I imagined.

"Does Isenkhebe Nefrusobek require my attention?"

The old priest Qeb-ha stood just outside; only the filmy weave of the drapes separated us. The last thing I wanted was the attention of an old, useless eunuch—useless at least to me.

"Qeb-ha, how far do you judge we have sailed?"

My real question was how much longer before I could get back to Thebes and River God.

"We will be at Abydos by Ra's entry into the Underworld, Isenkhebe. The Gods favor mooring there for the night."

"Would the Goddess not prefer we hasten? We might sail through the night to shorten our journey."

Qeb-ha straightened his shoulders to make himself taller, but his belly still hung over the top of his long skirt. Tiny drops of perspiration dotted the smooth scalp of his brown head.

"Isenkhebe is aware the Gods do not favor travel on the great river by night. Set sends evil into the world under the cloak of darkness. Hathor requires patience from us."

I guess he could see that I wasn't convinced—maybe he read my mind—because he went on.

"We must weigh our actions on the Great Balance; the Balance determines the Right Measure for all things."

His high voice deepened ever so slightly.

"A wind that is greater than its Right Measure, wrecks ships."

He had a great talent for finding the perfect saying. He knew I wouldn't risk a shipwreck.

"As always, Qeb-ha, I am humbled by your profound knowledge of the will of the Gods."

I was about to return to my divan when I saw Goliath over Qeb-ha's bowed head.

He was rising from the afternoon sleep; his skin shone like polished ebony. The muscles across his shoulders rippled as he adjusted his kilt and white headdress. His legs were twice as long as Qeb-ha's and powerful enough to break the eunuch's neck with one squeeze.

The pleasure from my River God was great beyond compare, but yesterday's drunkenness does not quench today's thirst.

"Qeb-ha." I tore my eyes away from the Nubian. "When we moor for the night, I wish to bathe in the Nile. The day has been long and hot."

Qeb-ha stepped quickly forward to the curtain.

"Isenkhebe Nefrusobek is aware that the God Set waits in the shadows for the innocent to lose their way."

"I shall take the Nubian for protection. He looks as if he could battle Set Himself and emerge the victor. Please arrange it."

"As Isenkhebe Nefrusobek desires."

But he couldn't resist a parting shot.

"It is in women that good fortune and bad fortune are upon the earth," he grumbled just loud enough for me to hear.

The afternoon faded into long shadows. I nibbled dates and pomegranates and drank watered sweet wine. Pehtes purred in my lap while I played endless games of *senet* with my ladies, throwing sticks and moving pieces around the safe and danger squares. The Sun God Re was low on the horizon when we pulled into the port of Abydos.

The city lay at the end of a canal from the Nile; I hadn't expected such a crowd at the riverfront. Boats of every size moored at the long stone quay. Sweaty dockers swarmed the wharfs like a colony of ants. Small fishing canoes made of bundles of papyrus cruised up and down the river, hawking tilapia and perch from the Nile. Qeb-ha was busy dickering over price. He needed several baskets of today's catch to feed the crew.

Everywhere I looked I saw clusters of merchants trading mountains of Egyptian grain for ivory tusks from Sudan or earthen jars filled with oils and wine from Cyprus. I saw no place I could hide in the rushes with the Nubian.

The moon had just risen when Qeb-ha came to the edge of my

pavilion. The night was absolutely still without a breath of moving air. Insects buzzed outside the netting around my bed. The reed curtains were lowered, and I was reading a papyrus scroll by the low light of an oil lamp. We had returned from a bathhouse near the docks only moments before. It was not the bath of my daydreams, but the perfumed water soothed my frayed nerves and calmed my fire.

"May I enter, Isenkhebe Nefrusobek?" Qeb-ha's high-pitched voice pierced my resting ears.

What could I do?

I nodded to my ladies, and they disappeared into the night.

"Isenkhebe is reading. May I inquire what?"

"I am studying the course of the river to Saïs and the cities along the way."

According to the map, we had sailed one, maybe two days to the north of Thebes. One or two days from River God.

"Yes, most wise. Sit-hathor would be pleased to see that Isenkhebe is using her time well."

"Better than at the river with a Nubian?"

If I shocked him, he didn't give me the pleasure of showing it.

"I am certain Isenkhebe's mother would advise her to enjoy herself with whom she wishes, as long as no fool joins her."

"Would that be me, or he who joins me, who would be the fool? Or would being with a fool, make one of me?"

He was not the only one who could talk in riddles, but he didn't rise to the bait and only shrugged his stooped shoulders, folding his hands neatly in his lap.

The air was milder now, pleasantly warm. My skin was cool and dry. A soft caftan folded along the curves of my body. The silver tassels in my short wig matched the thin bracelets around my ankles. I wondered if I could find a hidden corner of our narrow ship to pleasure myself with Goliath.

"We leave tomorrow morning for Khent-min, Isenkhebe."

"Khent-min? Why do we stop there? It is only a half-day's sail."

Qeb-ha only shrugged. He could be maddening. Seated across from me, with his legs crossed and his placid, enigmatic face, he was a Buddha with Egyptian *kohl*-lined eyes. Who knew what was really going on in his head. I think he enjoyed keeping me in the dark.

"Does it have something to do with my father?"

"Everything has to do with Isenkhebe's father. He is an Oracle, a God."

Qeb-ha didn't treat me as half-divine, but as half-idiot. But others must believe Sit-hathor's about story about her pure womb as well. No wonder people bowed wherever I went.

"What has happened, that after being absent all my life, he wishes to see me now?"

"He has not been entirely absent. He has chosen your tutors and insisted you were well-schooled in both mathematics and languages."

"And my life in the Temple? Who chose that?"

"The Gods choose our paths when we come from the womb."

The same words as River God. Surely not all Egyptians blindly follow the gods. Surely some at least question the messengers.

"You have not said why he sent for me."

"It is complicated, as are all matters of the gods."

"Explain it to me."

"The time is not yet ripe."

"How can time ripen? What does that mean?"

"Isenkhebe is a woman of no patience. She would hurry the moon to rise, so that it might set again. What of savoring the moonbeam that ripples on the black river?"

"There are many things that I savor, Qeb-ha. A mystery mission is not one."

"Isenkhebe will know all in good time. Until then, face the challenge of each day with fresh eyes. Live each day to its fullest. By completing the sunrise and sunset in Right Measure, one arrives safely at his goal."

I stared at him from under half-closed lids. I would get nothing more from Qeb-ha tonight.

Small waves lapped against the hull and the stone quays. Night birds called out and were answered. I heard the oarsmen playing *senet*. They gambled as usual, their voices animated and loud. The decks of other ships were also alive with raucous laughter and shouting; heat-weary men relaxed in the cool of the night.

"We must play *senet*, Qeb-ha; I would enjoy a meeting of minds on that battleground."

"It is in battle that a man finds a brother—or sister. It is on the road that a man finds a companion. It is my wish for both."

He seemed perfectly at ease with me. I was certain he couldn't probe deeper than the Isis who sat before him. His face was plump and remarkably unlined for his age. Did the lack of male hormones make him look younger the way it made his voice falsetto? The fat of his belly lay in rolls. His breasts were as generous as some women's.

Why wasn't Goliath with his glossy taut skin stretched over bulging muscles sitting next to me instead of this puffy old man?

"I am who I am, not by my own choosing," he said without a sound passing his lips. *"Man, even a godly man, cannot alter the life the Gods assign him."*

He had read my thoughts. My face went hot. I busied myself with a sip of wine, avoiding his eyes. Isis was a prejudiced bitch at times. Qeb-ha couldn't help being a eunuch. I'm sure he hadn't chosen to be castrated any more than I'd chosen to service the powerful in Hathor's Inner Sanctum.

"Good night, Isenkhebe Nefrusobek." He spoke out loud this time. "All good fortune is from the hand of the Gods. May the Goddess protect and bring sweet dreams."

And then he moved clumsily through the break in the reed curtains. I was left alone with my own idea of sweet dreams.

CHAPTER 9   WIZARD

The wind blew hot against my scorched skin; sweat evaporated into the dry brittle air before it could form beads. My parched throat burned; I was blinded by the glare of a golden disk filling the silver sky.

A cobra slithered into my path and raised his hooded head to glare into my eyes. His back curved in an S; his tail coiled upward. His forked tongue flicked my cheek. Clear drops of venom oozed from the spiky tips of two fangs. I tried to scream, but as wide as I opened my mouth, no sound came. It was a silent world.

With wings spread wide, a vulture swooped down, seized the cobra in razor-sharp talons, and carried him off in a cloud of red dust that blocked the sun.

When the swirling dust settled, a white-haired man in a blue gown with shining stars stood a stone's throw away. He raised a silver sword above his head; the rays of the sun exploded off the tip in a bright burst of white light. In his other arm, he cradled a rectangular green slab, engraved with words I couldn't read, no matter how hard I tried. I knew that I should follow him, but when I took my first steps, he was there and then he was not. I was alone again in a vast empty space. I was alone in the Universe.

The earth cracked; a massive gash yawned and green water rushed forth. A lake began to rise and rise, filling the whole desert until it reached my knees, then my thighs, and then my waist.

I struggled to wake up, but couldn't. I was trapped. Was I to drown in the High Desert? Could someone drown in a dream?

My mouth moved; my lips formed the prayer, *Hathor, my mistress, Gold-of-the-Gods, do not desert me!* But no sound came. It was still a silent world.

A falcon landed on my shoulder, and Hathor spoke in my ear.

"How do you expect to understand what is going on up in the sky, if you do not even see what is at your feet?"

I looked down; a hippo swam by my legs. I grabbed hold of her ears with both hands and pulled my body onto her back. The hippo turned her massive head with huge liquid eyes and whispered, "I am Hathor, my beloved Isis. Why do you not trust me to carry you to your fate?"

"Isenkhebe Nefrusobek! Come back to us!"

The only water was under the boat. There was no hippo, only the frightened face of Maia on her knees beside my bed. She was in her sleeping gown. Her head was bare, and her scalp glowed in the light of the clay lamp she held in her hand. There were no lines of *kohl* around her eyes. She was pale and looked scared, almost panicked. The others, sitting up on their mats in the corner, stared at me. They looked scared, too.

"My mistress was in the Land of Dreams. I feared she would not return. I called and called, but Isenkhebe Nefrusobek was too far away to heed my cries."

"May I enter?" Qeb-ha asked anxiously from outside the curtains.

I nodded numbly to Maia, who opened the slit in the reeds.

Qeb-ha rushed to my side. He took my wrist and placed his fingers on the pulse. My heart was pounding like a gazelle hunted by Berber dogs. Qeb-ha looked carefully into my eyes, seeming to reassure himself that I had returned.

His concern was so great, I wondered if some never came back from the Land of Dreams.

"Hathor was with me in the desert—" I started to explain.

"Do not speak of it. Words could summon the dream world to the real world."

"The Goddess was trying to tell me something, Qeb-ha, but she spoke in riddles."

"The dream could be a warning. The Gods created the dream to show the dreamer his blindness. A blind man will stumble on any path, even well-paved. How can he hope to navigate a road fraught with danger?"

Now that I was awake, the dream was fragmenting into vague bits of memory, pieces of a puzzle I hurried to assemble before they disappeared.

I called for papyrus and ink and began frantically writing down the images, struggling to recall the right sequence, but the details slipped away faster than I could write. I felt desperate to record the dream before it was lost.

No one spoke. They watched me as I wrote. They seemed frightened by my intensity. I don't think they were convinced I had completely returned. Or perhaps I had come back a different person.

Qeb-ha didn't leave until I finished. Maia brought me a cup of watered wine. I drank with great thirst in huge gulps, and lay back exhausted. I felt cold, then hot, then cold again.

Pehtes pushed her wet nose onto my cheek and kissed me with her dry, scratchy tongue. If I had been away in the Land of Dreams, she didn't know it. How simple life must be to a cat. How simple life used to be for me.

CHAPTER 10 TEMPLE OF MIN

Screaming baboons in a nearby sycamore grove awakened us before daybreak. Wood smoke blended with the morning mist; the sleeping jetty came alive. Workers hurried to make the most of the day before the heat rose. Our crew finished the rest of last night's broiled fish, drank beer, and ate beans with cone-shaped loaves of bread before casting off for Khent-min.

The winged-cobra sail unfurled against a fiery dawn sky and our barge began the next day of our journey. Marshy reeds and low desert lay on the West Bank. Low cliffs edged the East. Oars rising and falling, the rowers sang a rhyme that kept them in beat as the shore moved swiftly past.

The day turned breathless; there was no wind at all, unusual for the river at this time of year. Luckily, we headed north, downstream. The rowers pulled on their oars, and even with the winged-cobra sail slack against the mast, the current carried us steadily to Khent-min.

When we arrived at the port, a thick dust cloud hung over the city. The sound of the banging and clanging of stone construction carried as far as the docks.

"There are many wondrous sights in the great city of Min. May I suggest Isenkhebe visit the old temple of Ramses the Great with her ladies? The Pharaoh has ordered its complete renovation."

I was tired of our cramped cabin, and my ladies were more than eager to leave the barge. I agreed to visit The White Queen, a limestone colossus of Ramses' daughter-wife carved eight centuries before.

My ladies put on their best wigs, dyed their lips red with pomegranate juice, and painted thick lines of *kohl* around their eyes. I wore a simple linen gown covered with a beaded, fishnet tunic and a shoulder-length wig plaited with yellow silk tassels and doused with gardenia essence.

As always, Goliath accompanied me and chose two crewman, Ti and Wah, to guard my ladies. Women of rank don't go about the streets on their own.

We didn't stay long at the courtyard of the White Queen. It was noisy and dusty. Scores of workmen in stained loincloths and filthy headdresses hammered and plastered without pause.

"Please, Mistress," my ladies begged. "May we go to the market? They say Khent-min weaves the finest linen in the world."

The mammoth market square was as chaotic as the construction site. I decided Khent-min was a harsh place with no redeeming features.

A caravan from the Red Sea had just arrived with a shipment of rare spices from the East. The mob surged and was pushed back by a bearded man with a whip. He wore a bright blue turban loosely coiled on his head; I'm sure he'd slept in it for days.

In the southeast corner of the market was a slaughteryard. The stench of blood and urine mingled with dust and the pungent scent of incense wood. A tall Nubian slit the throats of one goat after another. With each slash, bright blood sprayed his chest and arms.

His nude body dripped in blood. Smelling the scent of death, terrified goats bleated, oxen bellowed and horses screamed. The air was filled with horrible sounds of animals dying. A panicked bull dragged four Nubian slaves to their knees.

At the center of the chaos sparkled tall mounds of glittering Sinai salt and snowy natron used in mummification. Around the perimeter of the white piles clumped makeshift stalls displaying linen, stone carvings and polished turquoise, carnelian and garnet beads strung into long ropes.

Vendors roasted nuts and grilled brochettes of goat meat. Clouds of flies swarmed the small, skinny boys hawking barley cakes sweetened with honey.

"Would the priestess care to trade a blessing for a fine statue of the God Min?"

The sculpture vendor gave me lewd smile showing black teeth. His hungry eyes didn't hide his lust. They travelled from my breasts to my ankles and up again before meeting my eyes.

"Give me that small basalt statue," I told him with a knowing smile. "And I shall bless you with a faience crocodile charm to make your Min rise. Let us pray one is enough."

He laughed. Even more black teeth showed.

The Min statue fit neatly in my palm. I stroked the smooth, glossy stone with my index finger. Jet black and naked, the city's patron god held a flail in his right hand and an erect penis in his left.

"The priestess has her own Min, I see," remarked the vendor with a smirk. He nodded his head in the direction of Goliath.

"If the Nubian is the lady's taste, she can find more like him at the Temple."

"Return to the ship in one hour," I ordered Ti and Wah.

I gave each of my ladies a handful of faience hippo, frog, crocodile and scarab amulets.

"Be careful," I cautioned, "to trade only for the best."

It was not difficult to find the Temple of Min. A wide, crowded street lined with billboard-sized paintings of Min with his sacred erection led straight to the pylon.

The Temple was eerily quiet after the din of the city—and dark. Long shafts of dust-filled sunbeams angled to a polished stone floor. Vast murals covered the walls. Most depicted the giant-phallused Min seated at a banquet table piled high with *cos* lettuce oozing white milk from its tall leaves. White bulls and barbed arrows covered a forest of square columns.

No one tried to stop me from entering the inner sanctum. Such a thing would be impossible in a Hathor Temple. Only the very highest rank of the cult is allowed inside the *naos*. But if the handful of Min priests busying themselves with offerings objected to my presence, they didn't show it.

A nine-foot statue of Min carved from a single block of black basalt towered over me; the Fertility God's phallus was as long as a man's arm and thick as a log.

Kneeling at the white marble altar, I placed a garland of lotus blossoms at Min's massive feet and sang a hymn of praise.

Min, Bull of the Great Phallus
You are the Great Male, the owner of all females.
The Bull who is united with those of the sweet love,
of beautiful face and of painted eyes,
The goddesses are glad, seeing your perfection.

The room was hot and the air thick with frankincense, but not thick enough to mask the smell of sex. Two priests in a trance ejaculated into silver bowls like the dozens already at Min's feet.

The worship of Min must take many enticing forms, the best hidden in secret sanctuaries, behind closed golden doors.

I wandered down a narrow corridor, lit by torches in niches peopled by basalt Mins with erect members. Goliath was never more than a step or two away. If I didn't stumble on an obliging priest, then I would find a private corner and measure the Nubian against the new standards set by these black statues.

We turned a sharp corner that dead-ended in a closed wooden door decorated with brass studs. I heard lyre and pipe music on the other side, and the sound of chanting. These voices were deep, not at all like the high-pitched chorus in Hathor's Temple. I quietly lifted the latch and eased the heavy door open a crack.

A dozen men or more, all nude, engaged in the worship of the almighty phallus. One bent over, a penis in his mouth, while a third penetrated him from behind. Another man penetrated the second and so on, forming a complicated endless knot of copulating men, who at the same time performed *fellatio*.

A low dais dominated the end of the small chamber; two men sat in low chairs. I recognized them at once as the Crown Prince and the Scribe who had shared me in Hathor's Temple. The Prince, his face in a trance, was being serviced by two pubescent boys. A thick wreath of lotus blossoms draped his nude chest.

The Scribe lounged in a chair of carved phalluses with a young child not more than ten between his legs. Their depravity had certainly not been cured by our ritual in Hathor's Inner Sanctum. The man moved the boy's head back and forth with his hand.

Maybe it was my thought of the Goddess that disturbed his psyche. I'm certain I didn't make a sound. But the Scribe suddenly looked straight at me. His eyes widened and he sat up, pushing the boy away. His evil rushed at me like a thousand buzzing hornets.

I shoved the door shut with my shoulder, leaning into it for just a moment to stop shaking. Heart pounding, palms sweating, I turned to Goliath to motion for us to get out, but it was not the Nubian who stood behind me. The metallic insignia of the Royal Guard flashed in the torchlight.

A hand went over my mouth; another grabbed my upper arm, dragging me around the corner and pushing me through an open doorway. There were no windows and no lighted lamps. It was black as the darkest night. The flicker of torches cast dancing shadows in the hallway outside.

I struggled to free my arm, but the weight of the soldier's body crushed me to the wall. Sobbing from terror, I tried to bite the hand on my mouth.

"Stop, Isis," the voice commanded in my ear. "This is no time for your foolishness."

O Hathor, I worship at Your feet for the gift You have brought me!
I looked into the face of River God.

"Say nothing, Isis," he urged. "Nothing at all."

I nodded, and he released his hand from my mouth. My whole body trembled so violently, I'm not sure I could have stood if he hadn't held me up against the wall. Instead of sobbing from terror, I burst into tears of relief.

"Sh-h-h! Listen to me carefully. I do not know what madness has brought you here, but the Scribe Setne is a dangerous man—capable of any evil. You must leave now. No hesitation. Now!"

I couldn't quite believe it was River God. He felt real enough. His scent was real enough. I touched his jaw and then traced his lips with my fingertip.

"But I thought you were in Thebes," I whispered.

"The Crown Prince is under my protection. We return to the Pharaoh in Saïs."

I heard the words but was only aware of his heat. I kissed the base of his throat, above his leather chest armor. He tasted of sweat and myrrh. I put my hands on the back of his head and lifted my face to his.

I could feel him hardening in spite of the tension. Our bodies were so taut that one flick of a finger would shatter us into a million shards. I was fragile as glass.

My life force flowed into him; I couldn't tell where he ended, and I began. His hard lips yielded; he was as tender as the night he held me at the Paris, as tender as the night at the Wynn.

Our need for each other bound us so tight, we might have been shackled in chains. But he had the strength to break away.

"Go! You were never here. Do you understand? You were never here."

He released me from the wall, took my arm more gently, and steered me down a new corridor, Goliath on our heels. I heard a voice in the distance calling out, "Guard!"

Bright sunlight blinded me when he pulled open a small red door in the rough stone wall. It was a tiny side street, not more than four feet wide.

"Do not speak of what you have seen to anyone, Isis. Do you hear me? Anyone."

He didn't follow us into the alley but closed the door without a word of goodbye.

O Hathor! River God and I traveled the same river. We both sailed to Saïs. The Universe wanted us together. My feet didn't touch the pavement all the way to the boat.

Qeb-ha had returned to the barge and was frantic with worry when he saw the ladies had returned without me. I didn't try to hide my thoughts from him. Two powerful forces had revealed themselves to me in the Temple of Min. I was both terrified and euphoric.

The evil of the Scribe had enveloped him in a black cloud of pestilence. I saw it from across the room, even in the dim light. But my River God loved me. O Hathor! He loved me. I could still smell his desire and need on my skin. His taste, honey-sweet, lingered on my lips.

"I think we should set sail, Qeb-ha. I do believe the Gods would approve."

To my surprise, Qeb-ha didn't reprimand me with a lecture on the dangers of Set in the night. He stood very still; I could feel him probing my mind. I didn't try to block him.

He studied the banners of the royal barge moored but a few hundred yards away.

"Yes, the moon is full, the river broad," he said at last. "There can be greater dangers than the peril of Set the Destroyer. I shall ask the Gods to forgive our arrogance that we sail tonight."

I finally noticed the young man by his side, dressed in the manner of the Canaanites, heavily robed even in this heat. He had the eyes of a gazelle, soft brown with long lashes; his luxuriant reddish-brown hair fell to his shoulders in tangled waves. He was wide-eyed. I must have looked a sight.

"This is Eben, Isenkhebe Nefrusobek. He will travel with us."

I had nothing to say about that. Too much had happened this day for me to question why this stranger would join us now. I knew that with Qeb-ha, there was a reason. I knew that with Qeb-ha, I wouldn't know until he was ready to tell me.

"You are welcome," I said simply, still in a daze.

I turned and entered my cabin, ordering the reed curtains lowered, closing out the sights of Khent-min. My heart told me to get away—and get away fast.

CHAPTER 11   THE FEAST

Time on the river stood still. Lone fishermen balanced in their shallow papyrus canoes and cast their nets onto the glassy Nile. We flowed past verdant fields more like clusters of gardens than farms. Laborers toiled naked in the hot sun, repairing the irrigation canals after the yearly Inundation.

I kept looking behind us, expecting to see a sail emblazoned with the Shield and Crossed Arrows of the Saite Dynasty, but there was no sign of the royal barge.

The boy Qeb-ha introduced as Eben was reading in the shade of a striped awning. Qeb-ha sat on cushions not far away, back straight with legs folded under him. A servant waved a palmiform fan to move the still air.

When I asked Eben where he came from, he told me Jerusalem and before that Babylon. I gave him a languid smile, slightly seductive, but not promising anything and switched to Aramaic, the language of the East.

"Your Egyptian is excellent, Eben."

Qeb-ha frowned; he didn't speak Aramaic. I supposed he still could read our minds.

"I have family, my Lady," Eben answered shyly. "In the Jewish colony in Elephantine."

He seemed reluctant to look on my face, and more reluctant still to meet my eyes. I don't think he had many conversations with women.

"What other languages do you speak, Eben?"

"I have studied Elamite and Greek, and of course, Hebrew."

"You speak Elamite? Is it not spoken only among nobles at the Persian court of Cambyses?"

"I trained as a scribe, my lady."

I flirted just a little, more playful than serious. Qeb-ha's eyes bored into me, but I chose to ignore him. Had he not told me that I should live each day to the fullest?

"If you were in Babylon, Eben, you must also have studied the stars."

"My father says that to study the constitution of the sky helps one understand the constitution of the earth. And if one understands the earth, he might, just might, learn something of the constitution of men."

The veins on the back of his hand were purplish-blue. His long waves of uncombed hair didn't hide the dark vein throbbing in his temple. A constellation of blemishes dotted his cheeks. A few scraggly hairs tried to form a beard.

I smiled at him a bit too warmly, eliciting another deep blush.

"Why do you travel with us, Eben?'

"It is for Qeb-ha to say. I am but a guest."

Qeb-ha and his secrets. He trusted me with almost nothing.

"You have done well, Qeb-ha," I said, switching back to Egyptian, "to include a young man of such education in our group."

Qeb-ha's eyes in his round face barely changed. The amethyst sparkled as it swayed back and forth. He looked at me, then at Eben and then back again to me.

The next hours passed with conversation about foreign lands and strange customs. Eben and I bantered back and forth in Greek, Aramaic and even the elusive Elamite.

He sang beautiful psalms in the lilting Hebrew of his tribe. He strummed the four strings of his lyre. The shadows grew long, and the air cooled. Having rowed through last night, we would stop for this one.

Re sank below the cliffs on the far bank. The sound of animals hunting and being hunted carried across the dark water. Camouflaged in the mud, great crocodiles lay in waiting, their eyes hooded and long thick bodies perfectly still. A herd of hippos upstream growled and thrashed about; they could turn ugly and lethal in an instant. An angry bull could crush a fisherman's bones between his massive jaws with one snap. Our crew would sleep on the boat.

The cook prepared the evening meal on small open clay stoves. The crew ate their regular diet of broiled perch, onions and beer. My ladies and I dined on salted oxen leg and cold roasted duck with cucumbers and goat cheese, dates, and watered wine. Of course, everyone ate bread, always bread.

Qeb-ha sat to one side and didn't join the idle conversation. Instead of his usual placid expression, his face was lined with worry.

"What do you fear, Qeb-ha?" I asked. "What do you see?"

"I see Isenkhebe is no stranger to trouble."

"But surely you can read my heart and see that it is pure."

"One cannot know the heart of a woman any more than one can know the sky," he grumbled.

"Do you truly fear what I might do? What of your pledge to be companions on the road and brother and sister in battle?"

"Isenkhebe is a reckless woman of little patience. That gives me much to fear."

The whites of his eyes gleamed in the starlight; his amethyst was only a tiny glint in the dark.

"Can I not convince you, Qeb-ha, that my faults lie only in small things?"

"Small things are also worthy of respect, Isenkhebe. The little bee brings honey. The little locust destroys the grapevine."

"It is a wonder I was chosen by the Goddess, if so unfit."

Qeb-ha for once had no response. Poor Eben seemed to shrink inside his heavy robe; our words were too personal for a stranger to hear. I'm sure he wanted to melt into the thick mist surrounding the barge.

Millions of jewel-colored stars twinkled in the vast inky sky. Restless hippos rumbled in the rushes not far away. Our crew slept, exhausted after so many hours of rowing.

The desert was black, no lights anywhere, on either side of the river. *Meskhetiu,* the Ox Foreleg constellation, pointed to the unchanging Star of the North. Legend told that Horus the god tore off the leg of the evil Set and hurled it into the heavens to guide travelers through Set's Land of Chaos—the desert.

Suddenly, Eben's pure voice rang out.

As you smile for us you light the Two Lands,
All of Egypt is filled with your presence;
Gods and men look to you,
No evil befalls them when you shine.
The sky with all its stars is dimmed by your beauty;
Lovely lady floating on the Nile, when a beggar beholds you,
he forgets his hunger.

As soundless as a shadow, Qeb-ha slipped away without his usual words of benediction. After Eben's psalm of devotion, he must find me more dangerous than ever.

"I am not worthy of your praise, Eben, but I am moved."

I kissed him gently on his cheek; his skin was warm to my cool lips. Hairs from his beard tickled my nose. The rose scent of my oils hovered around me in a heady cloud of sweetness and femininity.

I felt him tremble.

Sweet Eben would have to be content with that. He was too young and too delicate for a woman like me.

Four colossal stone baboons greeted us at the waterfront of Hermopolis, city of Thoth, God of the Moon and Healing. Their massive manes framed enormous muzzles under huge eyes staring over the port and across the Nile to the barren East Bank. On the West Bank, endless fields of golden wheat grew right up to the fifty-foot thick city walls.

Tall obelisks stood just outside the Gate of the Sphinx at the Pylon of Ramses the Great. When Ramses the Builder needed materials for the grand entrance, he ordered over a thousand decorated stones floated from Armana, the once glorious capital of the Pharaoh Akhenaton, heretic and believer in one god. A succession of pharaohs over the centuries had expanded Thoth's temple complex, slowly dismantling Armana to build mighty Hermopolis.

We docked south of the commercial district at a vast yacht harbor for luxury barges. Hermopolis was known not only as a center for great learning, but also great wealth.

Qeb-ha came to me with an invitation to a banquet on the west side of the city where merchant princes competed to build the most splendid palace. My ladies emptied the clothing chests to find exactly the right gown. The exquisite gossamer linen clung to my body like film. My skin, oiled and perfumed, had the sheen of a moonstone. Both my shaved mound and my nipples were stained dark red.

In honor of the city's patron god Thoth, I chose an amethyst and garnet necklace with dangling gold baboon charms. The intricate cloisonné design on my hinged armbands showed a bare-breasted Hathor surrounded by graceful nude dancers. The lapis lazuli ring, identical to Sit-hathor's, gleamed from my right hand.

More gemstones strung on gold threads twinkled in the glossy waves of a black wig. Turquoise stones decorated sandals too fragile for walking.

Maia outlined my eyes with thick lines of *kohl* and painted ground mica and malachite on my lids up to my brows. Accented by jet black bangs, my eyes glittered a startling green.

She drenched my body and wig in oil of gardenia. We held nothing back. Even those who saw me every day turned to stare.

I granted Maia permission to attend her first feast and loaned her a magnificent beaded collar of semi-precious stones with matching earrings. Her face glowed in excitement; she held her head high. Many eyes followed her, hungry for more.

Muscular Nubians, poles lifted to their massive shoulders, carried us in one-person litters hung with silver bells and colored tassels. The townspeople stopped and bowed low as we passed along wide avenues lined with shade trees and lavish mansions painted with murals of hunting scenes.

The feast surpassed all expectation. We gathered under the stars in a fountain courtyard surrounded by lotiform pillars with elaborate capitals painted in jewel greens and blue. Tall ceramic lamps cast star patterns. Nightingales in gold cages sang out to each other.

A naked servant girl with cobra tattoos around her nipples greeted us with garlands of cornflowers and olive leaves. We followed her to the head table flanked by low cedar chairs padded with yellow linen cushions embroidered with blue ankhs.

Qeb-ha was well-respected in this house. Our host Ankh-hor embraced him warmly and seated him at his right, with me on his left. He had a wide, ready smile that showed two missing teeth. His gold armbands looked too heavy for him to raise his chalice to drink. A broad pectoral of lapis lazuli and turquoise beads woven with filaments of gold covered his chest.

Musicians with finger cymbals, harps, and wooden pipes played from under a wide trellis dripping in white jasmine. Nude girls danced among the tables; gold chains hung round their slender hips and ankles, and gold serpents twisted around their upper arms. They wore elaborate wigs with tiny silver bells that tinkled as seductively as a *sistrum* when they dipped and swayed.

Hundreds of small lanterns cast a flattering light, but not bright enough to dim the night sky. The waning moon had just risen. A gentle breeze scattered the petals of myrtle trees growing in glazed pots. Purple snow flurries drifted to polished stone and floated on small rectangular pools of still water.

Ankh-hor, a high nobleman, spared no expense. Dozens of servants carried one golden tray of delicacies after another. First came ostrich and duck eggs, cucumbers and *cos* lettuce. We nibbled on olives from Cyprus and mounds of fresh cheese made from sweet goat milk. There were baked swans stuffed with smaller birds dressed with chopped dates, almonds and cracked wheat. Cranes fattened on grain pellets had been roasted in goose fat with sycamore figs.

Most treasured of all, and highlight of the evening, was roasted wild game seasoned with rosemary or cumin and garlic. Only the hunt could put ibex, gazelle and aardvark on the table.

I praised our host Ankh-hor for his generosity and exquisite taste.

"I cannot get my fill of the wild game, Ankh-hor. I relish the savage taste of the beast who has fed in the desert. The very air with its raw, heavy scent is captured in the meat."

"Then you shall hunt tomorrow, my priestess. It is my gift to you."

"Is that not exciting, Qeb-ha? I am invited to a hunt! May I tempt you to join us?"

I felt beautiful and powerful, not the woman Qeb-ha criticized. I had drunk too much wine, but in truth, I was more intoxicated by my own charms than by the grape.

Qeb-ha glared at me and squeaked something about 'duties.'

"Come, Qeb-ha my dear friend, do not be such an old man!" Ankh-hor put his arm around Qeb-ha's shoulder as one would when teasing a brother.

"A beauty like Isenkhebe Nefrusobek deserves to be spoiled. I shall send my son. The only thing he loves more than a beautiful woman is a hunt."

Qeb-ha waited for me to decline the invitation. I was delighted to see that Ankh-hor wouldn't take no for answer.

"You cannot refuse me, old friend. Would you deny me the promise of a thousandfold return on my gift at a feast?"

A guest could no more deny the wishes of his host than a host could refuse a guest. Qeb-ha's eyes pierced me like barbed arrows. I refused to look at him. He tried to speak to my mind, but I pushed his silent words from my head.

I was sick of the boat. I was sick of the river. I had not had a man in days. I could at least have a day of hunt.

I saw myself riding in a fast chariot, bouncing over the desert stones under a cloudless sky, hooves thundering on the hard ground with the power of the horses vibrating along the shaft and up through my loins to thrill me.

A fuming Qeb-ha didn't speak all the way back to the barge. I didn't need telepathy to know his thoughts. My ladies were undressing me when he slipped inside the curtains. He didn't ask permission to enter.

"Do not go on this hunt, Isenkhebe Nefrusobek."

"But I have accepted the invitation, Qeb-ha. What excuse could I give?"

"Say you are ill. Say anything, but do not go." In his fury, he addressed me directly, as an equal.

"It is you, Qeb-ha, who constantly remind me of my irresponsible behavior. Am I now to change my mind on a whim, and then lie?"

"What of our sacred mission?" His squeak was so high I thought his voice was going to crack.

"There is small risk in one hunt, Qeb-ha. I do not ask that we delay our voyage."

"A high-priestess should not hunt; a high-priestess should not kill. How dare you take this risk, when there is so much at stake? You disgrace your mother with your selfishness and arrogance!"

I'd never seen Qeb-ha angry. My ladies stood to the side with their eyes cast down. No one moved. No one breathed.

I deserved this hunt and a day of freedom. Still, Qeb-ha's disapproval weighed heavy on me. He saw things no one else saw.

"The Nubian will be at my side," I argued. "Ankh-hor's son will lead the way. There is nothing to fear. The Goddess has chosen me. You said so yourself. She will protect me."

Qeb-ha clenched and unclenched his fists. Would he strike me? That seemed impossible, but I had a small doubt. He turned abruptly and pushed through the curtains. The flames in the lamps flickered as his stubby body stormed past.

I knew he was right. I don't know why I wouldn't admit it.

When I travelled to the Land of Dreams I met a lion. He appeared from a raging wall of sand. Thick ropes of saliva oozed from his black gums. The spray from his roar showered me and the foul odor of decaying meat filled my breath. I gagged and closed my eyes, waiting for sharp teeth to tear out my throat.

Nothing happened; the world was still. Even the wind calmed. Then Hathor the falcon was on my shoulder, speaking into my ear, but no matter how hard I tried, I couldn't understand what she said.

CHAPTER 12   THE HUNT

Maia awakened me long before Re began to glow on the horizon.
I slipped into a plain linen shift, looser than my normal gowns
and not sheer at all. Wide sleeves covered my arms to the elbows.
My sturdy sandals had only the slightest decoration. The lions
tooled on the insoles said I vanquished the wild forces of the
desert. I pushed the lion dream from my mind.

I chose a simple gold chain necklace with small gold charms in
the shape of crocodiles, vultures and rabbits. I would be aggressive
like the crocodile, abundant as a rabbi and protected by the vulture.
Gold hoops with single amethyst teardrops went in my earlobes.
The brilliant purple would ward off evil spirits.

The stones reminded me of Qeb-ha's amethyst ear drop, but
I resisted all thought of him and his disapproval. *A high-priestess
should not hunt; a high-priestess should not kill.* There were many
things I did that a high-priestess shouldn't do. The plans of a god
are one thing; the thoughts of men are another.

Maia insisted I hang her Hathor *tiet* charm on my golden
chain girdle.

"Hathor will protect Isenkhebe Nefrusobek from all evil," she
said.

The protective *tiet* amulet dangled on my thigh. Butterflies
swarmed in my stomach. The old priest unnerved me more than
I wanted to admit, but I wouldn't let him win. As extra protection,
I slipped the precious Hathor lapis lazuli ring with golden horns
on my right middle finger.

At last, Maia brought my custom-made bow and quiver of
arrows and my hunting knife with encrusted hilt of ankh signs
crafted of semi-precious stones. The steel blade was sharper than
a razor.

I was ready to leave when Eben asked permission to enter.

"There is a scroll inside." His eyes begged me to accept a tiny leather pouch tied to a leather thong. "I made the talisman especially for this hunt, Isenkhebe."

I unrolled the miniature papyrus with Hebrew letters but couldn't read the meaning.

"It is words from Kabbalah, the power revealed to Abraham, my people's first prophet. Every Hebrew letter represents a number with secret powers."

"Are you a Kabbalist, Eben?"

I clearly saw Qeb-ha's interest in him and why we had stopped in Khent-min. Eben had fooled me with his gentleness; he didn't have the strength I imagined for a magician. I looked at him with new respect.

"Wear the amulet, Isenkhebe. Do not remove it. It offers protection and guarantees a safe return."

"Why would Hebrew magic protect an Egyptian priestess?"

"Our God is the god of all beings, whether they recognize him or not."

Eben's eyes were deep pools of still water. For a fleeting moment, I thought I might read the future there. But I looked away and held my hand out to Maia. She tied the scroll to my wrist with the leather cord while I shined my brightest smile on Eben.

"With the blessings of Hathor and Neith, I shall return with antelope for our late meal."

But instead of being cheered by my smile, Eben started swaying back and forth on his feet. His eyes went empty.

"Our meeting has been of the river," he muttered in a sing-song, chanting kind of rhythm. "Something stolen from another dream world. But this is not the beginning of the river. The water has been living for a long time, under the ground, in the mountains and among the songs of the desert."

Was this indecipherable murmuring more Kabbalah? I saw the green water of my Abydos dream, the underground river breaking its banks and spewing onto the sand, forming a lake. I didn't want to think about what he meant. Why did everyone have to talk in riddles all the time?

Ankh-hor's ferry pulled alongside the barge, and I was lowered in a sling to the small boat. Four oarsmen rowed Goliath and me across the river to the hunting grounds that Ankh-hor boasted were the best in all Upper Egypt.

The small lodge made of mud bricks with a palm thatch roof stood on the East Bank at the top of the first rise from the Nile. A thick grove of sycamore trees provided shade. Chariots with restless horses stirred up golden dust; the brass trim of the carts glittered in the bright rays of Re rising.

Built for speed, the chariots were so light that a single man could lift one easily onto a boat. Imported birch and elm formed the frames, wheels, and axles. The carts had leather fronts, decorated with paintings of date palms or rearing horses facing each other. Expensive as a Maserati, only the wealthy could dream of owning a hunting chariot.

Packs of long-legged Berber hunting dogs ran in circles, tongues hanging out. They snapped and growled but didn't fight. Groups of men in short white kilts and leather vests drank beer and ate barley bread; Re flashed off the tips of their spears. Their laughter loud and raucous, they no doubt exchanged tales of their conquests. I recognized some from Ankh-hor's feast last night across the river in Hermopolis. They saw me and grew quiet, bowing from the waist.

My heart pumped in excitement and the blood rushed in my ears. The nobleman Ankh-hor had promised me the hunt of my life. At this moment on the High Desert, Re coming over the hills, nothing existed save the stench of the horse sweat and the baying of hounds. The wildness went straight to my head.

"Welcome and Blessings, Isenkhebe Nefrusobek! I am Hetmus-hor, son of Ankh-hor, and honored to lead you in hunt on this most magnificent of days."

Hetmus-hor stood a head taller than the others and was covered in gold. His smile flashed perfect white teeth, rare among Egyptians. A white triangular headdress framed a bronzed face dominated by a high-bridged straight nose. His shining red-flecked brown eyes outlined in *kohl* took me in, without an ounce of shame, from head to toe.

He bent low and kissed the lapis ring on my hand. I could easily envision his broad shoulders wrestling a lion to the ground. I could easily imagine him wrestling me.

When he straightened, my eyes were on level with his wide chest clad in an elaborate leather vest patterned in gold sunbursts. Re coming over the mountains was not brighter than Hetmus-hor.

"I am giving you my best charioteer," he announced. "My chariot will be in the lead. You shall follow directly behind with your Nubian in third position."

He still held my ringed hand when he lowered his voice and leaned so close that his speckled eyes were only inches away.

"If that is agreeable to you, Isis?" he asked with a hint of tease. He dared use my private name, and he knew me not at all. Hetmus-hor was indeed a confident man.

I pulled my hand away. He was appealing—very appealing—but arrogant. He needed reining in.

"You move as fast as your chariot, Sir. Do not spend all your strength at the beginning of the hunt."

He laughed, a great booming sound, and beamed. It was all a game to him. He had been born to the hunt. There would be other moves.

"By Horus, I love a woman with wit. If you hunt as well as you speak, we shall come home with enough trophies for another feast."

Never dimming his smile, he took my hand again to lead me to the shade of the sycamore grove.

"Bring wine," he shouted. "Let us toast our honored guest, Isenkhebe Nefrusobek, who graces us with her beauty and intelligence."

Servants appeared with tin goblets of unwatered Delta wine. The morning air was splendid in the crisp sunshine; there was only a hint of the heat that would come.

Hetmus lifted his goblet to me and recited:

"May thou spend millions of years,
       thou lover of Thebes,
Sitting with thy face to the north wind,
       thy green eyes beholding felicity."

He had stolen the words of an ancient poem but substituted green eyes for me. He certainly knew how to flatter; his charming words came easily. "Charming as a courtesan" was how the woman with a knowing smile had described him at the feast.

"Many wives and daughters in Hermopolis attest that to be persuaded by Hetmus the Hunter is most pleasurable indeed."

I had no objections to being persuaded. I gave him the favor of a smile with a bold look that left the door wide open for possibilities.

"A toast to the kill!" a nobleman shouted.

Everyone, including the servants with the horses, cheered. I never felt more alive.

We flew across the sand and stone. I balanced on the rawhide flooring woven like strings on a tennis racket. Hares and wild dogs fled when we passed. Gazelle and oryx grazed until we thundered toward them, Berber dogs in the lead. Legs leaping through the air, horns high, the wild herds scattered to the winds.

I raised my prized bow, a composite made from layers of wood, sinew and horn. Its draw weight had been specially engineered for a woman's strength. I bent the bow to full shaft length and let fly an arrow with a barbed bronze head designed to kill. The arrow arched in the blue sky, then dropped with precision into the flank of a doe. She stumbled and fell. The dogs were on her at once.

"Behkai! Abaqer!" Hetmus barked the names of the pack leaders, commanding them in Berber to back off.

They circled the fallen animal, snarling, tongues panting, saliva dripping in long strings. The other chariots gathered around, horses snorting and pawing the ground, anxious to run again. Dust swelled up in great clouds. Hetmus pulled up beside me and extended his hand.

"It is your kill, Isis. The first kill of the day."

His red-flecked eyes glowed with pride.

I stepped down from the chariot and walked with shaking knees toward the wounded doe thrashing on the ground. Hetmus parted the snarling dogs with kicks and Berber barks, and I followed the path he blazed through the pack and the blood.

The female lay helpless, dark crimson flowed from her wound onto the golden sand. She turned her eyes toward me, big, brown and liquid. I saw Eben's eyes and stopped, not wanting to go further.

"Come Isis, give thanks to Neith and then put the animal out of her misery," Hetmus said gently.

His tender tone surprised me. There was more to this nobleman than charm. He nodded his head and smiled to reassure me. His eyes said, *You can do it.* Then he handed me a knife, but not my knife. I shook my head and drew my jeweled dagger from its tooled leather sheath.

After offering a silent prayer to Neith, goddess of hunt, and another to Hathor, asking her forgiveness, I went to my knees, took the doe's muzzle in one hand and drew the steel blade deep across her throat, from ear to ear. Hot blood gushed onto my white gown. I felt both ill and elated. My hands trembled.

"Isenkhebe, Isenkhebe, Queen of the Hunt!" the men cheered.

The dogs howled at the scent of fresh blood, and Hetmus smacked one with his spear to keep him away.

My charioteer hauled the carcass onto our cart and draped her over the railing, the head flopping down toward the ground, blood still pouring from the wide gash. Her eyes were open, but sightless. They were already drying in the heat. Flies swarmed in an instant; they must hatch in the very air.

Blood oozed from the flank wound and fell in droplets. Spots splashed on the tops of my feet and the hem of my caftan. The doe's heart no longer beat; the drops fell from the pull of gravity. By the time we returned to camp this afternoon, the animal would be bled.

The wind shifted suddenly and blew from the south with vengence. Horses spooked and pulled at their reins; charioteers used all their strength to hold them in check. The hounds, lapping up blood-soaked sand, stopped and raised their noses, sniffing the charged air.

My gown whipped around my legs. I clutched the chariot rail for fear of blowing off, looking around frantically for a cloth to protect my face from the biting sand. Holding on with my left hand, I bit the left sleeve of my gown and used my bloodied, jewelled dagger to saw off the cloth. In spite of the wind and the jolt of the chariot, I managed to wrap the linen around my nose and mouth.

I would have crouched down in the chariot, but there was just room for us to stand. My driver struggled with the horses; they reared up on their hind legs and kicked the air.

A brown wall approached, sweeping across the flat plateau as we stared. Hetmus shouted vainly into a wind that roared like ten thousand lions. He must be yelling to head back to the camp.

My driver pulled on the reins with all his might. The white steeds at last put their hooves to the ground, but when they did, they refused to turn toward the west. Instead, the horses bolted north in a desperate attempt to outrun the storm.

I hung on with both hands. The shouts faded behind us. The dead doe's head flopped wildly as we rolled over rocks and bounced high in the air. The wheels of our chariot scarcely touched the ground. My driver never took his eyes from the backs of the horses and the treacherous ground ahead.

The wind became impossibly more vicious, and the sand

enveloped us in a dense fog. I could no longer see the tails of the horses. Soon, I could not see the charioteer, who stood so close beside me that I felt his body movements in the thick dust.

He battled the horses and drove blind. We were thrown from side to side with such force that I would have flown from the cart, if not hanging on with both hands. I don't know how he could stand. The reins, taut in the pull between man and beasts, were his only anchor.

There was no time or space in the thick haze. I felt a terrific jolt when the chariot collided with something I couldn't see. Then we were flying, the wind swirling all around us. Had we been taken up into the sky?

We crashed in soft powder, and I was thrown from the chariot. I rolled, tumbling through a sea of sand, caught in swells as wild as any tempest on the sea. I tried to stand up, but the force of the wind and sand kept me on my knees. The more I struggled, the deeper I sank.

I stretched out on my stomach, my head pointing away from the wind, my arms up to shield my head, the other sleeve of my dress for cover. The blowing sand cut my skin like a thousand shards of glass.

I could barely swallow through the dust in my throat. Pursing my lips, I forced myself to inhale through my nose and not take sand into my lungs. A person could drown in sand. It had happened many times in such a storm. I could be buried and never seen again.

Where was the driver? He must have been thrown, too. I thought him on the other side of the chariot, although he could have been thrown forward over the horses.

The horses! Where were the horses? I could hear nothing but the howling wind. It went on for hours. Drowsiness overcame me. A hippo in soothing water swam by but didn't offer me a ride.

Why hadn't I listened to Qeb-ha? Why hadn't I listened to my own heart? Even a fool acts wisely if he follows his heart.

"Oh Qeb-ha, forgive me, I am a fool!"

My thoughts crawled through sand. My mind slowed to a standstill. A great silence engulfed me; I could no longer hear the wind. I was grateful. They say that silence conceals foolishness. I would hide and pray my fate would pass me by.

CHAPTER 13 THE GENERAL

I coughed once. Nasty brown phlegm came up. My eyes were dry and filled with grit. The weight of the sand lay heavy on my back and legs, but there was an air pocket around my head and I could breathe shallowly. I feared gulping dust into my lungs.

There was just enough space for me to lift my head; sand streamed from my face. My arms cramped from being in the same position so long, but I managed to use my hands to clear a tunnel to the surface. I could see daylight. Was it the same day, or had I slept through the night?

The sand weighed too much for me to rise, so I pulled myself forward, like a snake slithering out of a hole. At last, I crawled free and rose numbly to my knees. There was nothing to see around me except sand and the high sides of a *wadi*, a dry river bed now choked with a fine, gritty powder.

My skin raw, chaffed red from the blasting sand, was on fire. But I lived. My caftan, once snowy white, was filthy. Brown dust had settled in the fibers of the weave; a dark splotch covered the bodice. Blood. It seemed a lifetime ago since I cut the doe's throat.

The chariot had to be close. Had the driver survived? I saw no sign of the horses. Could creatures so large be buried out of sight? Nothing in the sand indicated a horse or chariot entombed beneath the surface.

I couldn't walk in the deep sand on my shaking legs so crawled on my knees in what I hoped was the direction of the chariot. I was unbearably thirsty; my tongue swelled and filled my whole mouth. My lips were cracked. When I tried to moisten them, no saliva came. The desert had tried to suck the life from me, but still I breathed.

My knee banged against something hard, and I touched the

shaft of the chariot in the sand. It must be standing on its end. The horses had simply disappeared. I clawed at the sand in a state of near hysteria; I couldn't bear the thought of being alone—alone in a silent Universe.

The hunting knife with jeweled hilt was still tied around my hips. My bow and arrow must be buried with the chariot. Water! We carried goatskins of water for a day of hunt. I dug and dug and never looked around.

They were on me without warning. One came up behind and grabbed me by the waist, just as I saw his shadow on the ground. I screamed, and my fear echoed off the rock walls of the dry river bed.

We struggled in the sand; my attacker kept sinking deeper. I fought as hard as I could, but was no match at all. One grabbed my feet, and another my shoulders, dragging me between them as they stumbled for footing.

Finally at the top of the ridge, they dropped me onto the rocky ground. They were angry, red in the face, hot from exertion, and humiliated that a woman could have caused them so much trouble. One kicked me in the side with his foot encased in a heavy sandal that laced up his foreleg.

"Stop! She's no good to us dead or broken."

A harsh voice. I recognized the guttural sounds of Aramaic.

One of them pulled me to my feet, and I stared straight at a golden lion insignia with massive legs and curled mane. The Lion of Persia! How could Persians be here, so close to the Nile? I had been too busy fighting to look at their faces. They had full beards decorated with colored ribbons, and real hair to their shoulders, not wigs. They were all of the same build, stocky and powerful, with the muscles of oxen. Their calves looked as big around as my waist.

They were on horseback; Egyptians prefer the chariot. The animals looked like their masters: massive chests, long manes braided with ribbons, and wild eyes. They constantly snorted and pawed at the ground. What did they feed them to make them so wild?

A soldier threw a filthy, coarse wool cape over my head and tossed me onto a horse. I hung upside down, belly across the felted pads used as saddle. I saw the doe draped across my chariot rail, her head bouncing as we rolled across the desert. This was swift justice from the Goddess.

The rider mounted behind me, and the horses thundered off. I couldn't tell in which direction, but felt certain they would not head west toward the Nile.

What of Hetmus-hor? Had he made it out alive? And Goliath? Had he lost his life to follow me on this folly? Or did they already search for me? Would they come, but too late?

I couldn't know that Hetmus-hor and the others escaped the storm. He hadn't shouted for them to head west for the Nile, as I thought, but to form a circle with the chariots, flip them over, and then corral the unhitched horses in the middle. They crouched in their shelters and lasted out the fury. When they dug their way out and calmed the animals, Hetmus was sobered and grim. Isis had been in his charge. He couldn't return to his father and say he had lost her in the desert. Not only was the life of the priestess, but the honor of his family at stake.

But it was much more than that. He remembered her shining emerald eyes when she made the first kill, and how her eyes clouded over when she saw the animal's suffering. Yet she had the courage to draw the blade in one movement, without hesitation, deep into the doe's throat. There was much to admire in her. This priestess awakened new feelings. He had known and forgotten a thousand beautiful women, but no one like Isis.

Hetmus allowed the hunting party some of the water and refreshed the horses. Most of the dogs had perished in the storm.

Then he ordered the hitching of a chariot and called for Goliath.

"Return to Hermopolis for help. Go to my father Ankh-hor."

But instead of mounting the chariot, Goliath stood with his feet apart, massive shoulders back, and head down.

"Why do you stand here? Go, I tell you. We have no time to waste."

Goliath shook his head, his eyes still lowered.

"Nubian! We have just survived the storm together! Do not force me to use the whip."

Goliath raised his eyes and looked straight at Hetmus.

"The whip is nothing. I have lost her. If I cannot find her, I wish for death."

It was the anguish in the Nubian's eyes that moved him—and the terror, not of the whip, but of the loss of Isis.

"Stay, man," Hetmus said, putting his hand on Goliath's shoulder. "Stay and find your mistress."

They explored the desert in quadrants, returning at regular intervals to organize a new grid. There was no sign of the chariot or Isis. The desert had simply swallowed them up. The sun god Re began his descent for the night; the last hot rays cast long shadows on the rocks.

Hetmus-hor himself came upon the tracks in the sand. Horses. There were several, and with riders. The trail headed northeast. He backtracked to the edge of the *wadi* and saw where the riders dismounted. There were too many footprints crisscrossing over each other to be sure how many men, but he guessed five or six. An indentation in the sand at the bottom of the *wadi* signalled something buried there. A chariot?

He climbed quickly down the side. There were signs of struggle, and of digging. Then in the last rays of sunshine, he caught the glint of gold. Lying on the brown sand was the gold girdle with delicate Hathor *tiet* charm that had dangled on her thigh.

Isis had survived the storm. She had tried to dig out the chariot.

But she had been seized by men on horses. Who were they and why would they take her? They couldn't be Egyptian; she would never have struggled.

The report to his father could hardly be worse. The High Priestess Isenkhebe Nefrusobek, daughter of Sit hathor, the highest priestess in the land, had survived the sandstorm but been carried into the desert by unknown men on horseback.

Ankh-hor was responsible for arranging the hunt and persuading the old eunuch Qeb-ha to let her go. She had been given into Hetmus-hor's care. Who knew what wrath would fall on their house? Sit-hathor was a powerful woman known to crush opposition. The foolish believed that she had given birth to a god's child. Hetmus knew that was nonsense, but her power couldn't be underestimated. It was said even the Pharaoh feared her influence.

Returning to the others with the gold girdle in his hand, Hetmus sent another chariot back to the Nile, this time for armed reinforcements. His party of rich nobles was equipped to hunt antelope—not men. They were short on food and water, but he wouldn't return without Isis, or at least without knowing where to find her. The horsemen couldn't be far ahead; he turned to follow the trail northeast.

He prayed he wasn't too late to gods he didn't believe in. He entreated Horus, Thoth, Hathor, and every other deity that came to mind. He prayed last to Set to set aside his evil for just this night.

I lost track of time, but don't think we traveled that far before we stopped. Feet, belonging to man and horse, were all I could see. I was so thirsty. I had never imagined such a thirst; the pain was beyond bearing. I would sell my soul for a sip of water.

Rough hands dragged me from the horse and threw me over a shoulder. I had no strength left to struggle. We were in a camp; I could tell by the sounds, but couldn't see much beyond the dusty ground. The earth had been churned up in a mad pattern of footprints and horse hooves.

We swept through wool panels into a tent. I was tossed down on thick carpets like a sack of old rags. My captor prostrated himself beside me.

"What is this?"

The rough voice was more growl of a beast than man, but the Aramaic was clean; I guessed an educated man. I thanked my father for my language tutors. I was terrified, but at least I understood what was being said.

"We found her in the desert, General, after the Great Storm. She was alone, her chariot and horses buried in the sand."

"Idiots!" The General's voice was deafening. "Why did you not leave her there to die?"

The prostrate man beside me kept his face buried in the carpet. I could see his trembling hands out of the corner of my eye.

"Show her to me."

A rough hand grabbed my arm and dragged me to my feet. The foul-smelling cape was pulled away, and I stood as straight as I could, considering the beating my body had taken. Every muscle screamed from bruise and dehydration.

I faced six standing officers around a wooden table covered with scrolls. Their shoulder-length hair was entwined with colorful ribbons; their beards were carefully groomed into long curls. Military leather waistcoats, armored with metal mesh and emblazoned with the golden lion of Persia, covered their bull chests. A double-edged *akinaka* thrusting sword hung from each belt.

I could tell by their bearing these men were high-born. This was no small raiding party.

An ogre with bulging eyes and thick lips moved so close to me, I smelled his foul breath and the sweat under his perfume. He appraised me from head to foot, like a man in a brothel before making his choice.

"She is no ordinary Egyptian, my General. Look at her jewelry.

There could be a fine ransom here."

"Idiots!" The General roared even louder. "If she is a woman of importance, do you not think they will be searching for her? Do you suppose she was in the desert by herself, driving her own chariot?"

More than one man quivered.

The General himself came to stand just in front of me. When he fingered the necklace of gold charms and lifted a tiny crocodile, his hand grazed my chest and my skin crawled. But I knew his character by that choice of the crocodile. This was a man who lusted, and not only for power.

I forced myself not to flinch, but stood immobile, concentrating on breathing slowly, ignoring my pounding heart.

"Well, she is here now. There is no changing that." His face turned thoughtful; he studied me from under half-closed lids.

"They will be looking for her. Place extra guards. Follow the tracks backwards and erase them. Post sentries five miles down the ravine toward the southwest."

Three soldiers left the tent immediately.

"You made a stupid decision." The General spoke to the prostrated man without taking his eyes from mine. "You have endangered the mission."

I stared back, determined not to blink or show fear.

"But perhaps these emerald eyes bewitched you. I shall decide your fate when I decide hers."

The man beside me slithered forward on his stomach and kissed the General's feet. My green eyes had saved his life for the moment—and mine.

"Get her cleaned up. Get her out of those rags. Feed her." He turned his back and returned to the scrolls.

They were not going to kill me, at least not right away. He wouldn't have ordered me to be fed. I had no idea how much time had passed since I had eaten, but I couldn't feel hunger when my need for water was so great. A person can live a long

time without food, but without water, the desert sun can suck
life away in one day.

Three women, one just a young girl, came to me when I entered
the tent. The guard grunted instructions about bathing and food,
and then turned and exited without a glance back.

They touched the soft linen of my spoiled gown and rubbed
it between their fingers to appreciate the delicate texture. They
removed my wig and passed it around, fingering each golden
trinket. A woman with slanted eyes put a small piece between her
teeth and bit down. Her eyes grew wide when she recognized gold.
They toyed with the amethysts hanging from my ears, shrieking
when they realized they weren't glass.

Exhausted, I couldn't stand. I hurt everywhere. Purple bruises
from the struggle at the chariot marked my raw skin. It would
take days to heal, but I didn't know if I had days. I didn't know
if I had hours.

When they took my ruined caftan, I noticed my gold girdle
was gone with the *tiet* amulet Maia had given me for protection.
I took it as a sign that I would never see her again. Hathor had
deserted me. I sobbed and sobbed, rocking back and forth like
Eben in one of his trances.

The women ignored my anguish; misery must fill every moment
of their lives. They tried to untie the leather thong that held
Eben's Kabbalah amulet on my wrist, but I slapped their hands
away. That shocked them. They stepped back. They were afraid
of angry green eyes.

A servant brought water at last, and I gulped it down so quickly
that it came right up again. The next time I sipped slowly, small
swallows with time in between to settle. I began to feel human
again. I told myself that I would survive even this.

Hot water flowed from brass jugs into copper basins. The
women sponged me from the crown of my shaved head down to
my henna-tipped toes. They wore their own hair. How did they

keep clean and free from vermin in these stuffy tents with no bathing pools?

The young girl with a perfect oval face smeared balm on my cracked lips. Her touch was soft, timid, like Maia. Sweet Maia who didn't want me to come on this hunt. Qeb-ha, Maia, Eben—all had feared for me, but I refused to heed their warnings. I refused to hear my own inner voice.

The other two women oiled my bruised body; my skin soaked it up like a sponge. They polished my nails with a pumice stone, smoothing out the broken edges. My beautiful hands! Cut and blistered raw.

Gold gleamed from the horns in the ring that matched my mother's. It gave me strength to see it on my middle finger, a reminder that I was Isenkhebe Nefrusobek, High Priestess of Hathor.

I didn't let myself think about how I would get back to Las Vegas, back to Barb, back to the 21st century. I vowed if I ever got home again, I would get rid of the Red Mirror.

At last I was clean, oiled and perfumed. They brought me a splendid robe of floral-patterned yellow silk. But even it was painful against my skin; I shuddered when they slipped it around my shoulders. A long sash with golden tassels and tinkling bells went around my waist.

The woman with slanted eyes and high cheekbones put delicate slippers on my feet, curled-up toes in front, open in the back. They had been woven from thousands of red silk threads.

The hot tea was very sweet, generous with honey. A platter appeared with rice and mutton stewed with figs and raisins. I choked down the vile meat. No Egyptian of status ever ate the flesh of a goat.

Finally, they brought me a small pipe with sweet smoke. I coughed and pushed it away. My eyes drooped. I floated above the rich carpets and drifted between the poles of the tent.

I don't know how much time passed before a rough guttural

voice broke through the trance. Two soldiers with curved daggers in their belts stood over me.

"Come," they growled in crude Aramaic, and hauled me to my feet.

CHAPTER 14 ISHTAR

"On your face, Egyptian whore, before the great General Sher, lion of the desert and beloved of Cambyses, King of the World."

The guards pushed me first to my knees and then shoved my face into the dusty carpet. The General reclined on cushions, his uniform replaced with a robe, silk like mine, but deep green.

"Bring her up to her knees. Let us see her face washed of desert filth and tears."

They pulled me to rest on my haunches, the gown flowing around me, shimmering gold in the yellow of the oil lamps. The women had cleaned my wig and covered it with a long scarf of emerald silk, woven with gold thread in an intricate arabesque pattern. It cascaded around my shoulders in stark contrast to the yellow of the gown. My amethyst earrings swung back and forth.

The same officers were there and still in uniform. They stood while the General lounged. Unlike Egyptians, the *kohl* was drawn to make their eyes appear perfectly round. They stared at me, both lust and hatred on their faces.

They talked to each other without looking away from me. They spoke Elamite-Persian, not the Aramaic of the soldiers. They discussed if I should be killed now and taken down to the plain and dumped. They reasoned that a search party would find me and take my body home. They would have time to finish their mission for Cambyses.

The General rose from his seat. The others fell silent. He loomed over me, a great bull with a massive chest and legs like the thick columns of a temple. I looked up into his eyes and saw a slight spark of something human. I stared straight at him and refused to blink.

Seconds passed, and no one spoke or moved. The wicks in the

lamps sputtered, making small hissing sounds like a thousand serpents.

"Leave us."

He never took his eyes away from mine. We had locked into battle; I didn't imagine him a man accustomed to defeat. I forced myself not to waver.

When the last man had exited, his face relaxed just a fraction; an ironic smile curved his lips. He stared at me, and I stared back.

It was he who finally turned away. He reached for a goblet on a brass tray set on a short wooden tripod and sank again onto his cushions, contemplating me from across the carpets.

"I shall call you *Ishtar*," he said idly in Persian. "You are the glittering evening star in a lavender desert sky."

"I am worth much to my people," I said in fluent Aramaic. I wouldn't let him know I understood Persian, the private language of noblemen.

My voice rang out strong and clear in the small space of the tent; it reflected none of the terror I felt.

"They will pay well for my safe return."

The General sputtered into the wine cup he held to his lips; he looked stunned.

"You speak Aramaic? But are you not Egyptian?"

"I am from Thebes, your Excellency, but speak several tongues."

I thought it wise to use a title of respect. This man held my life in his thick fingers. He studied me for a few long, silent moments. His fat eyelids drooped. He sipped from the goblet with his meaty lips. I was deciding if I dared speak again when his eye went to my hand.

"What does it mean that you wear the ring of the Goddess of Love?"

"Hathor is more than the Goddess of Love, esteemed General," I answered, hoping to convince him of my importance. "She is the Solar Goddess, the Gold-of-the-Gods."

"Do not presume to instruct me about the inferior gods of

Egyptian dogs," he snarled. "Why do you wear the ring?"

I couldn't afford to anger him. When I answered, I was careful to modulate my voice, keeping it low and respectful.

"I am a high priestess in the cult of Hathor. There are only two rings such as this; I am one of two who may wear them. I assure you the Temple will pay whatever you demand for my return, safe and untouched."

"And if you are *touched?* What then, High Priestess of Hathor?"

He smirked. One eyebrow arched. He was amused. I thought I saw the hint of a twinkle in his eye.

There was no amusement on my side. I didn't answer but met his eyes directly, unflinching.

Morphing before me, his eyes went cold and hard. The General was a chameleon, a hybrid of bull and lion, with only occasional glimpses of man.

"I am not in need of a ransom from effeminate Nile priests." His voice was as frigid as a winter wind.

He sipped his wine, studying me over the rim of the goblet. He waited for my response. Everything depended on the next moment—my future and my life.

I met his look boldly with more than a hint of promise in my eyes.

"Is it possible for a lion of Persia to have needs not met?"

I saw his pupils dilate, even surrounded by the coal black orbs. His eyelids jerked slightly; I had touched a nerve. He tried to keep his face stone, but revealed all in the blink of his eye. No matter his words, he was a man of many needs, some never met.

The General took a sip from his goblet and drew smoke from his pipe. I smelled the same sweet odor as in the women's tent.

"I have a proposal for you, Ishtar," he said casually. "I sense you like challenge."

I waited.

"I hear that certain priestesses of Hathor have—what shall we say—special talents? Your reputation reaches as far as Persia."

He hesitated only long enough to gauge my reaction. I showed him nothing.

"If you please me, you will belong to me and me alone, but only for as long as I am pleased. When you no longer please me, I shall return you to the women's tent, where you can please the other men. And when you please them no more, I shall have you killed."

I watched his lips move in his impassive face. How easily he talked about my inevitable death. It had been decided; it was only a question of when.

"But because you are a high priestess, I shall return your body to your temple, so that the priests can mummify you, and you can live forever in your Egyptian dream of eternity."

Silence.

"What do you say to that, Ishtar?"

Not more than one minute passed. Instead of answering, I rose from my knees to my feet in one movement. I no longer felt the pain in my body. I moved slowly toward him. The emerald scarf slipped from my head to the carpet; the gold in my black wig glittered. The bells on my sash jingled seductively, like the tinkle of the *sistrum* in the temple.

I fixed my eyes on his and knelt at his feet. I took the goblet from his hand and placed it on the brass tray beside his cushions.

They taught us in the temple that there is a sexual power inside us that when summoned, oozes from our pores. It's an animal energy that conjures up base desire. But the magic of Hathor is special; it transforms raw lust into a promise of pleasure and satisfaction known only by the gods.

I turned on the Power. My body radiated animal sex mingled with the potent allure of intense sensuality—and deep mystery.

"I have secrets," my aura teased, "wonderful secrets that only I can share."

Electricity sparked in the air. Great sensuous waves rolled over the General. Mesmerized, he barely breathed, his eyes fixed on my every movement.

I slowly untied the purple silk sash of his robe. I pulled it free in one long motion and dropped it carefully next to the pillows. He felt its slick slide across the small of his back.

I opened the front of his gown, folding back the cloth without hurry. I never took my eyes from his. His breathing came shallow and fast.

He was nude under the robe. I let my eyes wander. I caressed him with only my gaze, appreciating the muscles of his broad chest with its mass of thick curly hair like a beast.

With my eyes only, never touching him, I followed the line of hair down his hard belly. It crossed his navel and descended into a great black bush. His thighs were thick tree trunks. His manhood stood erect and hard, an obelisk to the sky.

I leaned back on my heels to study him. The man was truly a bull. He watched my every move, seeming not to breathe at all.

I started with the sacks. I took one in my mouth while I gripped the other in my hand—hard. The General gave an involuntary cry. The rougher my touch, the more he moaned.

When I felt him near the edge, I massaged him gently with a new caress, airy and ethereal. My fingertips were lighter than butterfly wings.

One hand held the shaft; the other was on his balls, pulling and kneading, first rough, then gentle, then rough again. He thrust his hips for me to go faster, but I stayed in control. I took my time, tormenting him with his own urgency.

The General twisted and panted. Each time he came close to exploding, I stopped. How many times could I bring him to the edge before I let him go over?

Putting my knees between his thighs, I forced them apart. I lowered my mouth onto his manhood and took him in as far as I could. And then when I sensed he was just there, I pinched his erect nipple hard and put my finger at the lip of his anus and plunged in.

He erupted with a powerful shaking and bolting like a wild

horse until he collapsed and breathed in great gulps.

He had never touched me. I had never opened my robe. He lay spent, his massive chest rising high and falling. I rolled back on my haunches and to my feet, standing over him. I said nothing.

The General opened his eyes, looking up at me. There was something new there. Just a flicker, but it was a start.

Reaching down slowly, I folded his robe across his bare chest and loins. I handed him his goblet of wine and stepped backwards, folding to my knees again on the carpet, in front of him. Not one word had been spoken since his life-and-death challenge to me.

I waited. I looked straight at him, unblinking. I believe my face was expressionless. I tried hard that it was. Inside I quaked. I had given it everything I had.

Shouting outside of the tent broke the spell. A guard called out, begging permission to enter. The General jumped to his feet and tied the sash around his waist.

"Enter," he roared. "This had better be good!"

A captain prostrated himself at the General's bare feet.

"Speak, damn you! Why do you keep me waiting?"

"The outward guards have spotted Egyptian chariots, Excellency. They camp for the night."

The General was instantly alert.

"How many? How far away?"

"Eight, sir. They are not military. They have not entered the canyon area."

"A search party. It is just as I said. They are looking for her."

He paced back and forth.

"Have you covered our tracks?"

"Yes, Excellency. The trail is wiped out."

"Keep watching them. Do not let them see you. If they do not find the trail, they will turn back. If they discover the trail, kill them all and bury the chariots. They must not see us and live to tell."

His eyes flashed with cold fire.

"But, hear this," he threatened. "I do not desire more Egyptians disappearing into the desert. We cannot have their army join the search. Our work is not finished here."

He was fully in command; it seemed not passion nor fury clouded his thinking. I could see why he was so feared.

"Call my staff and have them here at once."

"Yes, General. At once."

"All this for a woman!" he fumed. "Damn the Gods."

His aura was black and evil. I despaired that all my efforts were for naught.

He turned on me. Would he kill me right here, right now? The flush on his angry face faded slightly. When he spoke, his voice was almost human.

"You have gained yourself a night, Ishtar. The reputation of Hathor is well deserved." A spark of delight twinkled in his eye. "Maybe even more than could be imagined."

He started to dress.

"Go to the harem and sleep. No one will approach you."

A soldier appeared to take me to the women's tent, but not before I saw something glint on the table. It was the jewel-encrusted hilt of my dagger.

Chapter 15   The Sash

I had no way of knowing that the news of my kidnapping spread quickly. When word reached River God, he immediately requested leave from the Crown Prince to go to Hermopolis.

"The taking of a High Priestess is sacrilege," he said. "The Pharaoh would command me to find her and bring her back—or avenge her death."

"Yes!" shouted the Prince. "An excellent idea!"

The woman's kidnapping was a gift from the Gods. He now had more days—and nights to sample the pleasures of the Temple of Min.

"Do your duty to Hathor, Commander, and bring glory to Egypt."

River God chose twenty of the best oarsmen, ten to a shift, to row round the clock. The promise of double pay soothed any qualms about the dangers of Set and the risks of traveling by night. He sent word by carrier pigeon to the governor of Hermopolis to have a company of mounted soldiers ready to leave immediately upon his arrival.

He puzzled during the long hours on the river over who could be so foolish and so brazen to take an Egyptian woman of rank. The desert people knew the price for kidnapping a noblewoman, much less a priestess. The tribe would be decimated, their animals confiscated, their women and children sold into slavery.

He told himself to stay focused. He didn't allow himself to think the worst, or at least, not to linger on the possibility. He refused to think of what might be happening to her at this moment. Isis was foolish at times and a slave to her senses, but she was strong-willed. Whoever had taken her must have done it for ransom. They would not harm her.

If properly prepared and in the correct state of mind, he would be ready when the time came—ready for anything. Anything except what he feared most. He would never be ready for that.

Never once did he think of the Persians.

The Governor staged the expedition from the hunting lodge. More than two hundred horses stirred up dust, snorting, pulling at their tethers, ready to run. Servants gathered quivers of arrows, goatskins with water, and sacks with bread, salted mutton and dates. The men sharpened the broad blades of their iron swords and the bronze tips of their spears.

When River God's ship was spotted, they chanted as one, "Avenge Hathor! Avenge Hathor!"

River God was off the ship before the rowers pulled up oars. The East Bank was shallow with no quays. Dozens of small boats anchored at the river's edge. The crew unloaded supplies in a chain, some standing in water to their chests, the last among the reeds on the shore. They all sank in black mud to their knees.

The cavalry greeted him with a roar when he topped the rise of the bank.

"Hail Commander! Loved by the Pharaoh! Loved by a God! Live long! Live long!"

Singing his praises, the horsemen waved short killing swords in circles above their heads. Sunlight flashed on the metal studs of the round crocodile shields slung across their backs.

Waiting for him was Eben.

"Who are you, Hebrew?"

"I come from the priest Qeb-ha, Commander. I have horses and two men."

"You will slow us down. Go back to your prayers."

"The stars tell me that I shall find Isenkhebe Nefrusobek," Eben insisted.

Then he repeated word for word what Qeb-ha had told him to say.

"The Fate and the Fortune that come, it is the Gods that send them. I come with the blessings of the Goddess."

It took River God less than ten minutes to access the troops and confer with his captains. A groom rushed forward with a glossy black stallion, long mane and tail brushed smooth and braided with silver. He mounted and whipped the horse to a gallop, Hetmus-hor's man at his side. Two hundred armed horsemen and Eben raised a cloud of dust that could be seen across the river in Hermopolis.

Would this be the last dawn of my life in this world? A soldier shook my shoulder and barked to get up. I still had on the yellow gown, my wig on my head. Sleep had taken me the moment I lay down, and if I journeyed to the Land of Dreams, I was too exhausted to notice.

He took me to a place to relieve myself, and finally I could see the camp. Tents formed regular rows in a narrow canyon with steep walls. The approach was from only one direction. Horses were tethered in one spot, outside the camp perimeter at the mouth of the ravine. I saw only one guard posted there.

The General's tent stood apart from the others with its back up to the canyon wall. Deep tracks carved by erosion etched the cliff surface. When I looked more closely, I spotted small trails at a much shallower slope. They could be the paths of mountain goats or maybe shepherds. Bedouins lived in these rocky hills.

When we came to the General's tent, the guard pushed me roughly through the flap. I immediately prostrated myself. I didn't want my face shoved into the dusty carpet again.

"Up!"

I came to my knees and faced the General.

He was drinking hot liquid from a ceramic cup, his monster feet clad in heavy sandals propped on a cushion. He had on his leather tunic with a short kilt. Did the man ever sleep?

More of the rice and a pile of dates filled the platter in front of him. I was ravenous and thirsty. He saw me glance at the food.

"Come, eat, drink." He motioned me over with a dismissive wave of his hand.

I rose and settled again on the opposite side of the dish. He handed me a cup filled with tea, sweetened with honey. I smelled mint. It was too hot to swallow more than small sips. I fought my urge to down it all at once.

He watched me, detached, as if observing a prized mare feeding in the stable. I scooped up rice with my right hand, and using my fingers and palm to craft a small ball, put it in my mouth. I willed myself to chew. My hunger was like a dog; I could have swallowed each chunk whole.

"Persians never eat with women. Did you know that, Ishtar? But you are Egyptian. I am curious to see if you are different."

I had no comment. What could I say? How many ways are there to eat?

"Women must chatter while they chew. They cannot be silent. It is distasteful to see."

I was silent.

"Perhaps you are different, after all. I sense your mind working, but your lips are still. Would I dread your words, Ishtar, if I could hear them?"

I had no idea where he was going with this idle chatter. I continued to eat and looked at him only when he spoke.

I took a date and nibbled around the pit, then drank deep of my tea, which had cooled.

"My officers want me to kill you, Ishtar. They say you are endangering the mission. What do you say to that?"

His tone was lazy, as if he casually mused over the fate of a goat.

Still I didn't speak. Did he want me to beg for my life? Would that elicit pleasure—or scorn? One should not give way to the tongue when not asked. I would not give way to my tongue, until

I knew why I had been asked.

He continued in the same casual tone.

"I told them that it would be a pity to destroy such a creature as you. But then, they do not know you as I do."

He waited. He expected a response. I had to gamble. I had no choice. I modulated my voice carefully in a tone confident with the hint of challenge.

"You said that I would be yours as long as I pleased you. Have I not pleased you? Or are you not a man of your word?"

He actually laughed. He threw back his head in a roar of a laugh. He smiled at me. His eyes crinkled in the corners.

"I am certain, Ishtar, that there are few men you would not please."

He refilled his cup and mine and settled back; he appeared totally at ease.

"I value beauty, and I value brains, but I value talent most of all. And you, beautiful and clever Ishtar, have been given a great talent. It would be a crime to waste it."

I thanked my mother for developing my special abilities with all the skills of her cult. My father had given me language, so I could understand and spar. And of course, I thanked Hathor for giving me the Power. I owed my life today to all three.

I waited for a signal, a clue to what he wanted next. He wouldn't tell me, of course. He played the cat to my mouse. He wanted me to squirm, and then he would pounce with his great paw when he was ready.

The General watched me, never taking his eyes away. I looked all around the tent. Neither of us spoke, each waiting to see what the other would do. I saw a whip—the kind Persians use on horses—on top of a pile with saddle pads and a bridle.

I moved the tray of food between us to one side. His pupils dilated. He stopped smiling. I stood up before him and untied the sash of my robe. The gown fell open in front, not all the way, but enough that he could see the curve of my belly, my shaven mound, and a hint of my breast. Taking the sash in my hand, I doubled it, forming a loop.

As fast as a striking cobra, I slipped the loop around his neck and yanked hard. I caught him completely off guard. The little bells tinkled; the tassels swung back and forth. He went wide-eyed with shock. I released the pressure so he could breathe.

"You go too far!" He bellowed like a bull.

My voice cut through the air.

"I have not begun."

I held onto the end of the noose with one hand and reached for the whip with the other. My robe fell open when I stretched, revealing my full breasts, crowned with dusky roses. He didn't try to remove the sash from around his throat.

Gripping the whip, I lashed him across his biceps; the leather thongs stung his flesh. I jerked hard at the noose at the same time.

A great moan heaved from his bull chest. His manhood rose under the kilt. I lashed him again, on the other arm, harder this time. Angry red welts came up on his skin. His erection grew larger still.

I whipped his thighs, still tightening and releasing the noose with each stroke. He snorted like a wild bull. I expected him to rise up and paw the ground.

I only struck a half dozen times, but each blow was more forceful than the one before.

He grabbed the whip with one hand and seized my hand holding the noose with his other. He pulled me on top of him. My soft breasts crushed into the leather of his vest; the metal lions and mesh imprinted a pattern on my skin.

He flipped me forward on my knees like I was a loaf of bread and dragged me backward. I felt him deep in me. Thank Horus, he had chosen the canal of my womanhood and not the other. Could I survive such a weapon?

But he exploded the moment he entered me. He lost control.

He held my hips flush against his groin and breathed hard like a runner after a race. Then he released me, shoving me face down on my stomach while he fell back onto the cushions.

I could see through a crack at the base of the tent that Re had vanquished the serpent of the underworld and begun once again his journey across the sky. I wondered again if this was the last sunrise I would see.

The women bathed me and dressed me in new gowns. The first layer was a blue-green caftan, the color of Sinai turquoise, with elaborate embroidery in gold around the neck, cuff, and hemline. Over that they placed a delicate open robe in a rich lapis blue.

Persian women always cover their hair. They chose for me pale lavender silk with thousands of shimmering silver threads. When they brought the red slippers with turned-up toes, I asked for sandals.

They looked at each other and shrugged; the one with slanted eyes came back with Persian leather sandals that laced up the leg. I took them into the folds of my gown and put the slippers on my feet.

They watched me but said nothing. I hated looking into their empty eyes; I couldn't see their souls.

A guard came for me, and I returned to the General's tent. The officers were all there, very animated, gesturing wildly with their hands. Persians are rumored to drink copious amounts of wine when making decisions, but wait until they are sober to act. I prayed to Hathor they would not act now.

The men fell silent when I entered and prostrated myself. Hatred sucked the air from the tent. They needed only a word from the General to slit my throat right there on the carpet.

"Go to the bed," he commanded, not even looking in my direction.

I rose and went to the mattress with silk pillows and settled myself on my knees. Conscious of each movement in my body, I did everything to suppress the Power. This was not the time. My eyes avoided the group of staring men; I tried to fade into the patterns and shadows of the tent.

They soon forgot me and spoke rapidly, some of it military jargon, words I didn't know. But I understood 'supply lines' and 'direction of attack.' They talked freely in Elamite, unaware I could follow, outlining the weakness of Egyptian defenses and mocking the ailing Pharaoh and his son, Crown Prince Psamtik.

For the first time, I heard the Pharaoh was near death. The Persians laughed at the Crown Prince.

"It is a gift from the gods," said the man with ogre eyes, the one they call Zavan the merciless, "for such a weakling to face Cambyses, the Master of All Lands."

They spoke of invasion and the King of Persia as the next Pharaoh. Egyptian power was at an end. Persian gods, superior to the weak gods of the Nile, would rule a new world.

My fear grew with each moment, but I feigned a look of boredom as I picked at the threads of my dress. Images of peaceful Nile temples with green fields and lush gardens played in my mind. I saw them invaded and trampled by these beast-men with perfumed beards and icy hearts.

Worry and fear overwhelmed my desire to remain strong. I began to think of dying as preferable to this unknowing. When worry such as mine arises, the heart seeks death itself as escape. Still I was jolted when I heard them switch to talk of killing me.

Their eyes pierced me like twelve deadly daggers. I forced myself to stare at the golden threads frayed by my nervous picking.

"Kill her now. Smother her so the fool Egyptians think she died of thirst. We can dump her body——"

"Enough!" the General growled. "No more talk of this. When the time is right, I shall act."

They didn't speak of me again, but their hatred was palpable in the heat of the stuffy tent. Did these people ever need fresh air?

The language switched to Aramaic when a captain appeared

with a report.

"The Egyptians are on foot, your Excellency, exploring the canyons. There is no sign of reinforcements."

"They do not take their horses? Then they are low on water."

The General tapped a whip against his thigh. I recognized it as the one I had used on him in the morning.

"But reinforcements are coming, of that I am certain. They do not leave. They expect more men and supplies."

He fell silent. No one else spoke. I ventured a look in his direction from under my lashes. He stared at me, but I couldn't read his face.

"Bring my horse," he ordered. "I want to see for myself. And bring the woman whatever she needs. I want her here when I return."

It wasn't until he left that I realized I had been holding my breath.

I was alone in the tent. I waited a few moments, then rose to my feet and went to the table. Some of the papyri were maps, but I also saw long lists and official-looking documents. I moved a scroll and uncovered my jeweled hunting knife.

After putting the dagger in the folds of my robe, I replaced the scroll exactly where it had been. The table looked undisturbed. I hurried back to the bed and hid the knife with the Persian sandals.

I was on my way back to the table when the guard entered with a platter of rice, some meat and a water jug.

"Do you have any bread?" My voice showed no fear.

He looked surprised; he wasn't used to women or prisoners asking for anything. But he returned with a flat, round loaf of dark bread, the kind Bedouins bake in the sand under a campfire.

The bread went with my knife and sandals. The green scarf from last night had fallen between two pillows; I added it to the hidden pile.

I had no real plan. I moved on automatic. The only way out of the camp was past the horses, through the narrow canyon mouth. It was bright day with soldiers everywhere.

The wind must have loosened one of the flaps from the stake in the back of the tent toward the cliff wall. A thin line of dusty sunlight appeared at the ground and then disappeared again. I went to my knees, lifted a corner, and bright light poured into the dim interior. The cliff wall was about six feet away. I saw no guards; they stood in front.

I forced myself to eat the food, choking down the foul mutton, drinking some of the water. A small stack of goatskin water bags was neatly arranged not far from the table of scrolls. I took one from the middle of the stack and filled it with the remaining water from the jug. I put that with my secret stash and went back to the bed to await the General's return.

CHAPTER 16   THE BITE

Covered in dust and stinking like a stable, the General stomped into the tent, his hungry eyes searching for me. I sat up and looked for my death sentence in his face. If he had decided I must die, I couldn't see it there. He hurried towards me, shedding his armor with each step.

"You smell like a horse," I said calmly. My strength came from somewhere outside me. Inside, I quaked from anxiety and fear.

He stopped short—speechless, his leather vest half on, half off.

I relaxed on one elbow, slightly on my side, accentuating the curve from my shoulder to narrow waist that rose again along my hip. My legs stretched out, ankle resting gracefully one on the other, knee slightly bent, toes pointed. The blue silk folded on every contour of my body. I stared at him boldly from under half-closed lids and dialed up the Power.

"Water!" He bellowed. "Bring me water for a bath. And food."

He pulled off his thick sandals and tossed them aside. Spread-legged, bare monster feet planted firmly on the ground, he faced me in his loose tunic and kilt. His arms hung at his sides. If he had bent only slightly forward, I would have imagined him a gorilla. His thick fingered hands visibly itched to touch me.

Sweat made rivulets in the pale powder of desert dust on his skin. Stripes from my whip flamed fiery red on his arms and legs. I wondered what his men thought when they saw those.

Pots clanged and voices rose as the camp prepared for the evening meal. The wind had died. Re was retreating under the western horizon. Other night sounds echoed through the canyon, subtle but different vibrations that went with the changes of texture in the late evening air. I felt it slightly cooler in the stifling tent.

The General grabbed a jug of water and poured a stream down

his throat. The water spilled into his beard, caked with dust. Why don't Persians shave like civilized people? All that hair is so unclean.

The food arrived first. He sat on cushions in his foul shirt and kilt, stuffing slabs of fatty meat into his mouth. Bits of it clung to his beard. And he says it's distasteful to eat with women who chatter while they chew.

I saw him as raw animal. I envisioned him returning from battle, covered in human blood and ravenous for the taste of rare meat.

Twilight had settled when they brought the stacks of coarse cloth, large copper bowls and hot water in brass jugs. Embossed silver flasks of perfumed oil stood on a round brass tray.

"Do you wish me to bathe you?" I asked politely.

"Do you see anyone else here?" His voice was gruff but not threatening.

I took several lengths of the cloth and spread them over cushions.

"Lie here," I told him.

He called the guard.

"Do not disturb me. Do not enter unless there is news of the Egyptians."

The guard fixed on the General when he spoke, but I could tell he looked at me out of the corner of his eye. I wondered what gossip spread through the camp. There must be wild speculation about the power of the Egyptian sorceress who had bewitched their General Sher, Lion of Persia.

The General settled on the cushions, his massive frame bending with a grace I wouldn't have thought possible in a man his size.

I removed his shirt and put it aside. Then I removed his kilt and put it on top. He was already erect, but I ignored it.

Beginning with his arms, I wiped the layers of dust away. I moved to his thighs and stroked downward to his calves and ankles, dipping the cloth from time to time in water. When the cloth became too brown, I took a clean one. When the water became brown, I poured fresh.

"What is that leather strap around your wrist?" His voice was almost soft, not demanding, just idly curious.

"It is an amulet, your Excellency. I never take it off. It protects me from harm and gives me strength."

"I hope that is true, Ishtar. I really do."

I rinsed his hair and long beard and wiped the grime from his face. I washed his feet and between his toes. I bathed him as I would a small child. I did not turn on the Power.

His body relaxed; the erection melted. He closed his eyes, and I thought him asleep. But when I started to move away, he opened them and asked, "Where are you going?"

"To get more towels and the oil, Excellency."

I dribbled scented oil into fresh water and swabbed his whole body, now clean of dust and sweat. Only when I gently washed his testicles and penis, did the erection come back.

It had to be dark now. The lamps in the tent gave off a mellow glow. I could hear the camp laughing around the cooking fires, eating the evening meal, enjoying the soft night after a fierce day.

When finished, I set the water basins and dirty cloths aside. I put clean fabric by the bed. The General lay with his eyes closed, relaxed. I brought him his pipe with the sweet smelling smoke and lit it for him. He leaned up against the pillows and drew deep drafts. The muscles in his face calmed even more. He was quite handsome really, in a brutish way.

I slid out of my robe and pulled the caftan over my head; both tumbled to a lush pile. Deliberately, slowly, I straddled him.

I kissed him deep and caring, my tongue probing the inside of his mouth. No urgency, just languid, very tranquil. The last hint of tension in his massive bulk evaporated into me and then flowed through me into the thick, hazy air.

My nude body lay full on top of him. The warmth of his skin burned into mine. The beat of his heart reverberated into my chest. My lips pressed softly on his again. He floated up from the cushions.

I kissed him on his broad chest, everywhere, in a language that said, "I adore you."

I kissed the red welts on his arms. I kissed his hands and put them to my breasts. He squeezed me, but gently. Expecting pain, I got tenderness.

His hands moved up and down my body, stroking me; his palms were rough and calloused. My skin, chaffed from the blasting sand, was velvet compared to his battle-worn flesh.

I whispered in his ear, "Let us go to the bed."

He picked me up while still reclining and then stood. My legs draped across his massive arms; my feet dangled in the air. He kissed me as he lay me down. The power and sensibility of it surprised me. I was breathless.

He began to make love to me, not animal sex, but a kind of raw passion with tender emotion that moved me. I stirred; I couldn't help myself. He was overwhelming me.

I stretched my neck so that he would find the trigger points that ignite my fire. He found them. He found them all, and he tasted them all with his wet lips, thick tongue, and sometimes his teeth.

It was building in me. I didn't want to believe it. The low growls of a lioness rumbled in my throat.

No more touching. My hand found his manhood, so thick I could scarcely close my fingers around it. I guided him to me and placed him at the gate. He filled me and stretched me, and still I wanted more. I couldn't get enough of him. I hung onto his broad neck while he pounded me amid cries of pleasure, his and mine.

"Deeper," I pleaded. "Deeper!"

My words electrified him. He came to his knees, lifting me with him. He had the strength of ten bulls. He stretched his legs out and held me in his lap, rocking me back and forth. I could only hang my head backwards and plead for mercy. But when he slowed, I begged for more.

When I could bear it no longer, a fireball erupted up through my cervix and out the crown of my head. Contraction after contraction pulsed in my womb. It went on forever; I wanted it to go on forever. I held onto his massive arms, my nails digging in his flesh. Riding on a comet, I would not let go.

He lay me down and moved inside me, slowly. I stopped swirling and came back to earth, stretching for his neck with my lips.

I bit him in that place that is my own trigger point and tasted a drop of blood.

It was the bite that brought him over. His body convulsed; a long, protracted howl escaped his throat. I feared the guards would come, but they didn't. They knew now was no time to enter.

He collapsed on top of me, struggling to catch his breath.

"You are too heavy. I cannot breathe," I whispered into his chest.

He rolled off me and lay spread-eagle on the bed. His eyes closed. His massive chest rose and fell. His manhood lay limp against his thigh.

The jeweled hilt of my dagger was cold to my hand. I didn't think; I didn't hesitate. I grabbed his beard and plunged the blade deep, drawing it across his throat from ear to ear. It took all my strength.

My hand found the green silk scarf, the one that matched my eyes, and I stuffed it in the gaping hole. He choked. His eyes were immense and bewildered. He stared at me in utter disbelief.

"I'm sorry," I whispered to his lips quivering in death throe. "I'm so sorry, but you would never have let me go."

I covered his nude dying body with a blanket. I wanted to dress him, but didn't dare take the time.

Grabbing the sandals, I hurriedly tied them to my feet. After pulling the caftan over my head, I stuffed a scroll, the first one my hand touched, into a cloth with the water bag and bread.

At the last moment, I threw the General's dark cape around me; it would blend into the night. I ran to the back of the tent, opened the flap and crawled through. I was out.

Stars filled the night sky. The moon would rise soon and turn the rocky hills white. I found one of the trails in the cliff face that ascended more slowly and began picking my way through the rocks, as silent as I could be. The crunch of my sandals on loose gravel exploded in my ears. I hardly dared breathe.

The sounds of the camp, the laughter and talking of men, echoed through the ravine. They might even be joking about the General, making lewd suggestions about the Egyptian witch who pleasured him. Of course, they never imagined in their wildest fantasies that he lay dead in a pool of his own blood.

I clutched the bloody dagger in my right hand. If captured, I had to drive the blade deep into my own throat. My own fantasy was not wild enough to imagine what the Persians would do to me now.

CHAPTER 17 EBEN

I stumbled over stones and tripped in small holes, but kept to my feet and kept going. I could not risk hiding; they might find me. My water and food wouldn't last long. I had to keep on the move. But once I climbed over the hill and out of sight of the camp, I wasn't sure which direction to turn.

Desert and wild mountains lay to the east ending at the Red Sea. More desert and mountains lay to the south with miles of wilderness before meeting caravan trails. The Persians had arrived from the north. There could be more Persians; there could be a whole army of Persians. I needed to go west, toward the Nile. But west was the direction they would look for me.

I must be as far away as possible by daybreak, but had no bearings without the sun. Was I going in circles? Hundreds of trails wound through the rocks and gullies. I didn't know which one to take. I panicked that, after hours of trekking, I might end up where I started.

In a moment of despair, I leaned against a large, smooth boulder and tried to calm my panic. The stone still held traces of today's scorching sun; my hip and shoulder warmed. Maybe I could rest for just a few moments. I lowered my hood and adjusted my wig.

It was then I noticed my left amethyst earring, one of the pair meant to ward off evil spirits, was missing. First Maia's Hathor *tiet* charm, and now the earring. What did the loss mean? Did it have meaning? Qeb-ha wore one amethyst drop. Now I did too. Perhaps it was a good omen. I was desperate for a sign.

Gripping the leather amulet, I forced myself to breathe slowly. When my heart slowed, and the panic subsided, I heard Eben's voice as clearly as if he sat next to me on the barge.

"*Study the constitution of the sky, Isenkhebe, to learn the constitution of the earth.*"

Even with a bright moon, the canopy of stars over my head blazed. I spotted *Meskhetiu*, the Ox Foreleg, pointing the way to the Star of the North. *Help me Eben, show me the way.*

I wondered if Hetmus-hor survived the storm. I wondered if River God looked up at the stars now and thought of me. River God. It seemed lifetimes since I tasted you on the Nile. I came back through the Red Mirror for you. Where are you now?

Alone. I was so alone. And it was all my own doing. *This is no time for your foolishness,* River God had told me.

What of my Abydos dream? Hathor had saved me then.

Please, Hathor, do not desert me! I have been foolish, but I have learned. Give me another chance!

The moon was enormous with intricate etchings of deep shadow, as if the ridges on its surface reflected the barren landscape around me.

A black dot, barely visible, appeared in the white glow of the moon. I watched it grow larger until I could make out the silhouette of wings. As if gliding on a moonbeam, the falcon drifted toward me. Hathor's voice was barely a whisper as she flew past my ear.

"Follow me, Isis. Trust me to lead you to your fate."

Perhaps I hallucinated, but I didn't care if the falcon existed in this world or the land of dreams. I would follow wherever she led.

Not that many miles from where I stumbled through the rocks, River God stopped at the ravine and studied the tracks. *Wadi* walls protected the site from the wind; footprints and the signs of digging still showed in the sand.

He retraced her attack and struggle. Why had she been alone, without protection? Had the fool Hetmus-hor no sense of duty? But River God's anger was cold, not hot. Emotion led to mistakes. There could be no mistakes.

At the top of the ridge, he bent low to the footprints of bulky sandals and tracks of horses.

"Impossible," he murmured.

But the weight of the horses, the size of the prints, and the telltale pattern of hooves bound in leather, all indicated Persian animals.

Persians this close to the Nile! He must alert the Pharaoh at once.

His swiftest rider turned back with the tiny papyrus scroll that pigeons would carry from one post on the Nile to another until reaching Saïs.

Persians in region. Number unknown. Alert Pharaoh (glyph Amasis II).

He remounted and veered northeast, the two hundred horsemen raising another cloud of dust visible for miles.

The messenger on horseback thundered into the camp, his horse in full lather with white foam frothing at its mouth. The sentry and he stood outside the General's tent and begged for permission to enter.

"Your Excellency, a vast cloud of dust is moving toward us."

There was only silence from within.

"General Sher, your Excellency. We fear it is Egyptian cavalry, sir."

Still there was only silence. Neither dared make a move. But the General had been clear. Do not enter unless there was news of Egyptians. The sentry opened the tent flap and stepped through.

Sher lay alone in his bed; there was no sign of the Egyptian witch. When he came near, he saw the General's open, glassy eyes. When he pulled the blanket back, he saw the green scarf black with blood at his slashed throat. Blood was everywhere.

Panic set in at once. A great shouting went up around the camp that the General was dead. Men stumbled from their drunken sleep to their feet.

At first the officers could only stare in disbelief.

"The whore!" howled Zavan. "The Egyptian whore! I shall tear her to pieces with my own hands."

"Sentry! Where were you when this happened?"

The man fell to Araxa's feet.

"The General gave instructions not to be disturbed," he begged. "I but followed his orders, Excellency."

Araxa responded by grabbing a pointed *akinaka* from the belt of a soldier next to him and bringing the iron sword down full force across the back of the sentry's neck, severing his head from the spine. A bright red fountain sprayed their legs.

The head rolled to stop against the messenger's foot. He would have jumped back in horror, maybe kicked the head away, but too many eyes were on him. Only minutes had passed since the sentry and he stood together outside the General's tent, begging to enter. Sightless eyes stared up at him.

"We must organize search parties and find the woman now, before she goes far," raged Zavan.

Spit spewed from his thick lips when he screamed. His eyes bulged. His face was fiery red. The tendons in his neck stood out like ropes; a black vein in his temple throbbed.

"Your Excellencies," pleaded the messenger, tearing his eyes away from the dark lake spreading out from where the sentry's head used to rest on the shoulders. "May I speak?"

If he didn't speak up now, his own death might not be as merciful as the sentry's.

"What is it, man? Make it quick."

"Many men and horses are moving toward us, Sir, and moving fast."

"The whore! All of this because of that slut of Hathor."

The officers shouted at each other in their secret Persian, each with a different plan. The soldiers didn't understand a word, but they saw that no one was in charge. The General never doubted what to do. He never allowed shouting and arguing like this, at least not in front of the men.

Outside the tent, soldiers gathered in small groups; the buzz grew louder and louder. The General was dead. The Egyptians were coming. Would they fight or flee?

"Order! Get control of yourselves!" shouted Araxa. "Do you not know that I, brother in battle to Sher, want nothing more than to chop this woman into pieces and take my time about it? But we must wait. She will not be able to hide when Egypt is ours. She will pay. These Nile slugs will not soon forget Persian justice."

"And I, Zavan, shall dream every night of that lesson; it will be worthy of the General. She will beg for death, and still I shall see that she lives to suffer more."

"I swear to you all, on my sacred birthright as Araxa, servant to the King of all Kings, that we shall have our revenge on these Egyptian dogs. But not now. We cannot begin the war before Cambyses is ready."

"Break camp immediately," he ordered. "Leave men behind to sweep the area of tracks. And kill the women. Strip them and dump their bodies into a ravine for the vultures and jackals. The Egyptians will find only bones, if they find them at all."

The exhausted noblemen and servants had cheered with relief when they spotted the cavalry approaching. After days of searching first on horseback and then on foot, with no food and little water, help was here at last.

River God's feet hit the ground at the same moment his stallion came to a halt. Even before he emerged from the whirlwind of dust, they felt his fury. Instead of gathering around him in welcome, they pulled back. Coming out of the black desert, burning hot with anger, he might have been Set himself.

"Hetmus-hor!" he roared. "Which of you is Hetmus, son of Ankh-hor?"

The others melted to the side, and Hetmus stood alone, next to the fire.

"I am Hetmus-hor."

"So, you are the fool that lost her!"

"Bide your tongue, soldier! No man speaks to me in such a manner."

"I give respect to a man worthy of it. What man would let her out of his sight on a hunt?"

"A man overcome by Set's storm. The horses bolted. We came, but it was too late."

"Too late! Do you realize she was taken by those animals, the Persians? Do you have any idea what they are capable of? We may wish her dead, rather than face what they do."

Persians. The word echoed around the fire. No one had thought of the Persians. River God might have said the Gods had come to earth.

"Yes, Persians! Did you not see the tracks?"

Of course Hetmus had seen the tracks, but never thought of Persians. Ibex or wild boor. That was the spoor he knew.

"Say something!" shouted River God. He'd managed to keep his anger cold during the long ride, but his hatred now boiled over into rage.

Hetmus could think of nothing to say. What could he offer other than excuses? Guilt crushed him. He hadn't slept except in fits and spurts since the storm. His perfect world had shattered. All around him were shades of gray. There was no color anywhere. He saw his family's honor destroyed. But most of all he saw Isis among butchers. The Commander was right. She was better off dead.

"I said, say something!" River God roared.

His world went black, then red, and then exploded with horrible visions of Isis at the hands of Persians. The stench of his fury was in his sweat.

He grabbed Hetmus by the throat, his hands around his neck,

his thumb pushing into the windpipe. Hetmus-hor wasn't a soldier, but he was strong—and almost a head taller. His hands went to River God's throat and pushed him backward a step.

"Stop!" Eben shouted. "You do not help Isenkhebe. Control yourselves!"

They kept their hands on each other's throats, but stopped pushing. The shadows in the men's faces lightened and deepened with each flicker of the campfire. Contempt etched deep lines around River God's mouth and from his cheekbones to jaw. His eyes blazed with hatred.

Hetmus-hor was ready to defend himself, but those who knew him well saw a man naked, filled with self loathing. His friends looked away, not able to bear his shame.

More than once, they had wished to go home and leave the fate of the priestess to her goddess, but they knew well what was at stake. Clans rise and fall in crises like this. They had stood by Hetmus-hor as they knew he would stand by them.

The only sound in the desert was the snorting and labored breathing of the cavalry horses. The night was calm, with no wind. Millions of jewel-covered stars lit the sky, but no one noticed.

"Think of Isenkhebe!" Eben forced himself between the two men. His huge eyes peaked through long tangly hair. The straggly beard barely covered his chin. In the bulky striped robe, he looked slender and fragile as a gazelle.

"She is alive. I know it. It is her destiny to live. The power of Kabbalah will give her strength and show her the way. "

A long moment passed. Hetmus relaxed his grip first and dropped his hands. River God held on just long enough that it looked like he wouldn't quit. When he did release Hetmus, his fists stayed poised at his sides, ready to strike. They still stood almost toe-to-toe, glaring into each other's eyes.

"We can save her," Eben reasoned, "but only if we work together."

"And who are you, Hebrew, to spin tales of your magic?" mocked Hetmus-hor.

"I am one who cherishes Isenkhebe and is willing to do anything to get her back. Are we not brothers?"

"I do not believe in superstitions and omens."

"Isenkhebe shall be saved," Eben insisted. "It has been promised to me."

On the second day, they found the canyon where the Persians had camped. Faint spoors told them that many men and horses had been here, but it proved impossible to assess the exact number. They fell silent when they stumbled upon remnants of women's clothing tossed among the rocks.

The Nubian brought them the amethyst teardrop earring. Eben and Hetmus recognized it at once; they had last seen it sparkling in the sunshine, dangling from her earlobe. Isis had been here. The knowledge brought both relief and sorrow.

Not long after, a soldier discovered the deep ravine with the bodies of the women, mangled and half-eaten. Hetmus-hor, Eben and River God stood a long time on the side of the chasm, looking down, not speaking.

Finally, River God gave orders to descend, and he and two cavalrymen rappelled as far as they could on lengths of sedge rope tied together.

Hetmus-hor watched in a stupor. Once proud and erect, his shoulders slumped; he might have been as old as Qeb-ha.

"I had a dream last night, Hebrew," he said glumly. "I saw Isis on the back of a falcon. I don't believe the future is seen in dreams, but I woke with hope. That hope is now gone. We make the future ourselves. I have created this future. It is born of my error."

"The Kaballah is the Light. Trust."

"Your Hebrew Light," Hetmus shot back, "will have to shine bright to salvage this nightmare."

The sides were steep, and there were few footholds. At the bottom of the ravine were five bodies, broken and naked among the sharp rocks. When the lengths of rope were too short, the three were forced to climb up again.

River God sat on his haunches on the edge of ravine and stared blankly. He didn't see the rocks or the sky, only visions of the broken women. This is what he had feared since he first saw the Persian tracks. No matter what it took to get her body up, he would return Isis to the Temple to prepare for her *Ka's* journey to the afterlife.

"Commander."

"What?" he snapped. "What now, Hebrew?"

If it had been Hetmus-hor who sat next to him, he would have pitched him over the edge.

"When you were nearest, could you see if any of the women have a shaved head? From here it appears they all have long hair."

He closed his eyes. The images of the women were immediately there, and he saw clearly why the Hebrew asked. Relief. He could have cried from relief.

"By Horus, you are right!" he shouted. "They have hair. Isis is not among them! How could I not have thought of it?"

"Your heart is ruling your head, Commander. I told you Isenkhebe needs you to be in control."

He let the rebuke from a Hebrew pass. Nothing would lessen his joy and relief. He didn't know if Isis still breathed, but he knew she was not lying at the bottom of this gully for the animals to feed upon.

"I had a vision, Commander."

"A vision. What kind of vision? Did you see her? Is she alive?"

"She is alive, and I have a plan. It was revealed to me in a trance. You will search, but leave three men with me. One must be Goliath."

Eben climbed to the summit of one of the deep gorges that honeycomb the mountains. Standing at the edge, he tested the wind. With his hands cupped around his mouth, he shouted "Isis!"

He could hear the echo repeated a dozen times as it faded into the east.

"Isis! Isis! Isis!"

He paused between each set to let the echo reverberate on the rocks. His voice became hoarse. He drank water and called out again. Then he moved to another ravine and started all over.

He continued, not because he thought Isenkhebe would find them by the echo, but because she would hear and draw strength from the knowledge that she was not alone.

He didn't know if it was the best thing to do. He didn't allow himself to doubt. His instructions came from the Light, and so he followed without question.

CHAPTER 18   FALCON

I traveled in the cool of the morning and rested in the shade during the heat of the day. I needed to conserve water. I was sheltering in a small cave high on a rough hillside when I saw the dust of many horsemen headed northeast at full gallop.

The Persians were leaving! There were so many men, it had to be them. Had they left behind a search party? I thought not. They rode at top speed. Perhaps the General's death had caused them to break camp. But whatever the reason for their retreat, I dared hope. I thanked Eben and Hathor and even Set the Destroyer. If I kept my wits about me, I would yet make it out of this hell.

The falcon circled overhead. She seemed distant, too. I felt alone in the universe. The goatskin water bag was near empty; I had long ago eaten the bread. My feet were cut and bruised; pains shot up my legs with each step.

I could hardly remember the time before my misery. Everywhere I looked, I saw the General's eyes and the red of his blood against the green scarf. The image was strongest when I closed my own eyes. I fingered the amulet and spoke to Eben as if he were in front of me.

But it was the words of Qeb-ha that gave me greatest strength. *By completing the sunrise and sunset in Right Measure, you will arrive safely at your goal.* The phrase became my mantra; repeating it over and over kept the possibility of survival alive.

Lying back on the rocks, in a tiny shaded crevice, I drifted back to the Nile. It brought me peace to summon the warm, damp air of the river and the sound of the water rushing past.

When I dreamed, two giants lifted me with four hands and lowered me gently onto the East Bank, under the sycamore trees by the hunting lodge. The baboons made a great racket and flocks of white herons rose to the sky. It seemed that my life had begun there on the edge of the river, that everything before that morning was just a dream. Before I woke, I saw that the faces of the giants were River God and Hetmus-hor.

When I first heard 'Isis' ricocheting across the vast spaces, I thought I still dreamed. But the echo continued, and I dared to believe that someone who knew me well called out my private name. I couldn't tell from which direction the sound came. It echoed through the hills and bounced off the cliffs.

I stumbled down a steep incline to a *wadi* that wound through the hills toward the west. The ground was flat and less rocky, easier on my bruised feet and tired legs. The falcon circled overhead in wide arcs. I was afraid to answer the echo. Who knew what evil lurked?

The sun burned down without mercy. At least there was no dry wind to suck the last of the moisture from my battered body. The General's heavy cape around my shoulders protected my skin from the sun and kept my perspiration from evaporating. It covered the silk caftan which would have flashed bright turquoise for miles. As much as I wanted to be found, my life depended on it being by the right person.

More in a stupor than awake, I willed my feet to keep moving forward. I was alone in the stillness of the canyon; I saw no other life. The falcon circled in a white sky.

I came around a deep bend in the river bed and instantly flattened myself against the cliff.

A group of men rested just ahead; they wore the heavy robes of desert people, no matter the heat. Their heads were wrapped in turbans fashioned of colored cloth, all blue like the sky, except one man whose turban was red.

They took shelter from the heat of the day in the shadows of large boulders and strange-looking brown bushes. They didn't talk. The stillness hummed in my ears.

They were a ragtag lot, too few for a proper caravan, and caravans don't roam the wild mountains. Traders follow routes that lead from oasis to oasis. The men must be hiding, like me.

I eased backward slowly until hidden by a sharp turn in the cliff. My body was glued to the canyon wall. I closed my eyes and took several deep breaths. I couldn't go forward and couldn't go back. Behind me stretched miles of *wadi* leading away from the Nile. The cliffs were too steep to climb out.

"Isis! Isis! Isis!" My name echoed eerily, coming from nowhere and everywhere at the same time.

It had been quiet for a while. I wondered what the men thought of the sound of 'Isis' cascading through the *wadi*.

The men shouted and argued. Their harsh voices carried in the absolute quiet. I caught a few words; they were from the Island of the Arabs, the land that lies between the Red and Persian Seas. Beastly sounds joined the men's voices—nothing like the high whinny of a horse or complaining of a donkey. In the brief moment when I glimpsed the men, I saw no sign of animals.

Inching slowly forward, I stretched just enough to see around the corner. The brown bushes were not bushes at all, but camels—monstrous beasts with humps on their backs, lying with bellies on the ground, their legs folded at the knees, bent forelegs tethered with rope.

Deep throaty complaints rumbled from their foaming mouths as the men beat them with sticks and pulled them to their feet. Their thin legs with knees like ghastly skin tumors ended in enormous padded hooves. One camel spit a long trail of saliva and bared his teeth. Another spread his legs and urinated, the stream shooting backwards through his hind legs.

A few camels had a chair-like saddle on top of the hump, secured by straps tied around the belly. Each man climbed into a chair and whipped the camel's rump with a slender rod. First the back legs extended; the men tipped at a sharp angle toward the ground. Then the front legs straightened and the men sat perched high in the air.

I panicked. Were they travelling toward me or away? I looked around for tracks and saw a wide trail of freshly disturbed sand in the center of the *wadi*. I'd been too dazed to notice; I needed to be more alert. But the tracks meant we were going in the same direction. I could follow them out of here.

Led by the red turban, the caravan waddled down the riverbed away from me, blue heads swaying as if they rode the swells of the sea.

I waited until they turned the next bend in the *wadi* and then started after them, always hugging the edge of the sheer cliffs.

The shadows grew long; I could no longer see Re from the bottom of the canyon. The sky was the deeper blue of late afternoon, but the air was still stifling hot. The falcon glided in giant circles above my head, not flapping her wings for long periods of time.

Vultures also circled the ravine. Could they smell my hunger and thirst?

One step, then the next, followed by another. If I allowed myself to think of the pain in my feet and legs, I would give up and lie down to die.

The loose stones of a landslide tripped me, and I stumbled. A cobra curled not three feet from my bloodied sandals. He reared his head; only his tail remained curled on the rock. His hood fanned out around his open mouth. The forked tongue flicked in and out between sharp fangs. I didn't move; I didn't blink.

His swaying head mesmerized me; I heard the whistle of the wind as a snake charmer's flute echoing down the *wadi*. Tiny droplets of clear liquid glistened at the tips of his fangs. Tall as me, he stared straight into my eyes.

The slightest flinch, maybe only a blink, and he would strike. The venom of the cobra brings death quickly. It would paralyze my lungs; I would be dead in less than an hour.

My breathing was shallow, my chest barely moved. My dry

tongue was fat and filled my mouth.

A shadow fell across the rocks. The movement distracted the snake, and he turned his head away from me. I leapt to the side, throwing my heavy cape over my head and arms. The cobra should have struck, but the vulture seized him in her talons and carried the snake high into the sky.

My feet carried me blindly over the rocky sand; I saw only the forked tongue and sharp tips of fangs. When my sandal sank into a hole, I fell into terrible images of eyes: the cobra, the gazelle, and finally the General.

It was dark when I woke. Animals scurried around the rocks, coming out in the cool of the night to feed. I went forward, but not far.

The men gathered around a fire, eating their evening meal. They had to have water. My tongue was as swollen as when I dug my way out of the sand at the chariot. My lips were so cracked, I could taste blood when I tried to moisten them. If I didn't get water, I would die. I might not last another day in this heat.

My hand touched the dagger still tied around my waist, under the turquoise silk caftan. Wait until they sleep, and then sneak into camp. It was a wild plan, but I was desperate. I refused to die of thirst in this burned-out ditch.

The fire burned to embers. There was no moon. The Arabs posted no guard. All was quiet except for snoring of men and occasional low grumbles from the animals.

I arranged the thick cape around me so that my form was as tight and controlled as possible. Edging cautiously along the rock wall, I blended into the shadows. When opposite the dying fire, I stepped away from the side. Impossibly quiet, my feet walked on a cushion of air.

A goatskin water bag lay on the ground close to a camel; I couldn't believe my luck. I lifted the sack an inch at a time. The camel snorted and grumbled, and the nearest man stirred. I stood perfectly still, watching him. He rolled over and farted, but didn't wake. He lay no more than six feet from me.

My stomach growled with hunger, but I had to be content with water. I didn't want to press my luck. I backtracked to the edge of the *wadi*, and then remembered my footprints in the sand. Retracing my steps, I bent from the waist and brushed the edge of my cape against the loose earth, spreading it over the imprint of my sandals.

I would have made it away but for the jackal at the top of the ridge who stepped too close to the edge. Pebbles cascaded down, loosening more and more rocks the further they tumbled. A shower of stones fell all around me. Some hit me on the shoulders and back.

The racket of the falling rocks woke the camels first; they pulled at their tethers, trying to stand, making hellish noises. The men might have slept through the rock slide, but not the camels. I suppose the Arabs feared ambush, because they were instantly alert.

I froze, hoping the General's dark cloak blended into the black contours of the cliff. But they saw me almost at once.

The air exploded in wild shouting, and they rushed me with raised knives. Starlight glinted on the blades.

I threw the hood back so they could see my face and wig. I prayed that, even in the dim light of the stars, they would recognize an Egyptian woman.

They moved to encircle me, as natural as a wolf pack, no word spoken between them. The man facing me had the yellow eyes of a wolf jackal.

They had to have heard my name echoing throughout the day.

"I am Isis!" I shouted at them in the little Arabic I knew. "I am goddess woman!"

They were visibly shaken. The tribes of the desert are a superstitious lot. They believe a beautiful witch lives in the mountains and steals men's souls while they sleep. They were frightened of me. I took advantage of it.

"I go home. Big gold."

They relaxed slightly and glanced at each other; they definitely liked the mention of gold.

I stepped forward one step and the yellow-eyed man in the red turban stepped back.

"Egypt big happy. Give gold very big."

Summoning just a whisper of the Power, I started toward the embers of the campfire. Red Turban moved aside and let me pass. My feet felt as large and heavy as those of the camels, but I walked with shoulders back and head high.

I eased to the ground beside the campfire and took a drink from the goatskin bag. Drawn from a desert well, the water was brackish, but tasted sweeter than honeyed tea to my parched mouth. I took small sips, giving it time to settle.

They stood around the embers and stared at me; some dared whisper to each other.

"Give me food," I commanded.

Bread appeared, and I ate.

"Tomorrow ride camel."

Wrapping my cloak tight around me, I lay down beside the coals and pretended to sleep. So far they seemed awed by me. I wanted to keep it that way. I would show them no fear.

No one came near. They melted away. I heard hurried whispers. They must have agreed on something, because soon it was silent. Then I heard soft snoring again, and I allowed myself to sleep.

CHAPTER 19   RESCUE

My little caravan of twenty camels wound its way down the *wadi*. Riding atop the hump was much more difficult than it looked. The saddle chair swayed back and forth as on a rolling sea. Heat shimmered off rocks and sand.

If I closed my eyes, I was overcome with nausea. When I opened them, white light blinded me. Tiny particles of gritty dust coated the inside of my nose and mouth. But I would have endured anything to be off my bleeding feet.

When the echoes of 'Isis' began again, the Arabs spooked. They stared at me when they thought I wasn't looking, but turned away quickly rather then meet my eye. They probably still feared I was the witch who could steal their souls.

After midday, the caravan left the bleak mountains and began the long, dusty trek across the desert plateau. We stopped for the heat of the day, and I napped in the shade of the camel's hump. Before I closed my eyes, I saw the falcon circling overhead.

In the Land of the Dreams, I visited my temple garden with the song of the nightingale, the sweet scent of gardenia and the moist tongue of River God. But his face kept changing from River God to Hetmus-hor and back again.

Goliath was the first to see the cloud of dust approaching from the east. It was not a large group, not the cavalry or the Persians. He studied a thin black line moving away from the hills, watching the specks inching across the flat plain until he made out a train of camels.

Nodding his head, he pointed to a tiny dot circling in the

white sky. Falcons avoid the heat of the day like any animal with good sense.

Eben sent riders with instructions that the Commander and Hetmus-hor were to rendezvous with the Nubian under the falcon.

They had barely ridden off before Eben rocked back and forth from the waist in time with the wild rhythm of a Kabbalah chant.

A horse approached; I felt the thunder of its hooves in the hard earth. The rider drew closer and closer; my eyes strained to see in the white sunlight. Waves of heat rose up and distorted the shape. Was it a mirage?

Dust blew in my eyes and blinded me. The pounding of hooves stopped, and I heard the heavy breathing of a winded horse. When I looked again, Goliath was leaping to the ground.

"O Hathor! Thank you! Thank you!"

I rocked back and forth, hugging myself like Eben in a Kabbalah trance.

Goliath rushed to me and then stopped; he had never touched me, not even to brush against me. I went to my knees and grabbed his ankles, my lips on his feet. I would have cried a river on those feet that looked to me as massive as those of Min, but the desert had sucked the last tear.

The Arabs kept their distance; I was vaguely aware of them talking in awed tones among each other. The sight of the mountain witch kissing the feet of a Nubian slave must have spooked them even more.

I tried to stand, but the pain was so intense, I collapsed. Goliath lifted me into his arms; he was careful only to glance at my face before looking away. He stood, eyes straight ahead, like a giant basalt statue of a Nubian pharaoh carved for a temple in Aswan. I held him so tight, I don't know where I got the strength.

More horses approached and suddenly, as if they rode straight from my dreams, River God and Hetmus-hor thundered up and dismounted together. The two stood side by side, Hetmus-hor half a head taller than River God. Goliath, holding me in his arms, was taller still.

For what seemed like an eternity, no one moved. The shadow of the falcon circled all of us.

"Isis!" Hetmus-hor shouted. "You are alive!"

He rushed forward, pulled me from Goliath into his own arms and crushed me to his chest. My bruised and bleeding feet dangled in the air; I clutched his neck as if I would never let go.

I'm not sure I was really aware of who held me. At that moment, it didn't matter. The nightmare was over. I couldn't control my sobs of relief.

I raised my face, and Hetmus kissed me full on the mouth. I forgot my blistered lips and drank in his strength. He had saved me. Hetmus had saved me. I kissed him with the passion of gratitude.

Then over his shoulder, through my dry tears of thanks, I met River God's wounded, angry eyes.

Music and laughter carried in the desert air long before we could see the hunting lodge and the flotilla of pleasure boats moored in the rushes of the Nile. Every nobleman and priest from Hermopolis must have been on the East Bank to greet us.

Ankh-hor, Hetmus' father, was the first. He stepped into our path, flanked by six slaves in shimmering white kilts and blue-and-yellow striped headdresses. Ankh-hor himself wore so much gold, I was nearly blinded looking at him.

"Welcome home, my son, Savior of Priestesses, to your victory feast!" he shouted.

A great roar went up when the crowd saw me seated with Hetmus-hor on his white stallion.

"Hetmus! Hetmus! Hetmus!" they chanted. "Long Life! Long Life! Long Life!"

All around was the smell of meat roasting, but it only made me nauseous. Whole oxen, oryx and even hippopotamus turned on spits. Low wooden tables piled high with breads, cheeses and fruits were arranged in long rows. Judging by the shouts and swaggers, the party had long ago started on the sea of *amphorae* of wine.

After the silence of the desert, the clamor deafened me. There were too many people. I was exhausted. My head pounded.

"Let me pass! No one shall see my Isenkhebe in such a condition."

The crowd parted for my mother Sit-hathor dressed for a temple ritual in the tall headdress of solar disk, horns and ostrich feathers. She even wore the sacred beaded *menit* around her neck. A small army of priests trailed her. Four slaves carried an empty litter.

Ankh-hor stepped aside and bowed low.

"Out of my way," she menaced. "You are responsible."

"Yes, my lady, but we have brought her back," he begged.

He looked terrified, as well he should. Sit-hathor was not a woman you crossed.

I looked around for River God.

He was still mounted on his black stallion with its long mane and tail braided with silver twine. His men gathered around him, sunlight flashing on their swords, singing their Commander's praises, competing with the chants for Hetmus-hor.

River God glared at me over the heads of the crowd as if it were my fault that Hetmus held me, that it was my fault that the crowd praised Hetmus for single-handedly rescuing me. Why had River God not acted first? I could be in his arms now.

He hadn't spoken to me during the trek to the Nile, but rode silently in front, leading the way, never looking back at Hetmus and me on the white horse.

When I asked why River God wasn't traveling with the Crown Prince to Saïs, his captain told me that as soon as the Commander received word that I'd been lost in the desert, he had commissioned the fastest boat in Khent-min and drove the crew to row round the clock to reach Hermopolis. The cavalry spent days searching in the desert until the falcon led them to me.

I saw the Persians flee. Never did I imagine it was from River God.

Waiting inside the great tent Sit-hathor had set up for my arrival were Qeb-ha and Eben. I kissed Qeb-ha's hand and begged for his forgiveness. How could I ever have disdained him for being a eunuch? How could I have been so foolish not to see his true worth? *On the road one finds a companion,* he had said to me in Abydos. *In battle one finds a brother—or sister.* But I had wanted neither from him.

"I am only a priest," he said kindly. "The Gods know the impious and the pious man by his heart. The Goddess has judged Isenkhebe to be pious. Why else would Hathor appear as a falcon to lead Isenkhebe out of the desert to us?"

Eben rocked back and forth from the waist, muttering his incantations. Qeb-ha explained that the idea of the echo had come to Eben in his meditations.

"But it was Goliath, Isenkhebe, who first saw the falcon circling in the midday sky and knew it to be a beacon."

The heat, the thirst, the pain, the fear, the desolation, the panic—everything crashed on me at once. I'd never known such exhaustion.

I lay on the bed and wept for what seemed like hours. My mother held me and wouldn't let anyone near. Maia brought herbed water to soak my swollen and cut feet, but my mother took the bowl and cleaned me. The great Sit-hathor herself shaved my head tenderly with a new copper razor.

"Burn this foul wig," she commanded. "And burn this wretched cape and these sandals as well."

But she fingered the smooth silk of my turquoise caftan in the same way the women in the camp had touched my linen hunting gown. She studied the delicate embroidery and the superior quality of the fabric—the turquoise color still sublime, even stained by the dirt of the desert.

"This smells like an animal! But perhaps it could be cleaned? I would like to learn more of the weaving and the thread."

She touched it longingly. Beauty has the power to surmount impossible barriers.

"Keep it, but get it out of the tent now! I want nothing of those Persian beasts near my Isenkhebe."

When she started to take off the leather amulet, I wouldn't let her touch it. I would never take it off.

Sit-hathor shaved me and bathed me and massaged the best fragrant oils into my chapped skin. She fretted over the bones in my hips and urged a warm duck broth down my parched throat. A gown of the finest weave in all Egypt was pulled past my shoulders, tender and raw from coarse wool chaffing against sunburned skin blasted by sand.

The party outside was loud now with singing and the sudden shouts of gamblers. I wondered if River God was still here. He hadn't tried to see me.

Hetmus-hor had come to the tent but been turned away. Sit-hathor let him know that she held his father and him responsible for everything that had happened—for the desert, for the Persians. She gave orders to the priests that no member of Ankh-hor's family be allowed near me.

She didn't ask me anything about what had happened in the camp. No one asked me how I escaped, not River God, not Hetmus-hor. I think they didn't want to know. I wanted to forget, but couldn't.

Bathed, oiled and dressed, a full and glorious new wig on my head and my eyes painted with mica and *kohl*, I lay on the low bed unable to see anything but the shock on the General's face. My lips were too cracked to stain red with pomegranate juice. It was painful to speak, but I did.

"Mother, I must tell you."

"Yes, you must tell all, but later. Forget the desert and be joyful you are safe with us. Hold only happy thoughts in your head and beautiful visions before your eyes."

"But I have visions that won't go away. They are before my eyes when open, and they are there when my lids close."

She sighed and waved everyone away.

"Then speak, my beauty; speak of the horrors if you must. But wounds must not be picked too soon. They need time to heal. And remember that this evil happened to your body, not to your soul."

"My wounds *are* to my soul."

Her eyes widened ever so slightly. She took my hand in hers. Our twin Hathor rings flashed in the light.

"Then we shall call upon the Goddess," she crooned in her voice of liquid gold. "Hathor delivered you from the desert; She shall deliver you from this. But once the words are spoken, purge them from your mind. Those memories will no longer be part of your life."

As she spoke, the Hathor energy flowed through me. I felt the General again—the pain and the ecstasy—and then finally the ride on a comet. I shuddered and exhaled all the air in my lungs; my breath rattled my chest and vibrated in my throat. To my ears the sound was a wail.

"I killed the General, Mother," I whispered. "I made love to him, and then I cut his throat."

Her black eyes first grew round and then narrowed to slits. She exhaled a long hiss not unlike a serpent. Her curled upper lip exposed small yellow teeth worn on the edge.

"He bled to death. I watched his *Ka* leave his body."

My voice took on a flat quality devoid of emotion. I heard myself speak, yet I was detached from the meaning of the words.

"His blood spilled down his chest and onto my hands. It was everywhere. I tried to staunch the bleeding with a green silk scarf."

"Listen to me!" Sit-hathor's fingers dug into my upper arms. "Do not *ever* speak of love with this animal again. You owe him nothing, do you hear? Nothing."

"He had to die, Mother," I sobbed, "but I did not want him to. I did not want him to die!"

Sit-hathor leaned forward until her face nearly touched mine. I'd never seen her eyes so glittery, like black glass.

"Stop Isenkhebe! He was a monster. I forbid you to have feelings for him."

I closed my eyes. I felt dead myself.

"I had no choice." I said flatly. "It was him or me."

She released the pressure on my arms and kissed me lightly on the forehead. When she spoke again, her voice was matter-of-fact, as if she commented on a household chore.

"Of course you killed him, my daughter. And I hope you cut off his filthy balls and stuffed them in his vile mouth."

I felt safe. Everyone thought I was safe. I assumed the Arabs had been paid off and were satisfied. They accepted a large sack of gold amulets and giant chunks of roasted meat from the feast. I didn't know the man in the red turban understood a few words of Egyptian—*priestess, Persian, escape.* Just enough words for him to roam the banquet and catch small phrases from the tales that grew more fantastic with each telling.

I didn't know he already plotted how this Isis of the desert might bring yet more gold.

CHAPTER 20 FORTUNE-TELLER

I heard the pounding of hammer on stone, never ceasing. They must be carving a column just outside my bedchamber.

My ears rang. I felt drugged and disoriented. A door opened; I heard voices. Then Barb rushed in. The property manager followed with a ring of keys in his hand.

"Are you okay?" she asked, her voice filled with alarm. "Do you need a doctor? Should we call 911?"

The manager had his cell phone out, ready to hit send.

"No! Don't call! I'm fine. I was just…sleeping. I didn't hear you knock."

"Sleeping? What is wrong with you?" Barb collapsed on the floor beside me and took my hand. "I've been calling you for *two* days. Your office has been calling you. Why haven't you answered your cell? We thought you'd been kidnapped—or were dead."

I looked at her and wondered how she knew.

"I'd like some water. Would you bring me a glass of water, please?"

The manager walked into the kitchen and opened a cupboard.

I whispered urgently to Barb, "Get him out of here and I'll tell you everything."

"Thank you." I emptied the glass in one go.

The manager studied me for a moment and then asked, "Do you mind if I have a look around? Make sure everything is okay?"

He didn't wait for my answer but tested the sliding glass doors. They were locked. He stepped into my bedroom. I heard him check the glass doors to the terrace and then go into the walk-in closet and my bathroom. Finally, he checked the second bedroom and bath, and then came back and stood looking down at me.

I still sat on the floor, the empty glass in my hand.

"Everything seems fine." His tone said he didn't believe it. "If you're sure you're okay, then I'll get back to my office. I'll have to file a report, though."

"I'm fine. Thank you so much for your help. I'm so sorry to be such a…bother." I tried to sound cheerful and normal so he'd leave.

When he finally closed the door behind him, I got up off the floor and headed straight for the toilet. Barb followed me to the door.

"What the hell is going on?" Barb sounded just like my mother when I was in junior high, and she caught a boy in my room.

"Remember I told you about the Red Mirror?"

When I finished, Barb sat motionless and silent on the red modern sofa she hated because she said it hurt her back. Her wheat-colored Dutch boy hair gleamed in the light. She clutched a polka dot throw pillow in her long, thin arms. I had a brief doubt that she had heard me at all. I had doubts that she actually sat there.

Barb looked over at the Red Mirror and then back at me.

"You know," she said quietly, "if I hadn't seen you and Rasheed—*River God*, you say—at the Stirling Club and the connection between you—right from the first moment—I'd think you were out of your mind."

Barb believed me! I never expected anyone to believe me. I could hardly believe myself.

"Thank you, Barb. I know it sounds insane and impossible… but I don't think I'm capable of…of dreaming something like this."

"No, not even you could dream this up."

Down-to-earth Barb seemed willing to fly a little.

"Do you want me to stay with you?"

I shook my head. "I need some time to…process everything."

"We'll get together later. Keep your cell on and don't go near the mirror. Promise?"

I nodded my head.

"Say it out loud."

"Yes, I promise. Cell on—and no Red Mirror."

I checked my missed calls. Besides Barb, there were a string from my boss. Ed was pissed off. I couldn't deal with that, at least not yet, so I continued to scroll.

Carla had called yesterday, twice. She answered right away.

"I'm having a party!" She sounded excited, her voice high with happiness. "I want you to meet my new boyfriend. He's a doll. I'm in love."

Carla fell in love easily and out again just as fast. Beautiful and rich, she had the kind of money you work for, not a trust fund, not easy. She owned a penthouse with a heart-stopping view of the Strip. At the top of her game, she was mature enough to be taken seriously, but young enough to have muscle tone.

Jewish, with shiny black hair cut short like a pixy, she had grown up in Rio and spoke English with the same rapid fire speed as Portuguese. Her mind, too, moved at the speed of light.

I wished I could be more like her. Carla always knew exactly what she wanted and got it. She was spoiled, but she spoiled herself. .

"Tonight, darling. Come by after nine. It's intimate, just a few friends."

I knew what that meant. Carla had a lot of friends.

"May I bring someone?"

"Of course! Is he good-looking?"

I laughed. I always laugh a lot with Carla. One of her parties was just what I needed to calm my nerves.

"It's my friend Barb. I promised to see her tonight."

"Of course, bring her along. It's dressy; be sure and tell her that."

Carla didn't need to remind me. I don't think she ever threw a casual party.

On an impulse, I called Elaine back in Pennsylvania. We'd been roommates in college and friends ever since. She was married with two kids and lived in a wonderful two-story colonial on the edge of Amish country.

"Elaine, you believe in reincarnation, don't you? That you've lived other lives?"

"We live many lives. I believe our souls progress to higher consciousness by the lessons we learn from our experiences in each lifetime."

Her voice was calm; Elaine always seemed so tranquil. She reminded me of the nurturing side of Hathor, the benevolent aspects of motherhood and fecundity.

"Do you believe you meet the same people in other lives, but they're different and yet the same?"

"We encounter the same souls over and over until we learn the lessons we need to teach each other."

"Have you known me before, Elaine?"

"Absolutely. We have known each other before, and we will know each other again."

Rasheed said exactly the same thing the morning he left me in the Wynn.

"You haven't told me why you're asking me all this. What's happened?"

"I'm just sorting some things out. I'll tell you all about it someday, but there's too much to explain right now."

"I'll take the time, if you need me."

"No, that's alright. Thank you. Thank you, so much, Elaine. You're a good friend. Say hi to Steve and the kids."

My electric toothbrush washed away two days of crud. My hair was a mess; I took a long shower, and then grabbed a rice bowl from the freezer, stuck it in the microwave and thought of my breakfast with the General.

Everyone was dead now: River God, Hetmus-hor, Qeb-ha, Maia—all dead. The Persians were dead. Even the camels were dead. All the drama seemed so pointless. When looking back from 2500 years, it doesn't really matter at what age—or even how—you die. But I felt inexplicably sad. I missed them all. Well, not the Persians. But the General still haunted me.

It took a long time to decide what to wear to Carla's party. I dug out a snug, low-cut white top and a long white clingy skirt. At the bottom of my closet, I found gold sandals with turquoise-looking stones embedded across the straps. My feet looked so bare. No henna patterns. I'd seen lots of girls with tiny tattoos on their toes and ankles and always thought it silly. I wasn't so sure anymore.

When I looked into the Red Mirror, I saw Isis in my face. I wet my hair, parted it down the middle, took out the scissors and cut bangs straight across my forehead. It surprised me how much I looked like Isis then—Isis in her wig, of course.

I fastened a heavy gold chain low on my hips, and then remembered a necklace my aunt had brought back from one of her trips to Israel. Three golden chains fell across my collar bone with strings of turquoise beads in between. Not quite Egyptian, but close enough.

Barb waited for me in the lobby of Carla's high-rise. The valet whisked my car away, and the doorman opened the glass doors into the marble foyer. She looked at me and didn't say a word until we got into the stainless steel elevator.

"Well, you really are playing the part. Did you cut your bangs?" It was a silly question, and she knew it.

"You look great, Barb."

She did, too. Her flaxen hair glistened. She wore hot pink and yellow. I wondered when we had known each other before.

The maid answered the door and took our coats. Barb followed me down the parquet hallway into the living room with modern paintings in bright primary colors. A broad terrace furnished with white outdoor sofas and heat lamps stretched outside the open glass doors. The lights of the Strip blazed in the background.

Brazilian jazz played through hidden speakers, Two cooks were busy at the gleaming Viking range, and the aroma of *empanadas* hung in the air.

The kitchen was crowded with handsome young men in black suits and T-shirts, their hair short and spiky. Most of them were speaking Portuguese. This was Carla's group of Brazilian friends. Their dates, gorgeous girls in the shortest of skirts, balanced on the highest of heels.

You had to be beautiful to attend Carla's parties—or rich.

A bartender in a white jacket served drinks. Barb and I took flutes with champagne and wandered out onto the terrace, looking for Carla.

I spotted her at the edge of the balcony, talking to a small group. Her black pixy hair barely reached the shoulder of the man she leaned into. We maneuvered our way through the sofas, and I eased up beside her.

"Oh my god!" she gushed. "I didn't even know it was you! You look just like Cleopatra!"

She kissed me on both cheeks and beamed. She was positively radiant. Yes, Carla was in love.

"Meet Hector," she said triumphantly. Her black eyes glowed.

"*Encantada*," he said with a wide smile of brilliant white teeth.

I took his hand and smiled back.

"Hello, Hector."

He held onto my hand just a second too long. Carla looked from my face up to his and back again.

"Do you two know each other?"

Hector remained cool, very smooth, but his smile was full of secrets.

"*Si*, but from a very long time ago."

He had the natural confidence that comes with being tall, handsome, and privileged. What had Carla said about him? Something about Argentina and polo?

Barb had a look on her face that shouted, "Oh no, not again!"

I pulled my hand away.

Carla put her arm through Hector's and snuggled against his biceps. Whatever had gone on before, he was hers now.

"Now tell me how you know each other," she insisted. "No secrets allowed!"

She beamed up at Hector and actually batted her lashes. Hector smiled at me a little too warmly.

"It was long ago, Carlita, in another life."

He kissed her lightly on the cheek and said, "Please excuse me while I get another cerveza. *Más champaña,* Ladies?"

With another gracious smile and slight bow of his head, he excused himself, "*Con permiso.*"

I don't think anyone noticed his sideways glance into my eyes as he squeezed by me, his dinner jacket brushing my arm. Carla's starry eyes followed him.

"Isn't he gorgeous? He's a perfect gentleman, but not too much, if you know what I mean?"

Her eyes twinkled, and her dimples deepened. I knew just what she meant.

A handsome couple joined us. They knew Barb and started to talk real estate. I slipped away.

The hallway to Carla's bedroom was empty. The door to her bathroom opened with a blaze of bright light. A man with white hair and a tuxedo came out and smiled.

"It's all yours," he said gallantly.

Hector waited by the picture window in Carla's bedroom. The Stratosphere looked close enough to reach out and touch.

"Hello Isis."

I walked right up to him, put my hands on his chest and leaned my head back. He was just as tall.

"Hello Hetmus."

Hector showed not a trace of the teasing, arrogant Hetmus-hor the morning of the hunt. He was like a man who had thirsted on the desert for days. He took me by the shoulders and pulled me tight to him, my hands still on his chest, my elbows crushed between us. He kissed me with such force that I had to use the muscles in my neck to keep my head from bending all the way back.

He wrapped his long arms around me, nearly lifting me off my feet, kissing my lips, my neck, my shoulders, my throat, everywhere he could find flesh. He buried his face in my hair and breathed in. His whole body sighed.

If he held me tight enough, I wouldn't disappear. An image of him devouring me flashed in my mind; he could have swallowed me whole.

I smelled starch and the faintest scent of soap. He was rock hard against my waist.

With no effort at all, he lifted me into his arms just as he had held me in the desert under the shadow of the circling falcon.

"I've waited a few thousand years for this," he breathed in my ear as he carried me to the bed.

"Hector! Stop! Are you crazy? You can't do this! We can't do this. This is Carla's bedroom. Stop!"

He lay me among the pillows and pile of fur coats and ran his long fingers down the length of my body from my face to my ankles, his eyes soaking up every curve.

"You are perfect, Isis. I could never tire of touching you."

He kissed me again, long and hungry.

"Leave with me," he breathed into my ear.

"I can't do that to Carla. She's my friend."

I could see by his face that meant nothing to him. I sat up to the edge of the bed. Hector put his feet on the floor beside mine. The bed was low; his knees poked up at an angle, but he still easily and gracefully pulled me onto his lap. My legs dangled from his thighs. He held me like I was a child.

"I will fix it with Carla. She is nothing to me. I like her—I liked her. But I will not lose you again."

Barb appeared in the doorway. She looked so much like an angry headmistress; all that was missing was her hands on her hips. Waves of rage rolled through the room.

"I, uh, hate to break this up, but Carla is looking for you, Hector."

She spoke to Hector, but glared at me, her eyes shooting daggers. *What are you doing? Have you lost your mind?*

"Go to her," I told him. "We don't want a scene."

Thank Hathor, it was Barb who had come in and not Carla. There was no telling what Brazilian Carla might have done.

I got up from his lap, and he stood. I straightened his jacket and reached up and smoothed his wavy chestnut hair. I placed my palm on his cheek.

"Go to her, please," I pleaded.

He kissed me lightly, just a brush on the lips. His eyes were warm brown with red specks.

"Don't leave without me," he said.

When Hector's back disappeared through the doorway, Barb looked at me with disgust.

"Bloody hell, could you be more obvious? Both of you disappearing like that. And in Carla's *bed?*"

"I need a drink." It was the only answer I had for her.

I ordered single malt with a splash, no ice. The bartender knew the code; he filled my short glass three quarters full.

Barb glared at me. I could read her thoughts. *Get yourself under control, girl.*

I thought she might lecture me right there at the bar, but a lush, busty redhead in a blue knit sheath squeezed next to me to order a glass of Chardonnay.

"Have you seen the fortune-teller yet?" she asked. "He'll blow your mind."

Barb went in first. I admit to being a little scared. My mind still dwelled in the past, the distant past; I didn't know if I could handle the future. When she came out, it was with a dazed expression.

"It's really, *really* strange. He told me things that nobody could possibly know."

I didn't think Barb had any secrets.

"Were they good things?" I couldn't bear any doom and gloom.

I was far too emotionally fragile for anything but good news.

The fortune-teller sat in a darkened room at a small table. A low lamp with a red shade burned nearby. He didn't look directly at me, but motioned for me to sit in the straight-backed chair on the opposite side of the table. The bare surface of the wooden top gleamed.

His suit was all wrong; it didn't fit him at all. Even his body language was awkward. The way he moved and the way he spoke made me think he wasn't all there, not crazy or retarded, but autistic maybe.

Taking my hands in his, he closed his eyes. His body swayed from side to side. The rocking reminded me of Eben when he went into a Kabbalah trance. I looked hard to see if the Hebrew mystic was buried somewhere inside this strange, lost creature, but I got no feel that Eben was here.

He mumbled. I couldn't make out anything he said. Should I ask him to speak up? Then he stopped rocking with a jerk, and sucked in a short breath. His hands tightened on mine. They were sweaty and hot.

"You are in great danger," he intoned.

His voice came from some distant place, the sound hollow, like a soft echo. I had the sense he wasn't here in this room, but far away.

"You think you are safe. Everyone thinks you are safe. But they are wrong."

I hated this. I didn't like it all. This wasn't what you expect at a party. He should be telling me that I would meet a tall dark stranger and that I didn't need to worry about money.

"You have to get out. To stay is more horrible than you can imagine. They will do terrible things to you, if they find you. They will find you, if you stay."

I pulled my hands away. I wanted to put them over my ears so I couldn't hear more.

He jerked again and opened his eyes, looking straight at me for the first time.

"You have to go back, Isis. You have to go back, or you will suffer. You can't imagine the suffering."

I stood up so abruptly, the chair tipped over and hit the parquet floor with a smack. I don't know what terrified me the most, the words he spoke or his eyes.

Eben sat before me, trapped in this pathetic shell of a man. Eben's eyes pleaded with me.

"Go back, Isis. Go back and save yourself."

My heart exploded in my chest. I couldn't get out of the room fast enough. I fled through the door and leaned against the wall in the hallway, bending from the waist, gulping air.

Barb, completely freaked, held me tight. "My god, what did he say to you? It's just a party game. Nothing he says is real."

She forgot her own awe when she exited the room. People looked at me, probably trying to decide if I had drunk too much or overdosed. I heard '911' for the second time today.

I imagined how ridiculous I looked, dressed up like Halloween. Barb maneuvered me into the third bedroom and closed the door behind us.

"Sit down," she commanded. "Put your head between your knees. Don't move. I'm getting you some water. "

I was dizzy and felt sick, and hoped I wouldn't vomit on Carla's Marimekko rug.

Voices conferred outside the door, but no one came in. Barb reappeared with a glass of water and made me take sips. Then Carla was there.

"What happened? Did you drink too much? Why don't you lie down? You can sleep here tonight." She was distraught and caring at the same time.

I had a hard time understanding; voices sounded thick and syrupy, as if played on too slow a speed on a tape recorder. Hector came up to me and bent on one knee. He took my hands in his and leaned so close that only inches separated us.

"I am here for you," he whispered softly. "Whatever it is, I am here."

Carla looked at us in bewilderment. Barb was so apprehensive, I could almost see her wring her hands. There was no sign of Eben, the fortune-teller.

I pulled myself together. Isis wouldn't sit paralyzed on the edge of a bed.

"I think I'm okay now. In fact, I know I'm okay." My voice sounded strong; I almost convinced myself.

"I feel so stupid. I can't believe I caused such a scene. I hope you'll forgive me, Carla."

Hector appeared with my coat and bag and announced he was driving me home. Carla stared hard at him and then at me. She knew. She'd have to be an idiot not to see. But she could never imagine the real truth.

Once the excitement was over, everyone else went back to the bar.

Rage and jealousy seethed in Carla's eyes when the elevator doors slid shut. Well, there goes that friend. I honestly didn't think it was my fault. Blame Isis. Blame Isis for everything.

Blame Isis for my going back.

Hector started in as soon as the valet shut the car door.

"I feel I have known you forever, Isis, *pero* each time I find you, I lose you."

He had moved the seat back all the way. His head brushed the convertible top. Then suddenly he was Hetmus-hor with a white headdress and a gold collar.

I blinked, and then Hector was back. I didn't know which world I was in.

"What happened, Hector, when you first saw me on the terrace?"

I didn't recognize Eben in the sad body of the fortune-teller until I looked into his eyes.

"Strange visions rushed through my mind *como*—"

He snapped his fingers to show how rapidly the images came.

The sound was incredibly loud in the small space of my little car.

"I had never thought of you before. Not even once. But when I saw you, I knew I had been looking for you all my life."

"Do you believe in reincarnation?" I asked.

"*Yo?*" He laughed. "I don't believe in magic things."

But then he sobered. "Maybe that is not true anymore."

The light at Koval turned red. His face turned red. Even his eyes flashed red.

"*No importa* how we know each other. I have never wanted a woman—no!—*needed* a woman—like I need you. I care nothing for the reasons why. I will do whatever it takes to have you. *Cualquier cosa.*"

I believed him. But that's what scared me. I remembered him taking me from Goliath's arms. He had held me tonight like he held me then; no force of nature could tear him away.

He must not know about the Red Mirror. I couldn't tell him about Eben the fortune-teller. If I did, he would never let me do what I needed to do.

The doors to the elevator slid open. Hector stopped me as I stepped out.

"I will tell Carla that you are someone from my past, that we left things unfinished years ago, and I realize it is not over."

Yes, good idea. Always stick to the truth. It makes lying easier.

When he opened the door to my condo, Aisha was there immediately, rubbing against his legs. He picked her up, stoking her black fur. She didn't struggle at all, but relaxed into his arms and purred louder.

"Don't say anything to Carla, Hector. Please. Not yet. It's too soon."

I kept seeing the anger in her betrayed eyes. I understood her perfectly. I'd be furious too. It wasn't fair, but it was nothing any of us could have foreseen. I never intended for it to happen. I never even imagined it could happen.

"It is not too soon for me, Isis."

He was so open. I could see to every corner of his soul; his heart was on fire.

His honesty made me ashamed. I wanted to be honest with him, but couldn't.

This time he held me without crushing. His lips lingered on mine, his tongue gentle, but not devouring. He didn't stroke me; he didn't explore me. He didn't use his hands at all except to hold me.

But I felt the need all through his body; he was rock-hard again. My body responded with a will of its own; the heat of a sudden flush warmed my skin. But even as the safety of Hector's cocoon tempted me, my mind was clear.

I wanted to please him. I wanted him to please me. But not now.

"Hector, I'm not ready."

He was gentlemen enough to stop, but I could see he was confused and frustrated. And why wouldn't he be? My body had signalled a green light.

"Give me time, Hector. Please. So much has happened. It's too...soon."

He took my face in his hands and raised my chin so I looked straight into his eyes. The little red specks sparkled in the brown.

"It could never be too soon for us, Isis."

He stroked the side of my cheek with his long fingers, then stroked once across my forehead as if to wipe the tension away.

"Put every worry out of your mind. Nothing will happen to you when you are with me."

He kissed me lightly, just the brush on the lips like in Carla's bedroom, and then whispered in my ear, "*Hasta mañana.*"

He closed the door, and I went straight to my laptop and googled 'Egypt Pharaohs.' The list covered more than three thousand years with dozens of dynasties. I started at the beginning and scrolled almost to the end before I found it.

'Saite Dynasty. Psamtik III. 526-525 BC.'

The Crown Prince became Pharaoh Psamtik II but only for a

few months. The next dynasty was called the 'First Persian Period. 525-404 BC.' Cambyses was the first Pharaoh of the new Persian dynasty.

Next I googled 'Cambyses.' The Persians routed the Egyptians, and Psamtik fled to Memphis where he lost everything, almost 2500 years of Egypt, to the Persians. Cambyses sold Psamtik's daughter into slavery and chopped his son into pieces before his eyes."

What had been River God the Commander's fate? What had been Isenkhebe Nefrusobek's—my— fate?

Everyone thinks you are safe. But they are wrong.

If I didn't leave Egypt, the Persians would get me in the end.

Go back, Isis. Go back and save yourself.

Finally, I slept. I dreamed of a party on the roof of Carla's building, the blaze of Las Vegas Valley stretching for miles all around, ending in dark mountains at the edges. The car lights on I-15 were an endless strand of sparkling diamonds coming toward us, and fiery rubies moving away.

I danced with Hector, my head on his chest; he towered over me. Carla danced with someone I knew. When he turned his head, I saw it was Rasheed. She flashed me a triumphant smile.

"You have my man, but I have yours."

Her eyes glittered as bright as the lights stretching into the horizon behind her.

Barb was there too, dressed all in black. Her hair looked like moonlight. She was on the arm of a bull; the man's silhouette was broad and powerful like a linebacker. When the light fell on his face, I saw the General.

I wanted to warn Barb of the danger, that she had to get away, but a sudden sandstorm swallowed up all forty stories of the building. I closed my eyes to keep out the grit. When I opened them, I was alone, buried in fine golden dust to my waist.

"Barb, I have to do this. I know you think it's insane. Please help me. *Please*."

"Don't do this to me! What if something happens to you?"

"Something will happen if I don't go."

"Listen to yourself! Isis is dead. She's been dead for thousands of years. Does it really matter when or how?"

"It does to me."

"We don't know anything about this. Maybe you're only allowed so many trips."

I didn't have any answer. I'd already thought of that myself. The cell was quiet until she uttered the forbidden words.

"What if you can't come back?"

"I have no choice, Barb."

Barb sighed. I could barely hear it across the airwaves, but I knew what it meant. She'd given in.

"Thank you, Barb. And thank you for being my friend."

"Don't say it like that! It's like you're saying goodbye."

"I'll be back, Barb. I promise. Just keep everyone away for a few days. Only a few days."

I tidied up, putting a couple of things in the dishwasher before turning it on. I gathered cat food and a bag of litter to take next door. Sonny had a cat; the two got along. He'd been fine with keeping Aisha. He hadn't even asked why.

Hector called for the second time, and I picked up. If I didn't, he might come over.

"Did you sleep well?" He put so much affection into mundane words.

It hurt to hear his voice. I dreaded lying to him. I was afraid he could see right through me to the truth. I felt transparent, like an x-ray.

"When can I see you?"

"I need to take care of some things. Can I call you when I'm done?"

So far everything was the truth.

"Are you sure you're okay?"

What if he could read my mind, like Qeb-ha? But not even Qeb-ha could do that on a cell phone. Well, I had no way of knowing that for sure.

"I'll call you, I promise. I just need some time alone." I almost pleaded with him.

There was a moment of silence before he answered.

"*Bueno*. I am here. I am here when you want me. I am not going anywhere."

"Hector, did you tell Carla?"

He sounded surprised at my question.

"Do you believe I could go back to her and say nothing?"

No, he couldn't do that. He was as open and honest as a child. How did he survive in the real world? Is there a real world?

"Thank you, Hector, for last night. I'll call you. Promise." I wanted to get off the phone before I said too much.

"Isis," he spoke clearly, without any hesitation. "*Te amo*. I love you."

I hung up and leaned against the kitchen counter, closing my eyes. He had said the words I had waited for all my life. I just didn't know if I wanted to hear them from Hector—at least not now.

I posted on Facebook, Google+ and Twitter and checked my email for the last time. I changed the message on my cell phone, put it on silent, and plugged in the charger. I made my bed, showered and changed into a running suit, and then checked that the doors were locked. The red lamp, on a timer, would be the only light at night.

The rags and the oil were still by the mirror. The metal strut that took me to Egypt was half polished.

Everything depended on time moving forward, even as I traveled backwards. I didn't want to end up in the desert, or even worse in the General's tent. That possibility broke through my defenses, but I pushed it away. Those thoughts would keep me from going.

The Red Mirror still leaned against the white wall. I considered hanging it, but decided there was no point. There would be time for that later. Or so I hoped.

CHAPTER 21 TEMPLE OF NEITH

It was unbearably hot. Heavy, moist air pressed on my flesh. I reclined on my sofa, sipping watered wine, watching flowering trees and naked farmers slide past. Stands of papyrus choked the river banks. There were no cliffs here or no golden sand dunes creeping up to the water's edge. We must be in the Delta. The lush fields flowed into the horizon.

Miles to the south, just past the ancient pyramids of Giza, the Nile had divided into seven narrower branches all streaming to the Great Green. We sailed the Rosetta Branch. River traffic was heavy here. With little space to row, our oarsmen relaxed against the wooden benches, joking and singing bawdy songs.

Papyrus, furniture and weapons factories replaced the green fields, and suddenly we arrived at the river port of Saïs. Round-hulled Phoenician cargo ships designed to sail into the Atlantic carried cedar and hump-backed cattle from Lebanon. Smaller Greek ships brought clay *amphorae* filled with wine and olive oil. Boats large and small jockeyed for positions at the jammed riverfront.

Dozens of obelisks dominated the city's skyline; their electrum- and gold-covered tips gleamed. Brightly painted temples sparkled like jewels—sapphire, emerald, ruby and citrine.

All along the wharf stretched a double row of painted carved columns supporting a stone roof. The marketplace that sheltered in the arcade's deep shade spilled out onto the quay. Merchants traded spices from makeshift tents; others argued and bargained in the blaze of the sun.

Metal clanged against wood and stone. The clamor of voices in dozens of languages rang in my ears.

Our oarsmen tossed thick ropes of braided sedge to Nubian dockworkers drenched in sweat; their muscles rippled across their broad shoulders and their black skin glistened. I looked fore and aft; I saw Goliath but not Hetmus-hor or River God.

Goliath waited near the carved bowsprit of bundled papyrus reeds, ready to be the first ashore. Standing close by him was Qeb-ha.

The old priest and I exchanged nods. His amethyst earring swung gently back and forth. I read relief on his face; his eyes smiled. Saïs, at last.

It is on the road that one finds a companion. It is in battle that one finds a brother.

A party of priests in long white skirts accompanied by armed Temple Guards in short kilts and blue headdresses arrived to escort us to the Temple of Neith. Thank Hathor, we wouldn't spend our days on this crowded barge in the noisy harbor. I sensed no imminent danger. I had time. Isis still had time.

A broad avenue between parallel rows of red granite stelae topped by winged disks led to the heart of the city. Sparkling fountains spilled into pools sprinkled with rose petals. Almond blossoms fell like snow on the green grass.

The boulevard itself was clogged with foot traffic. Phoenicians, wrapped in patterned cloth to their ankles, moved aside to let us pass, bowing their heads. Syrians in heavy striped robes brushed against us without a glance back. A tight circle of Lydians in turbans, belted tunics, and high suede boots shouted at each other, arguing as usual about money.

The number of merchants with colored ribbons in their beards alarmed me; I never dreamed there would be so many Persians in Saïs.

But most of all I saw Greeks, everywhere Greeks, almost as many as Egyptians and Nubians. Older Greeks wore long draped *peplos* with the right shoulder bare; younger men's *chitons* exposed muscular thighs and powerful biceps. Most were clean-shaven and wore their hair short with curls shaped by hot irons in Greek barbershops.

We passed through massive wooden gates from the madness of the street to the serenity of the Temple gardens. Clumps of rainbow hollyhocks, orange lilies and cobalt delphiniums bloomed among slim obelisks and fat sphinxes. Dark green lotus pads with white and blue lotus flowers carpeted dozens of still ponds. Here and there bloomed the ethereal pink lotus of Persia. Beauty from the beast.

The high-pitched screech of a peacock greeted us. The cocks roamed in the sunlight, tails spread in colorful fans while the drab peahens roosted in the leafy willows. Long-legged ibis, stork and snowy egret fed among the papyrus reeds. Iridescent dragonflies swarmed in the rushes.

At the heart of the parkland lay a sacred rectangular lake stocked with gold-speckled fish and white swans. The glassy waters reflected the blue sky and the main temple's façade of thick columns topped by elaborate floral capitals.

Armed with long spears and shields as tall as their torsos, Temple Guards stood at attention beside the pylon gate. The heavy cedar doors clanged shut behind us, blocking out the pandemonium of the street. Only the invited may enter this world; I prayed to Neith that the massive doors, two feet thick, would keep me safe.

Not far from those doors and not far from where we moored in the port was the tavern where foreigners gather. Along with Greek dishes and wine, the Cypriot owners of the Golden Falcon in Saïs serve up gossip and intrigue. A man might get anything he wanted for a price.

When a sailor tired of gambling, he could choose among the exotic women and young boys waiting in the curtained alcoves at the back of the room.

The place buzzed with news of the ailing Pharaoh. Gamblers

were busy placing bets on when the Persians would invade, and how long it would take Cambyses to defeat the effete Psamtik.

Two men huddled over a small table in a dark corner, talking in low voices. The larger of the two had the chest of a bull and round, *kohl*-lined eyes. Colored ribbons tied the ends of the long curls of his beard. The Arab in the red turban spoke rough but understandable Aramaic.

"The priestess is here. She stays at Neith Temple."

"Whore of Hathor!" barked the Persian. "I spit on the day the devil spawned her. She will pay for Sher's death. She and all the decadent Egyptian dogs who aid her."

The Arab shrugged. He had no interest in why the Persians wanted this woman; his only interest was the reward.

"The witch must be seized and brought to me. The Great Cambyses himself desires to oversee her death. Come back when you have her."

The Persian placed a small bag of Lydian coins on the rough tabletop, and the Arab quickly slipped it into the folds of his robe.

The man in the red turban went directly from the tavern to the Royal Palace and entered a hidden door in the thick wall surrounding the compound. A waiting guard led him through back hallways to the Scribe's quarters.

The Egyptian sat on a raised dais with twin boys about ten years-old curled on a blood red carpet at his feet. He motioned the Arab to approach, but stopped him before he came too close. He wasted no time on niceties. The man was one of those dirty desert people who never bathe and wear filthy turbans crawling with lice.

"What is the Persian interest in this high priestess?"

The young boy at his left knee translated into Aramaic.

"She killed General Sher," answered the man in the red turban. "They want revenge."

The boy translated the Arab's words into Egyptian.

"She killed him!" The Scribe considered this new information, stroking the boy as one might a cat. "That part of the story I had not heard."

The sharpening in his hawk eyes didn't go unnoticed by the Arab. *So the Scribe wanted the priestess for himself.* This woman could prove very lucrative. If he worked things right, he might get the Egyptians and the Persians both to pay.

"The Persians are offering a handsome sum for her."

The boy translated again. The twins wore their own curls, unusual in Egypt. The Arab guessed they were from the East, maybe even Persia. They stared at him with large, frightened eyes, pets abused by their master and unsure of what might come next.

"Are they indeed?" mused the Scribe, his own mind scheming of a possible exchange for his safe passage when the Persians arrived.

He pulled the boy's face around and trailed his fingers across the young lips. He dismissed the Arab without looking at him.

"Report back to me. I want to know everything, and I want the woman. I double any price the Persians offer."

Musicians played soft music from a hidden spot under the arbors. A cool breeze moved the palm fronds. Qeb-ha came to me after my bath, and we shared our meal on a marble balcony overlooking a pond surrounded by sunny chrysanthemums and fiery celosia. A flowering myrtle bloomed just out of reach. The Nile, noisy and crammed with boats, lay in the distance. All was peaceful here.

We dined on pigeon pie, cucumbers, lettuce, grapes, melon and bread. Our wine was from the temple's own vineyard. Made from grapes ripened in strong sunshine, black soil and intense heat, Delta wine is heavy and sweet.

"Qeb-ha, where are the Commander and Hetmus-hor?"

I looked at him directly with no attempt at guile. I didn't try to hide my thoughts.

"The Commander is at the Royal Palace, Isenkhebe. His duty to the Pharaoh is sacred and comes above all else."

"And Hetmus-hor?"

"Hetmus-hor is in Hermopolis."

"Hermopolis?"

"Isenkhebe perhaps thought that he might be here?"

He looked at me with amusement. I imagined him thinking, this woman will never learn.

"Isenkhebe Nefrusobek is a high priestess, bound to Hathor," he reminded me.

"I should not think that would hinder Hetmus-hor," I answered.

"Indeed, Isenkhebe. The Governor himself attempted to convince Hetmus-hor that his presence here would not be appropriate. But, such were the objections of Hetmus-hor that he was commanded to remain at the home of his father—under guard."

"Guard?"

Qeb-ha shrugged his shoulders and raised his eyebrows as if to say the follies of ordinary men were beyond his understanding.

"Hetmus-hor has difficulty accepting limitation. He is a strong-minded man, spoiled by his father, and unused to conforming to rules."

So that's how it was to be. River God had his duty, and Hetmus was days to the south under house arrest. Was I to save Isis on my own?

"And what of my father, Qeb-ha? When shall I meet him?"

"When the time is ripe, Isenkhebe. All things happen when the Gods ordain."

Qeb-ha took an amethyst-colored grape into his mouth and spit out the seeds; there was no use asking him more about the forbidden men in my life.

"I pray you forgive me, Qeb-ha, for my past foolishness."

"The Goddess has chosen Isenkhebe Nefrusobek who has done foolish deeds but also brave ones. The Gods lay the heart on the Great Scales to measure its final worth."

"You keep saying the Goddess has chosen me, but for what?"

"Patience. One cannot hurry the moon's rising."

He rose to leave and then turned back. I thought he was going tell me more, but instead he was silent while probing my mind. I sensed he was deciding his next step.

"Eben wishes an audience," he said cautiously.

"Do not fear for Eben, Qeb-ha. My taste runs to men, not boys."

"May the Goddess continue to favor Isenkhebe Nefrusobek with wisdom," he intoned.

"Thank you, Qeb-ha. You have proven a good friend."

"Did I not say that it is on the road that a man finds a companion? I wished for that from the beginning."

"You also told me that it is in battle that a man finds a brother. Are we brothers now, Qeb-ha?"

"The battle is not yet begun, Isenkhebe. But it soon will."

Eben strummed his lyre and sang Hebrew psalms. We sat together on the balcony, stars over our heads.

The night air was fragrant with the perfume of jasmine growing on trellises just outside my rooms. Nightingales sang in these gardens too, like at home in Thebes. Home. Thebes. I had a momentary thought of Las Vegas, but it slipped quickly away.

"Thank you for teaching me about the constitution of the sky, Eben. The Star of the North kept me going in the right direction. But most of all, it kept me from panic. You kept me from panic. Thinking of you calmed me."

I told him about my time in the camp, but not everything. I couldn't tell him exactly how I pleased the General to stay alive or exactly how I escaped. I was sensitive to his innocence.

"I drew strength from your amulet's powers. I am convinced of that. Thank you."

"It was the Light, Isenkhebe, that gave you strength."

He sat as close to me as he ever had, but never touched me. I was a goddess to him; he worshipped me, but knew it could only be from afar. I believe it pleased him that I was an ideal. It suited his poetic spirit. A real woman is messy, with too many imperfections.

"You Egyptians say that one does not discover the heart of a friend, if one has not consulted him in anxiety. You have discovered my heart, Isenkhebe. Now it is yours."

Sometime in the night, warm hands moved across my breasts and over my belly, caressing my hips and the slope of my thighs. Moist lips explored all of me, leaving no place unkissed.

There was a faint scent of myrrh. I moaned in my sleep. Pehtes purred in my ear.

"Isis," a low voice breathed my private name, but I wasn't sure who. "Isis. Isis."

I didn't open my eyes. I wanted it to go on; I didn't want it to be a dream.

Bright sunshine flooded the balcony when Maia came with my breakfast of fruit and *seremt*, a kind of wheat porridge liquid enough to drink.

"Why did you let me sleep so long?"

I stretched among the cushions and pushed Pehtes off my feet.

Maia put the brass tray on the balcony next to the low stools where Eben and I had talked. I remembered seeing the two of them on the boat, heads together, in deep conversation.

"Maia, do you not find Eben pleasing? His voice, his music, his presence are such a blessing."

Maia blushed deep and averted her eyes.

"He seems lonely here, so far from his people. I owe him much, even my life. It would please me greatly if you would befriend him. You should make him more welcome here."

She blushed deeper.

"Look at me, Maia."

Her eyes were huge and round. I couldn't believe how terrified she looked.

"You understand my meaning, Maia. You have my blessing. Who knows what the future brings? It is a pity to waste these years. Revel in pleasure, do as your heart desires."

I thought she was going to cry. Did her vows mean that much to her, or did she sense that the only life she had known was coming to an end?

I took her hand and said softly, "You were born to please and be pleased. It is your nature, Maia. Do not deprive its fruition."

Maia was finishing the final adjustments to my dressing when the message came. We had chosen a short wig trimmed with silver. Silver serpents with emerald eyes coiled around my bare upper arms and encircled my ankles. Matching silver serpents dangled from my earlobes. My long white linen gown of tiny pleats had broad straps covering my breasts.

The small scroll of plain papyrus with Greek letters said nothing except I should go with the guard. The blood drained from Maia's face; her black eyes were huge.

"Do you know anything about this?" I asked.

She only shook her head.

A lone Temple Guard waited in the reception room. He carried a spear but no shield; a short iron thrusting sword hung in his belt. He stood erect and didn't look directly at me. Goliath glared at the guard and kept his hand on his own sword.

"Fetch me the heart amulet, Maia. The one my mother Sithathor gave me in the Temple."

I followed the guard, and Goliath followed me. The Nubian would not stay behind, and the guard did not object. We passed through two open courtyards with porticos of papyriform columns covered in grape vines before entering a green granite chapel. The guard turned in the first vestibule and went along a deserted corridor ending in tall double doors. He knocked. We waited only a few moments.

A priest with a shaven head, long white linen kilt, and bare chest with a broad golden collar opened the door, but didn't speak; a leopard skin cloaked his stooped shoulders. His right hand held a torch. He was old, older than Qeb-ha. He smiled to reassure me.

Half of his teeth were missing; the remaining were dark as aged ivory. Enormous gold ankhs stretched his earlobes and grazed his shoulders at the bottom of his short neck. He motioned for me to enter.

The guard stepped aside; he wasn't going any further. When Goliath moved to follow me, the guard held the spear in his path and shook his head.

"He goes everywhere with me," I protested.

"The penalty for entering is death." The guard looked straight at me for the first time.

He didn't move the spear. The priest said nothing.

I nodded to Goliath, and he reluctantly stayed behind. The priest closed the heavy wooden door and bolted it from the inside.

We entered shadow and total silence. The narrow hallway with vaulted ceilings had no windows or doors. The long line of limestone blocks fitted so tightly that I could detect only a hairline joint where they met. Our footsteps in leather sandals echoed in the stillness. I had the feeling eons passed between visits here.

The passage widened into a small chapel area with a false door carved into the end wall. Torches flamed in niches on both sides. Through this stone door passed the *Ka* spirit to visit from the afterlife.

The priest bent to the floor; his fingers went straight to an unseen lever on the bottom of the carved door jamb. Stone ground on stone, and a draft of cool air blew across my cheek. The torches sputtered for a moment, then burned straight again.

He slid through a narrow gap where the short wall met the long, and I followed. He quickly shoved the stone portal closed behind me. Narrow travertine stairs disappeared into black. I counted thirty steps as we went down; we were deep in the earth beneath the temple. Our single torch lit a small circle around us.

The stairway cut through a domed ceiling painted midnight blue with strange white symbols glowing amid hundreds of yellow stars. I couldn't remember ever having seen the glyphs before. I certainly couldn't read what they said.

The steps ended in a perfectly round room, walls painted the same deep blue as the dome. Ebony doors etched with the same alien glyphs, this time in gold and silver, encircled us.

The priest inserted a heavy ankh-shaped key hanging from a golden cord into the lock of a door with a seven-pointed star above the lintel. A tunnel led to a black hole, and I followed him into the void.

The flame of our fire burned in utter darkness. How I wished I also had a torch. Moisture seeped through the sandstone walls and ceiling; the stink of mildew filled my nostrils. The only sounds were our footsteps on stone and the hissing of the torch. The tunnel turned and twisted until the priest finally stopped at a single wooden door. That door, too, opened with the ankh key, and our torch lit a spiral staircase twisting into the bowels of the earth.

The steps were steep with no railing. He moved quickly for an old man; his feet knew the way. I followed him cautiously, never taking my hand from the slimy stone walls, careful not to slip and tumble to the bottom. There was darkness above and blackness below.

A red door with a seven-pointed silver star at the apex waited for us at the bottom of the stairwell. The priest knocked hard and then soft. The door opened wide. I closed my eyes against a light as bright as the noon sun when exiting a shadowy temple.

A hand took my hand and led me inside, and the red door shut firmly behind me. I was deep in the earth and at the end of a maze. I resisted the wave of claustrophobia that washed over me. I resisted the feeling of being entombed.

Dozens of lanterns hung from stone arches. Thousands of scrolls filled niches in the walls. I had a vision of catacombs lined with bodies bundled in white. If interred here alive, the reading on these shelves would fill the days of a long life.

A tall man with long silvery hair stood beside a square wooden table covered with papyri. Seven-pointed stars, embroidered in silvery threads, shimmered in his blue robe. He was the Wizard from my Abydos dream. He had nothing in his hands though—no tablet and no sword.

With a smile that dimmed the lamps, he reached out both hands to me and drew me to him. His eyes were pale, almost without color; I didn't think it possible for him to go in the sun.

"I am Hermes , known as *Trismegistus*," he said in lilting Greek. "Welcome my daughter, Isenkhebe Nefrusobek, to the Library of Neith, the greatest Mystery School of all time."

CHAPTER 22   HERMES TRISMEGISTUS

My father's palms were large and square with almost no lines. Sit-hathor's gold heart amulet glinted against the smooth skin. Some say you can see a person's character and destiny in the lines and shape of their hands. Hermes had only three lines in his palm; his path must be very clear.

He gazed at the heart amulet; the ghosts of fond memories passed liked wispy clouds across his face. After a few moments in the pleasures of the past, he returned to me.

"I did not need the amulet to know you, my daughter. The beauty and strength of your mother are reflected clearly in your face."

"Come sit beside me," he said, patting the seat of a cushioned ebony chair with a high back. "You have been through a terrible ordeal, my daughter. I am sorry for that, but it has made you stronger."

Hermes touched my shoulder gently. His hand was warm and dry. He left it there a moment, not hurrying to take it away.

"I only recently learned of you." I tried to keep the accusation from my voice.

Why had my father been kept a secret?

"Yes, I regret that. A father and daughter should not be apart. But ours is not an ordinary family. And your mother is certainly not ordinary—not by any standard."

He chuckled to himself, again in the past with a kinder, gentler Sit-hathor than I had known.

"And not everyone has a god for a father," he continued. "*Hermes Thrice-Greatest* these superstitious Egyptians call me. 'Once-greatest' must be enough, I should think."

Hermes Trismegistus was a warm man who smiled easily. He put me at ease with idle talk about Sit-hathor and Thebes while he moved the scrolls aside, replacing them with three silver chalices filled with wine. He squeezed my hand in a loving way before passing me a chalice rimmed with stars and crescent moons.

"I hear you also have a sharp wit. I admire a woman with intelligence as much as I admire a woman with beauty. You, my dear, are blessed with both."

He turned his head and spoke into the shadows. "Do you not agree, Antinous? Is my daughter not both beautiful and quick?"

I was thrown a bit off balance that Hermes hadn't told me that we weren't alone.

"Your daughter is indeed beautiful, Hermes."

Antinous had the voice of an educated Greek, deep, musical, trained for oratory and theatre. He didn't seem ready to concede my wit.

I should have noticed that Hermes had set three chalices on the table. I felt at a disadvantage, as if I had been scrutinized and judged, and failed the first test.

The Greek leaned casually against a wall, his muscular arms lightly crossed at his chest. A blue *chiton*, belted at the waist, ended halfway up his wrestler thighs. The soft wool draped from his left shoulder across a broad chest. His right shoulder was bare as well as those gorgeous biceps and perfect forearms. The contour of his muscles ended in strong wrists and graceful hands.

His beauty was so perfect, he might have been sculpted from marble. A Greek statue, but clothed.

A mane of waves with streaks of gold crowned his head; ringlets fell on his brow and around his ears. He had hair you wanted to run your fingers through and watch the curls spring back. He had a body you wanted to run your fingers over and watch the gooseflesh rise.

When Antinous took the third chair at the table, I saw he was even more beautiful up close. His pale skin was flawless. I didn't think it possible for eyes to be so blue. He was reserved and just a little cool—very hard to read.

"Antinous is my trusted assistant. Everything I know, he knows."

And what exactly did my father know? I felt exposed and vulnerable. And definitely at a disadvantage. I knew nothing about Hermes—or Antinous.

Once Antinous joined us, Hermes grew more solemn. I sensed he was ready to move on to the purpose of our meeting.

"All knowledge is contained in these scrolls, including many secrets."

He swept his arm in an arc to point out the hundreds of papyri neatly stacked in the niches.

"Secrets?" I asked. "Is that why I am here?"

"I have heard you are both impatient and direct," Hermes said. But he smiled the indulgent smile of a doting father.

The lanterns hanging above the table cast a circle of warm light around us. The shelves, filled with scrolls, were almost in shadow. Antinous watched me a little too intently; he made me uneasy.

There was no sound other than our voices. I wondered how far underground we were.

Hermes didn't appear to be in a hurry. He settled back in his chair and took a sip of wine before continuing.

"So, Isenkhebe, what have your tutors taught you about Atlantis?"

"Atlantis?"

I was a little stunned at his question; I hadn't expected him to start out with a fable. There was nothing in his face to indicate he wasn't serious. Another test?

"Atlantis is a mythical land that supposedly sank into the sea?" I answered.

What other answer could there be?

"Let me assure you that Atlantis was, in fact, very real."

I glanced at Antinous. Both he and Hermes watched me—Hermes with a bit of amusement in his eyes. Antinous had a quite somber look. I felt he analyzed my every word. It was clear they expected me to respond.

"You called me here for a reason, my father. I assume it has something to do with Atlantis. Am I to guess, or will you tell me?"

"A sharp tongue like your mother!" Hermes laughed and poured himself more wine.

Antinous didn't laugh. In fact, his eyes narrowed just a bit, and a crease appeared between his eyebrows.

Hermes studied me for a moment. I sensed he was taking me step-by-step to judge if I were worthy.

"Atlantis was a very advanced culture many thousands of years ago. Much more advanced than ours. Yet in some ways, very much the same."

"More advanced in what way?"

"They deciphered the Cosmic Code."

"Code?"

"*Microcosm* and *macrocosm*. The world below and the world above mirror each other."

"I am not sure I know what that means."

"It means quite simply that the physical world is a reflection of the spiritual world. That form comes from thought. That one form of matter can be changed to another."

Images of medieval alchemists turning lead into gold flashed through my mind.

"The Atlanteans could lead a life of their choosing without labor. But like us, they were greedy and arrogant. They experimented with natural forces, breeding monsters that were part man-part beast. But the end came when they released a cosmic energy they could not control. It ripped their world apart in a runaway chain reaction."

"Were there any survivors?" I envisioned a massive nuclear catastrophe, one large enough to destroy a whole world.

"A very few. Some came to the Delta ages ago. The simple men living here made their man-beast abominations into gods."

Hathor with cow ears? Thoth with the head of an ibis?

The connection was suddenly obvious.

"The strange symbols I saw in the domed room. Are they

Atlantean?"

Hermes glanced at Antinous and nodded. They both looked pleased, and I felt relieved to have passed a test.

With the grace of an athlete, Antinous rose from the table and returned with package about the size of a very thick laptop. I wondered wildly for a moment if it were a suitcase bomb.

"The Cosmic Code must never fall into the wrong hands, my daughter. The power must be protected until the world is ready."

On cue from Hermes, Antinous reverently folded back the soft antelope skin. A tablet of polished green faience covered in Greek script glowed as if lighted from within. I recognized it immediately from my Abydos dream.

And the following to be the truth.
That which is below is like that which is above,
and that which is above is like that which is below,
in the accomplishment of the miracle of one thing.
And as all things came from the One,
through the meditation of the One,
so all things were born from one thing by adaptation.

I read quickly. Above and below reflecting each other like a cosmic mirror. Macrocosm and microcosm.

"What is the One?" I asked.

"Everything comes from the One Energy—both what you see around you and what you cannot see. We may seem separate, but only the form changes, not the essence. We all come from the One. We are all one."

"But if you know the secret to the cosmos," I asked, "why do you not just manifest a way out of the danger?"

"I have manifested, Isenkhebe. I have manifested the Emerald Tablet, and I have manifested you."

Hermes swallowed my hand in his. His energy flowed into me and filled me with calm.

"You are the chosen one, my daughter. It is your destiny to

protect the Tablet."

Me? Protect the Tablet? This was a little out of my pay scale. I came back to save Isis, not the world. I didn't feel all that capable of protecting myself, much less the Cosmic Code.

Hermes squeezed my hand harder. A slight buzz in my ears grew louder. I had no sense of my body. I no longer felt the chair. I no longer saw Hermes or Antinous, although I was vaguely aware of the oil lamps casting shadows on the rows and rows of scrolls. I drifted outside of time in a velvet sea—just as I had in my living room the first night with the Red Mirror.

"Surely you recognize your unique power, Isenkhebe." Hermes' voice swam through deep water to my ear.

I'd never thought myself powerful, but I was here; I had passed through the Red Mirror to this life. That must be unique. It certainly couldn't be common. I had another power, too. The Hathor Power.

"You must take the Emerald Tablet out of Egypt. There is very little time."

He squeezed my hand again, and I came back to my chair.

Hermes looked over at Antinous, and then back at me. This time he took my hand in both of his. His tone was soft, like a doctor giving a patient startling news and trying to deliver it in the gentlest possible way.

"You will be the wife of Antinous. He will take you home to Greece. Your new Greek name is *Isidora*, gift of Isis. All has been arranged."

Wife? I would have pulled my hand away if Hermes hadn't held it tight.

"A woman cannot travel alone. A woman cannot live alone," he said patiently. "This you know to be true."

What I knew is that I didn't know the Greek at all. He was handsome, even beautiful, but came across cold and aloof. I sensed wariness on his part. How convinced was he of this marriage? *Everything I know, he knows.* There was a lot about me not to like in a wife.

I wasn't even sure he was attracted to me. If he were, he hid it well. Would he expect me to be faithful to him? Surely they both understood that impossible for a priestess of Hathor. And I wanted River God. I still held out hope.

River God. Would I ever see him again in this life or our life in Las Vegas? Hermes claimed to know the secret to the cosmos. He must understand how souls could meet each other on both sides of the Red Mirror.

"Hermes, have we known each other before? Shall we know each other again?"

If he thought it odd that I so abruptly changed the subject, he didn't show it. He might even have expected my question. If we are all one, he might be able to read my thoughts. Qeb-ha managed to probe quite deep into my mind, and his powers seemed feeble compared to the genius of Hermes Trismegistus.

"We shall know each other until we have learned what we need to learn," he answered.

Elaine had said the same thing to me when I had called her to ask about reincarnation. She was the only person I knew who believed in reincarnating circles of souls. Until Hermes. But it turned out Hermes Thrice-Greatest had an even more complex notion of past and future lives.

"Do not think, my daughter, in terms of have known or will know; they exist at the same moment. Time is a continuum that loops back on itself."

Antinous had said nothing all this time. What secrets did *he* know? I couldn't read his eyes. His face was a mask.

There was no clock in the Library of Neith buried in the bowels of the earth. I couldn't tell how long I had been here. It seemed like a few minutes, but it could have been hours. Time. Minutes here could be hours on the surface. Hours in Las Vegas were days in Saïs.

Hermes reached over and touched the leather amulet on my

wrist with his index finger. He didn't have the hands of an old man. His skin was soft and pliant.

"The Kabbalist will give you a new amulet. He is devising it now."

I didn't bother to ask how he knew about Eben. Hermes knew things far greater than that.

I sighed. My choices weren't limited; I had none. And so I resigned myself to what must be, rather than what I wanted.

Eben the fortune-teller at Carla's party had been perfectly clear. If I were to save Isis, then I must leave Egypt at once.

"When do we sail?"

CHAPTER 23 ANTINOUS

I followed Antinous up the spiral staircase; we each had a torch. Neither of us spoke. Our future together had to be as much on his mind as mine. The tension between us sparked in the dark.

We hurried down the long tunnel, but he stopped at the bottom of the steps that lead up to the little chapel with the false door.

The torches in our hands blew a little sidewise. After the stuffiness of the damp tunnel, the air seemed almost fresh. Antinous stood inches away. White Atlantean symbols danced against the blue dome behind his head. He smelled of lamp oil and slightly of male sweat. No perfumed oils or myrrh. His skin glowed. I'd never seen a man so perfectly formed. He really was as beautiful as a statue of Adonis.

His eyes were the color of the sky over Thebes on a spring morning. His lashes were thick as brushes. Leather bands encircled his wrists; he wore no other adornment and no *kohl* around his eyes. The gold highlights in his curls shimmered in a halo around his face. His lower lip was slightly fuller than the upper, which was shaped into a bow; his mouth almost formed a pout. His chin had a deep cleft. A muscle in his jaw knotted and unknotted.

Antinous didn't speak; he didn't move. My breasts rose and fell as I breathed; the sheer linen clung to their curve. The emerald eyes of the serpents coiling around my arms glinted in the torchlight when I reached out to trace my long nail around his lips.

He put his free hand on the nape of my neck. His grip was more forceful than I expected; it didn't fit with his aloof demeanor. His eyes locked on mine, but I saw none of the hunger I always see in men's eyes. I could read nothing there.

My fingers combed through the short curls on his neck. I traced around his ear with my fingertips. My eyes invited him.

Finally, he lowered his face toward me, but didn't close his eyes until his lips were on mine. I opened my lips and took him in, sucking on his tongue in a gentle teasing way, urging him on. My heart raced; heat surged through my veins. I felt hot as the sun.

How far were we from the wall? I envisioned my back against the cool, damp stone, one hand guiding him, the other holding a torch. Would the torches stay lit if we lay them down on the stone floor?

But instead of responding to me, he drew back while still gripping my neck. His eyes stayed locked with mine, but I could read nothing there; it was as if his eyes were separate from his body and had no connection to the changes there.

He was my husband and my future. I eased the thin linen strap of my dress aside with the tips of my fingers; my breast was a pale mound in the torchlight.

Antinous looked down, blinked once and then looked again into my face. Taking his hand away from the nape of my neck, he slid the sheer fabric back into place, covering me, never taking his eyes away from mine.

I jerked as if he had slapped me.

He switched the torch to my right hand and then took my left hand into his right.

"Come." He said nothing more, but gripped my hand just as firmly as he had gripped the back of my neck, and led me up the stairs.

Antinous dropped my hand once we reached the top of the steps and entered the chapel. He didn't speak or touch me again but walked quickly with eyes straight ahead.

Goliath still waited outside the double wooden doors. He stood at attention when we exited. He looked sharply at Antinous and then directly at me, something he rarely did. He judged the danger to me by a brief glance at my face. I may have shown discomfort, but not fear.

We returned to my chambers in silence with Antinous in the lead. I followed him, and Goliath followed me. I replayed the scene in the tunnel over and over in my head. He had kissed me. I had responded. Were we not to be husband and wife? Had I violated some Greek taboo at the foot of the stairs?

Maia had sent for Qeb-ha, because he waited in my chambers. His face, usually placid as a Buddha, was etched with worry lines.

Eben was there, too. When we entered, he sat before his scrolls, reading his numbers and stars, stopping to rock back and forth from time to time, reciting hurried incantations.

Goliath kept his eye on Antinous and his hand on the hilt of his short-sword. Shame washed over me that I ever entertained thoughts of abusing him. He was totally devoted to me, and I would have made him miserable for my own pleasure. He was the one who first found me in the desert and cradled me like a child—the first man to touch me after my escape, after the General.

Both Qeb-ha and Maia were surprised to see Antinous, but concealed it well. I introduced him as Hermes' assistant. Nothing more.

Maia's eyes studied the Greek. She took in every detail of his tall frame and golden curls. She saw his beauty and bearing, and she knows me. I could see her thinking, *Who is this new lover?* I kept my face a mask.

"Hermes will send you a message very soon," Antinous said in the flat tone of a messenger with no personal interest.

"Do not go, Antinous. I wish to speak with you."

"Please leave us," I told the others.

Qeb-ha hesitated for the slightest of moments, then bowed his head, leading Eben and Maia from the room. Goliath went no further than just outside the door; his giant frame cast a shadow across the threshold.

Antinous leaned against the railing of my balcony, his elbow on the edge. His stance appeared relaxed, but not his face. As in the tunnel, the muscle knotted and unknotted in his jaw. His mouth formed even more of a pout.

"I do not consider it safe to talk here," he said.

I moved closer to him, and he shifted his weight; he was very ill at ease with me. He had rejected me in the tunnel, and I didn't know why.

"Am I not to know our plan, Antinous? I do not think myself unreasonable. My life is at stake, after all."

I thought perhaps he wouldn't tell me. His jaw set. The cleft in his chin deepened. When he spoke, his voice was so low I had to move right next to him. Again I smelled the scent of male mixed with burnt oil.

"Speak of this to no one, Isenkhebe. Do you agree?"

My first reaction was resentment that he thought me so foolish, but he was right to caution me. I would have told Qeb-ha and Eben. I would have told Maia; she had been with me all her life.

"A Phoenician ship waits at Rosetta, where the Nile meets the sea. We must sail north from Saïs without detection."

Antinous stood erect now, tense all over.

"Tell no one," he repeated.

He started again to leave, and again I stopped him. This time I put my hand on his forearm. His skin was pale next to mine. Even the tiny hairs on his arm were so fair they almost disappeared. He felt warm, but not damp.

"Antinous, did I offend you in the tunnel?"

It took some courage for me to ask. But Greeks have a reputation for favoring their male friends over their wives. If that were the case, I wanted to know now.

He stared out at the temple grounds for a long moment. Re was sinking towards the west. The heat of the day had broken. Birds flocked around the myrtle tree blooming a few yards away; a peacock trilled his mating call. The high tinkling sounds of women's laughter carried across the garden like musical notes from a glass wind chime.

My breath caught when he turned his eyes back to me. They

were exactly the same color as the sky behind him, and in them I saw the yearning I am accustomed to see in men's eyes. But I also saw doubt.

"I know you can satisfy me, Isenkhebe. But can I satisfy you?"

Qeb-ha begged permission to enter as soon as Antinous left. Eben and Maia followed on his heels. Qeb-ha's eyes were wild; the amethyst earring swung frantically back and forth.

"Eben sees danger! Great danger!"

"But there is a tiny door through which you may escape," Eben interrupted. "Everything depends upon the correct action."

"Is there actually a door, Eben?"

Naturally I thought of the domed room deep underground and the circle of ebony doors with Atlantean symbols.

"We must leave at once for the South!" Qeb-ha's voice was impossibly high with angst. "We shall all travel to Elephantine, to the Jewish community."

When I didn't immediately agree, he grew more agitated. He almost begged.

"Eben can find shelter. Isenkhebe can disappear there."

"What do you see in your stars and numbers, Eben?" I asked.

"I cannot see clearly, but there is only one path to escape. You must be careful to chose correctly. The outcome is not yet written."

"Qeb-ha, you said Hathor chose me. Would the Goddess desert me now?"

"Who can understand the heart of a goddess?" Qeb-ha would not be consoled.

My nerves were the frayed ends of electrical wires with live current sparking out. A warm bath did nothing. The song of the nightingales did nothing. The breeze rustling through the palm fronds did nothing. Not the sweet scents of jasmine, not the heady waft of myrrh, there was nothing that could soothe me.

Maia brought me a draught of potent herbs to help me sleep.

I needed a man's arms around me, a man with two daggers, one sharp and within reach at the side of the bed.

Goliath was no longer an option. I couldn't use him or any slave for my own pleasure—not after the desert.

CHAPTER 24 THE COMMANDER

A hand pressed down on my mouth. I tried to sit up, but couldn't move my head. There was no moon. I could see nothing in the darkness except the form of a man directly over me. I kicked, and I thrashed, but couldn't dislodge him. Bile came up in my mouth.

"Sh-h-h, Isis," River God breathed in my ear.

I clutched him to me, digging my fingertips into his muscled back, hoping to draw strength from his power. His lips replaced his hand, and he tried to kiss me, but I sobbed too hard.

I felt his muscles tighten over the full length of my body. I wanted to melt into him, to become one with him. I could walk out of here, and no one would see me.

River God waited for me to calm. His lips and tongue traveled slowly down my neck, across the hollow of my throat and up to my ear. He took the lobe between his teeth, gently, and then sucked, long languid pulls that I felt right down to my womb.

His tongue was in my ear. He breathed warmth and life into me. He took his time, unhurried, savoring my need. His touch caressed me as tenderly as a breeze. My breath was so shallow, I scarcely took in air.

He massaged my lotus in his slow, languid rhythm that teased me to life, but never hurried to finish. No one had a touch like River God.

My hand found his hardness; I felt him swell. The muscles in his thighs and butt tightened, and he grew hard as the stone phallus of Min.

He took my face in his hands and kissed me. He was almost, but not quite, brutal. His warm, smooth palm pressed along my ribs, across my belly and over my mound. I opened up to him.

My hips rose and fell as his fingers possessed me. I rocked on the palm of his hand.

My cries must have wakened the household, but Maia didn't come. She knew those sounds well. Pehtes curled at the top of my bare scalp, purring a lion's roar, wallowing in the animal scent.

The sleeping potion fogged my senses. I floated above the bed, yet could still feel his touch. The night stars disappeared; the open balcony faded. Las Vegas sparkled through the tall windows of the Wynn.

In one breath, he was River God, in the next, Rasheed. Our souls glided back and forth between two worlds.

"Why did you not come back to me?" I whispered. "I came back for you."

Of course, he thought I meant I came back from the desert and not through the Red Mirror. River God knew nothing about the future. He stopped his caress and let his hand rest on my thigh for just a moment until he rolled onto his back.

"I came for you in the desert," he said in a flat, cold voice.

He put his hands behind his head. He looked up and not at me.

"But you allowed Hetmus-hor to take me from Goliath," I pleaded. "It could have been you. It *should* have been you."

He got up from the bed. The spell was broken, like the night of the bath in Thebes. Words are always the spoiler with River God.

His silhouette moved quietly in the room to find his sandals and his sword.

"You must leave Saïs," he said. "It is not safe for you, even here in the Temple."

I listened to his voice in the dark, telling me the real reason he had come.

"I have heard rumors at Court. The Persians will pay any price for your capture. Cambyses wants revenge for General Sher's death."

I closed my eyes and saw the General's startled face, eyes huge with disbelief, blood gushing from his slit throat and spilling onto my hands.

The Persians are masters of torture. It takes days for their victims to die. Eben the fortune-teller's warning screamed in my ears. *You have to go back, Isis, or you will suffer. You can't imagine the suffering.*

River God sat down on the edge of the bed. My eyes had adjusted enough to the starlight to make out the angles of his cheekbones and his lips tight with resolve and worry.

"I fear the Crown Prince and his vile Scribe are scheming to trade you when Cambyses invades."

An elephant stepped on my chest. I had thought the danger was from the Persians, but I wasn't safe even from Egyptians.

"You must leave for the South, maybe as far as Kush."

"I cannot go south."

River God gripped my shoulders and pulled me into him. I winced from the pain of his fingers digging into my flesh.

"You will do exactly as I say. Do you hear me? This is no time for your foolishness."

River God still thought of me as the pampered party girl I once was, but I was not the same woman. I had survived the desert. I had survived the General.

"Make ready to leave at sunset tomorrow," he ordered in his Commander's tone.

He dropped my arms and stood.

"Look for a ship under my banner."

River God didn't know the Persians would drive deep into Egypt, that not even Kush would be safe, but I did. I knew how the war ended. I had seen it from the future.

"The Persians will invade in the month of Payni," I said.

Maybe that information would save him.

"So soon! How do you know this? Has the priest Qeb-ha seen it in the Temple?"

River God certainly had great faith in his gods.

"Eben the Kabbalist has divined it. He says everything is written in the stars and his numbers."

I amazed myself with how easily the lie came.

"The Jew was right about you in the desert," he said grudgingly.

"What else does he say?"

"Don't trust the Greeks."

"Yes, I have heard rumors of Greeks who are allies with the Pharaoh, but will not pledge allegiance to his son."

"I myself do not believe in his son," he whispered. "How shall I worship him?"

Not to believe in the Pharaoh is the greatest of sins and high treason. I tried to imagine River God's anguish.

I rose to my knees on the bed and took his hand in mine, covering my mouth with it, drinking in his fragrance. He pulled his hand gently away and raised my fingers to his own mouth. His breath was hot; the tip of his tongue wet my fingertips. I wondered if this were the last time in this life I would feel his lips on me.

I had said nothing at all to him about Antinous and Greece; I couldn't. It was too dangerous. One couldn't tell—even under torture—what one didn't know.

So I lied to him with my silence.

"Make yourself ready" and not "I love you" were his last words as he headed toward the balcony.

"Why do you always leave me?" I cried out. But he was gone.

Maia came to me while I still slept. The sun god Re had barely risen; the trees were full of morning birdsong. She knelt on the yellow-and-green striped carpet beside my bed when I opened my eyes.

"What is it? You are frightening me. Tell me at once!"

"Isenkhebe Nefrusobek has not had her monthly bleeding."

I looked at her, stupefied. Of course, she would know that about me. She was responsible for everything that I ate, everything I put on my body. She was responsible for my laundry.

I closed my eyes and unravelled the crazy quilt of what happened when, and on which side of the mirror. I think I had known from the moment I saw Maia's worried face. The General.

"Is it the Persian, Isenkhebe Nefrusobek?" Maia looked terrified.

She would consider any child as sacrilege, but the bastard of a foreigner growing in an Egyptian priestess would be beyond bearing.

I didn't answer. I lay very still with my eyes closed.

"Isenkhebe Nefrusobek cannot carry this child. It is forbidden for a high priestess to bear children."

"What of me? Am I not the daughter of Sit-hathor?"

"That is different. Isenkhebe's father is a god. This father is a monster. The child will be an abomination."

I thought of the abominations that are the Egyptian gods

"We must do something now, Isenkhebe. This morning. It will be over in a few hours."

"No! I cannot be weakened in any way today. I must be strong. You must be strong. We all must be strong."

Maia sighed and dropped my hand. She looked so incredibly sad. She stood and bowed before leaving.

"Sit-hathor will be devastated. I cannot tell her. That is Isenkhebe Nefrusobek's task."

The day passed in sadness and goodbyes. I stroked Pehtes, who sensing change, never left my side. I considered taking her with me; a Greek woman raised in Cyrene on the Libyan coast could have a cat named Pehtes, Berber for "the black one." But I knew I must leave her behind.

I touched each piece of my jewelry, so beautifully crafted in gold, silver and electrum, and then opened each of my precious scrolls with their exquisite hieroglyphs in black and red ink. The medical papyrus contained a section on women.

Prescription to make a woman cease to become pregnant for one, two or three years: Grind together finely a measure of acacia dates with honey. Moisten seed-wool with the mixture and insert into the vagina.

Too late for that.

The steel blade of my jeweled dagger was razor sharp; again I saw dark red blood flowing from the General's throat and shocked betrayal in his eyes. His death haunted me. The desert haunted me. Were the charioteer and the horses still buried in the sand? Would their bodies mummify in the arid river bed and be discovered thousands of years from now?

In the end, I couldn't part with my necklace from the hunt—the one from the General's tent. I held it in the sunlight; tiny golden rays reflected off the delicate charms. The vulture saved me from the cobra in the desert.

The General gave me my first clue to his black heart when he took the crocodile between his thick fingers. I smiled at the fertile rabbits and thought of the General's seed growing inside me. Would I allow his child to live?

I could seduce Antinous as soon as possible and claim the child as his—but if he looked like the father, would Antinous believe me? I could tell him the truth, but I feared his cold rejection.

A fine start to a marriage already in peril. My options were all painful. The General managed to hold me prisoner even after his death.

Re was sliding toward nightfall. The fading light fell on the high walls of the rose granite *naos* at the other end of the garden; the sanctuary glowed golden red. Birds feeding on evening insects raised a deafening chorus.

I gathered Qeb-ha, Eben, and Maia in my bedchamber and gave each a pouch with amulets and jewelry.

"We must not travel together," I explained. "You will need these for bribes."

"Please give this to my mother," I told Qeb-ha.

His eyes filled when he saw the small box with my Hathor lapis lazuli ring, the one identical to Sit-hathor's, one of two in all Egypt.

"It is too dangerous for me to have it on my person. You understand that, Qeb-ha, do you not?"

He gripped my hand and didn't try to stop the tears. I remembered that first day in Sit-hathor's temple when he had waited for me in the shade among columns with heads of Hathor carved at their tops. I had despised his high eunuch voice then; now I yearned for the sound of it, never to stop hearing it.

"Thank you, Qeb-ha, my companion and brother. We shall all meet in Thebes. Then I can go south to Elephantine and further to Kush, if I sense danger."

He knew I didn't speak the truth, but chose to say nothing. *The fate and the fortune that come, it is the Gods that send them.*

Maia pressed a small vial into my hand.

"Take five drops each morning, three days in a row. It will be slower, but as effective."

We stood in a small circle, each of us lost in our worries and dreads.

"Do you have another amulet for me, Eben?"

I think it startled him that I knew, but he pulled a tiny leather amulet out of his robe; the pouch and strap were identical to the one on my wrist. I wondered what these words said. Did they grant me safe passage to Nubia? I didn't need that.

He removed the first amulet and tied on the second. His hands shook; he had trouble tying the knot.

"Isenkhebe, the amulet has no scroll."

"What do you mean *no scroll?*"

I counted on the magical spell of tiny Hebrew letters and symbols to save my life again.

"There is a vial instead of a scroll."

Eben's eyes were so full of anguish that I almost couldn't look there. I saw the large brown eyes of the gazelle as the life force left her the morning of the hunt.

"It will be over in seconds." He spoke in a dead flat tone.

Although none of us needed an explanation, he added, "If you are captured."

Goliath rushed into the bedchamber. His black eyes were enormous; the whites showed all around. Beads of sweat glistened on his forehead.

"The Royal Guard is at the pylon gate. Our guards have disappeared."

I kissed Maia on both cheeks and squeezed her to me.

"We are family. We shall be together again, I promise you."

Of course, she didn't know I meant in another life.

"Take Maia to Elephantine," I whispered to Eben. "Thebes will be safe neither from the Prince nor the Persians. Please do it for me."

I kissed Qeb-ha's old hand.

"It is in battle that one finds a brother," I told him.

"Happiness will come to Isis out of misfortune, after what she has undergone," Qeb-ha said silently. His final benediction, a prophecy from his gods, spoken without words, was our last intimacy.

"I hope so, Qeb-ha, I really do."

The heat of the day had passed. River God waited for me at the wharf to sail south, not knowing about Antinous and Greece, not knowing I would never come.

We didn't see the two Arabs, one with a red turban, hiding in the shadows outside the pylon gate.

"The Scribe means to cheat us out of our reward. He thinks to take the woman himself."

"Come. I know a way in, if we hurry."

The two scurried along the towering wall of the stone palisade and found the postern, a hidden door servants use to exit and enter. Temple Guards lock it every sunset; they had only moments to act.

They slipped through the green gate and passed the guard a small pouch with Lydian coins. He grunted, stuck it into his waistband and turned his head away from them.

They were on the temple grounds. Now to find the priestess.

CHAPTER 25 HECTOR

The plan was to meet Antinous at the double doors in the Green Granite Chapel. Goliath and I had just entered the first courtyard when a great weight hit the ground behind me, like the falling of a tree. The Nubian lay still; blood flowed down his face from under his white linen headdress.

I went to my knees to help him, but a hand came from behind and stuffed a cloth into my mouth. I tried to lash out; iron arms held me in place. A rough sack went over my head, but not before I saw the flash of red turban.

The sack had held grain; I breathed chaff up my nose. I gagged. Vomit came into my throat and then was sucked into my lungs. It would be a strange end indeed if I choked to death in a filthy bag before I could escape with the Emerald Tablet.

Hands lifted up the sack and threw me over a shoulder. I hung upside down and jostled wildly as my captor ran. The bag held me as tight as a swaddled infant. No way to kick or punch, I rolled my body back and forth, trying to throw him off balance. But I was helpless—helpless to move—helpless to reach Eben's vial.

We fell. I hit the ground with a smack. I could see nothing, but willed my body to roll sideways, over and over. I felt soft grass instead of stone and heard scuffling but no voices. My hands were not bound. I ripped at the sack to free myself but was picked up again, higher in the air, by a taller man who ran very fast.

My new captor entered a building; his footsteps and movements were the only sound. I felt hard stone when he set me down. The filthy sack was pulled off, and the cloth came out of my mouth. My vomit stained it. I gulped air. When I no longer felt sick, I dared look up.

Hetmus-hor crouched over me. I threw my arms around his

neck, sobbing with relief. Hetmus the Savoir—again. He held me so tight I thought my ribs would break, but never have I so enjoyed pain.

"Qeb-ha said you were in Hermopolis. That you were forbidden to come to me."

"I told you that I would do whatever it takes to have you, Isis. *Qualquier cosa.*"

I stared into his red-flecked eyes.

"Hector?"

"*Sí*, Isis, it is me. Your *amiga* Barb told me everything. When I crossed through the Red Mirror, I—or am I Hetmus now?—was under house arrest. I came as fast as I could."

Hector had come through the Red Mirror! I struggled to process first that he was able to pass through—that I wasn't the only one who could—and then that he did it for me.

"Did you think I would let you face this alone, Isis? You do not know me at all."

He kissed me lightly. His brilliant white smile flashed again.

"But you will."

Shouts rang out. I couldn't tell if they were outside or in. The thunder of feet pounding stone paths reached us even through the thick walls. I thought I felt the earth quake under the weight of an army invading the temple grounds.

"Royal Guards are searching everywhere for you; they were at your chambers."

Vomit came up in my mouth again. Gentle Maia. Old Qeb-ha. Sweet Eben. They would be forced to tell everything. But the Prince and his evil Scribe would never believe they didn't know my plans.

I rocked against Hector, the crown of my head banging into his chest, squeezing shut my eyes to push the nightmare visions of their agony from my mind. I saw then how right Antinous had been that I must tell no one.

"There is nothing you can do for them, Isis." Hector shook

me ever so slightly to bring me back. "We must get out of here now, Isis. Now."

More than ever I knew I had to escape. Just knowing me was a death sentence. What would they do to *me* if captured?

"I have to get to the ship! I must meet Antinous. Only he knows the way to the port through the underground tunnels."

"Antinous?" Hector's smile dimmed. "Who is Antinous?"

I put my hand on his bronzed forearm, just above the gold armband; he was warm, and his skin moist. I felt suddenly and inexplicably calm. The Universe had sent Hector to me. I was going to make it.

"There is too much to explain now, Hector, but Antinous will take me out of Egypt. It is the only way I am safe."

Hector rolled back onto his haunches and stared at me. The sparkle in his eyes was gone. I don't think saving me for someone else is what he envisioned when he went through the Red Mirror. But he stood up, took my hand and pulled me with no effort to my feet.

"Then let us find Antinous."

The tall double doors were closed and locked. No Antinous. We stared at the long empty hallway with no place to hide. We waited, exposed and vulnerable; I tried to control my panic.

Hector leaned against the stone wall next to the doors. I finally noticed the blood on his iron thrusting sword.

"My slave? Is he dead? Please tell me that he is not dead."

Last I saw Goliath, he lay in a pool of his own blood, his headdress bright white against the dark red. I never tasted his manhood, but I kissed with sheer joy his dusty black feet in the desert; they were the most wonderful sight I'd ever seen.

"The Nubian is a giant; he will live, but the Arabs are dead. I recognized the one in the red turban from the desert."

The Arabs! River God had said there was a price on my head. They could be working for the Persians—or even the Crown Prince or his Scribe. And they had dared enter the sacred grounds of the Temple. River God was right; I wasn't safe anywhere in Saïs.

I pounded on the wooden door. Nothing. I pounded even harder. Still no response. But when I raised my fist for the third time, the door opened. The same old priest stood with a torch in his hand.

He still didn't speak. He looked up at Hector, appraised him quickly, and stepped aside. The door shut behind us, and he bolted it.

"Where is Antinous?" I tried to keep my voice low and calm. I tried to believe that the Universe was on my side, but I was losing the battle with panic.

His shaved head bobbed up and down; the ankhs in his earlobes swung back and forth. He handed Hector the torch and began speaking with his hands. Sign language! My Greek tutors had overlooked that.

"He says Antinous left to go to your quarters."

I looked at Hector in wonder.

"You know sign language?"

"*Sí*, although I am not sure how. I am not quite used to being Hetmus." The twinkle was back in his eye, the charm in his smile.

Footsteps rang in the corridor on the other side of the doors. Not a few men, but many. Then came pounding with metal shields or the hilts of swords. We stared at the bolt rocking back and forth and ran.

We no longer cared if they could hear us. It was a race to get through the secret door before they burst through the others.

The priest pushed the panel and the wall moved an inch at a time. I thought my heart would burst from my chest. We slid through the crack, and Hector leaned against the stone slab. We could see no trace of the opening, at least not from our side.

"Someone must tell Antinous to meet us at the river." The terror in my own voice frightened me. I had to pull myself together.

Hector and the priest spoke with their hands. I looked from

one to the other and then at the crack in the wall, expecting it to open at any moment. The priest's face was solemn but held no fear. He took off the gold cord with the ankh key and handed it to Hector.

"The priest will wait for Antinous," Hector said.

"Thank you!" I sobbed in relief, kissing the paper-thin skin of the old man's hand. "Thank you!"

We could hear the muffled sounds of shouting and clanging metal on the other side of the wall. Hector grabbed my hand and took three steps at a time. I couldn't keep up. He scooped me into his arms, and within seconds was at an ebony door, but not the door that led to Hermes Trismegistus.

The priest nodded his head from the halo of his torch at the top of the steps. His giant ankh earrings swung erratically about his short neck in staccato bursts of light.

Hector inserted the key into the lock, and the door swung open into absolute blackness. He looked around the blue room, stood me to my feet, grabbed the only torch, and we stepped through. The door slammed behind us.

On the other side was silence and unending black. We ran down the damp tunnel toward nothingness, our lone torch spluttering wildly.

I struggled to keep up with his long stride. My sandals flopped and slid on my feet.

He stopped, not winded at all, passed the torch into my hand, and picked me up. My knees bent over his forearms; I hooked my arm around the back of his neck.

Hector moved fast now. His paces were long and steady. We sped through the tunnel. He may have been the spoiled son of a rich man, but he kept himself in shape.

The tunnel took a sharp turn and sloped upward, the incline not steep, but definitely heading to the surface. We ended abruptly at a small wooden door, rounded at the top, bolted on our side. Hector set me down, signaled for me to move backwards with the torch, and slowly slid the bolt open with only the slightest squeak.

Fresh air poured into the tunnel. The wind had come up since sunset; the flame of the torch bent sideways. It was dark outside, but not as black as the tunnel. The sky over the harbor lingered between twilight and night.

Hector showed me a knock, a pattern of hard and soft. I was to bolt the door and stay inside. An eternity passed while I waited. At last the knocks came. I opened the bolt; Hector stepped in and quickly closed the door.

"We are just across from the wharf. Soldiers are everywhere. There is a warship moored at the far end of the quay. It flies the banner of the Commander. No soldiers approach it but swarm over all other boats."

"The ship is for me to escape to the south." I gripped his forearm with all my strength. "But my only hope is north to the sea, to Rosetta."

This time we stepped through the round-top wooden door together. I was not prepared for the numbers of men in uniform that ran in all directions. What had I done to merit all this?

The General's dead eyes stared at me from a pool of dark blood flowing from his throat, and I knew. One does not kill a Persian general without being hunted.

We stood in the shelter of the doorway for a few brief moments. My hands trembled. I saw soldiers everywhere, but not close by. Hector stepped outside and kept his back to the wall. I watched his tall figure move away from me before I dared step out myself.

Just as I left the shadow of the doorway, a hand came out of the night and closed over my mouth. I started to scream, but stopped; I wanted no attention drawn to me. An arm pushed me back into the dark recess around the door. I struggled, but the man held me fast. Who now? I seemed forever to be shoved into walls.

A halo of pale curls glowed in the light from the harbor. I bobbed my head up and down rapidly and relaxed my body to let him know I recognized him. His hand dropped from my mouth.

"Antinous!" I whispered. "How did you find me?"

"Hermes. He has always said that we would meet here."

Hector didn't make a sound when he came up behind Antinous, but his long shadow fell across the wall behind me. Antinous pivoted to face the Egyptian, drawing a thrusting sword as he turned. I grabbed his wrist to keep him from striking.

"No, Antinous! He saved my life. But for him, I would not be here."

There was a long moment of tension, no one speaking, the two men staring at each other, measuring the other's worth. I gripped Antinous with my right hand and Hector with my left. Both burned hot.

I sensed that Antinous sized up one of my lovers with whom he must compete. Hector judged the man who would take me from him.

Finally, Hector said begrudgingly, "Greek, you are the luckiest man alive."

Then he smiled at me in the most sweet and tender way and put his palm on my cheek. His love flowed into me, giving me strength.

The Universe had sent Hector to save me again. I dared let myself believe that I was going to make it.

"Let us get you on that ship," he said.

Antinous carried a hemp sack with green wool, lengths of silken cord, and a Greek wig. I took off my black waves with gold ankhs and pulled the dark blonde plaits and curls over my shaved head.

While Antinous sorted the yards of wool fabric, Hector wiped *kohl* and mica from my eyes with my Egyptian linen gown. Then he took the green *peplos* cloth from Antinous and draped it around me expertly, fastening it in place with the pins and silk cords. When he saw my surprise, he flashed one of his blazing smiles.

"Hetmus-hor knew a few Greek ladies in his day."

I went in a sack again, but not upside down. I should not make a sound; no one must suspect anything. We hurried along the barricade wall, keeping to the shadows. I bounced in the sack and held my body in a tight fetal position. We left the search behind. The night grew quieter.

After a short distance, Hector laid me gently on the ground. His sandals crunched on the loose rock as he walked away. I heard only one set of footsteps.

Antinous stayed with me, but neither of us spoke.

He was here. He had lived up to his promise, but more than ever I was aware of his doubt. And he didn't even know about the General's child.

CHAPTER 26   THE GREAT GREEN

Gentle waves lapped against the stone wharf. Humming insects swarmed in the cool of the night. Night birds called from the trees. I barely breathed; my breasts didn't move.

Footsteps approached, and Hector heaved me up high again, over his shoulder. We left the gravel walkway and made little sound, only leather soles on the hard pavement. We crossed open ground, then walked along the river. I heard the creaking of a wooden ship against the stone quay.

Antinous walked beside Hector, matching his stride. Then Hector went ahead of Antinous, and the sound was leather soles on wood. We took three steps down before stopping. The footfalls on the deck of the ship sounded hollow; there must be a space below.

Quiet words were exchanged. I heard River God's voice, low, giving orders. We descended a short flight of steps, very steep. I could hear the river rushing past the cedar boards, then someone untied the sack and it fell around my ankles.

River God recoiled with shock when he saw me. I'd forgotten I wore the dress and wig of a Greek and no black *kohl* on my eyes. I must have been pale as white sand in the moonlight.

Hector smiled. The Egyptian priestess had morphed into a very convincing Greek. His eyes filled with the same pride as on the morning the men called out, "Isenkhebe, Isenkhebe, Queen of the Hunt!"

"Do not utter one word." River God's tone chilled me. "The sound of a woman's voice on this ship will carry all the way to the Crown Prince's ear."

His mouth was hard, and he clenched his fists. Jealousy blackened his face, but I saw longing under his anger. This time I was leaving him.

We stood in a tight circle, the four of us—blond and muscular Antinous, Hector so tall he could not stand fully upright in the low space, and fuming River God, rigid and tense in his military vest with the Pharaoh's golden insignia. And me, facing the three men who controlled my destiny.

Hector held out his right arm to River God.

"We are agreed? You will take Isis and the Greek north to meet the Phoenician ship?"

At first River God refused to look Hector in the eye. When he finally faced him, he didn't try to conceal his contempt for the man who had lost me in the desert and then was praised as my savior. And now Hector arranged my escape, but not to the south as River God planned.

Hector gripped River God's shoulder; his long fingers dug into the hard muscle. I thought for a moment he might shake River God to bring him to his senses.

"I know exactly what I ask of you, man. But there is no other way."

I really thought River God was going to refuse. The muscles in his jaw were so knotted I could see them flex even in the poor light. His left eye twitched as if he had developed a tic.

"Do you think I would give her up," Hector reasoned, "if I thought there was any chance I could have her?"

River God glared at Hector; his black eyes were as hard as obsidian. I thought him so handsome, but tonight the bones of his face formed harsh, ugly angles. His mouth, so lush when he kissed me, was tight and cruel.

I held my breath. I think we all held our breaths. At last, he gripped Hector's forearm, just below the elbow, and laid his left hand on Hector's shoulder to signal the pact. A man of his word, River God would not betray his pledge.

The air in the narrow space below deck was as charged as before a sandstorm. My heart raced, and my head pounded. Antinous kept silent; he was no fool. One wrong word from him and this scene could end in tragedy.

Hector stroked my cheek with the back of his fingers. He took my chin in his fingers and lifted my face. The red specks in his eyes were iridescent.

"I shall never find another woman like you, Isis."

Then he kissed me, long and deep. He didn't hurry. He was oblivious to River God and Antinous standing next to us. When he pulled away, he leaned down and whispered in my ear.

"You owe me one. *Hasta Las Vegas.*"

He kissed me one last time, lightly, just a fleeting touch of his lips, and then disappeared up the steps.

River God stood absolutely frozen, like a quartzite statue in a tomb. When he finally looked at me, his glare was full of accusation. I saw betrayal in his face and wounded pride.

I hadn't said anything to him about Greece—or Antinous, whom he ignored. He wouldn't even look in his direction. Raw pain sharpened the planes of his face.

I wanted to reach out and tell him this was not goodbye. I wanted to say the words he had said to me in at the Wynn. *We have known each other before, and we will know each other again.* But River God knew nothing of the future; he knew nothing of himself as Rasheed.

This was the last time I would see him in this life. I edged close to him, my body yielding, his more rigid than ever. I was desperate to reach him, so I did what I'd never before done with a lover. I summoned the Power.

My skin flushed with heat. A hot aura pulsed from my body; I believe my flesh glowed in the dim light.

"You told me in Thebes that the Gods set us on our separate paths," I crooned in the softest of honey whispers. "This is not the path I would have chosen; this is not the path I want."

Still he didn't respond, not to me, not to the Power.

"I would have lain in your arms until you left me," I breathed. "I would have been there waiting for your return."

Balancing on my tiptoes, my breasts pressing on his leather chest, I put my lips to his. Chiseled from stone by a master sculptor, they did not yield. My desire burned so bright, I would have lain with him right there on the rough planks, even with Antinous standing over us.

River God's pride wouldn't let him hold me. He stared straight ahead, refusing to look at me. Only the twitch in his eyelid gave him away. He would show no pain or weakness; he cut me out of his heart at the same time he cut my heart out of me.

Invisible fingers tore at the connective tissue in my chest. Not even the Persians could invent such torture.

He moved past me and up the steps, not looking back at me, never looking at Antinous. I couldn't bring myself to look at Antinous.

The warship pulled away from the wharf, oars moving crisply in the water. I heard the sail unfurl with a sharp snap, filled instantly by a brisk wind. River God was true to his word; we entered the swift current flowing toward the Great Green.

Antinous and I didn't speak. We didn't look at each other. I curled up on a bale of something and tried to sleep, even more exhausted than in Sit-hathor's tent, after the desert. I wondered how living flesh could endure such tension and pain.

Seagulls woke me. The scent of salt saturated even the stale close air below deck.

Antinous rose and went up the steps without a word or look in my direction. He should never have seen me with River God. Those images would burn forever in his mind. They would burn forever in mine.

He came back after a short while, curls tousled by the sea breeze. His cheeks glowed rosy pink, not the pale ash from months buried among scrolls beneath the Temple. He didn't speak, but motioned for me to get into the sack, and then tied the end and hoisted me onto his shoulder as easily as tall Hector had. That surprised me.

I don't know why I thought of Antinous as weak.

I could see nothing, but heard the sharp cries of the gulls and waves from the Mediterranean crashing on rocks.

Antinous dropped me down on the deck like a bundle of no value, not hard, but not soft. Did he show the others that the bundle meant nothing, or did he demonstrate what he thought of me?

Rough hands hoisted me over the side. Someone caught the sack and dropped me against hard boards. The dinghy pitched back and forth, banging up against the hull. I was leaving Egypt in a sack.

We rocked on the swells and rowed away from the ship. Another boat approached. There was a lot of shouting while the two boats were lashed together. Then I was picked up again and tossed to unseen arms. I made out a few words of Phoenician.

When we had sailed a short distance, fingers unloosened the knot and the sack fell away from my head. Antinous pulled me from the bottom of the boat to a seat beside him.

The sailors showed no surprise when they saw me. Paid to mind their own business, they looked at me briefly and then away. But if stories were told, they would be of a Greek noblewoman, not an Egyptian priestess.

We headed to a massive galley with the face of a giant yellow-and-green sea monster painted on the broad bow. The red sail flapped in an easterly wind. Bobbing like a cork in the rolling waves, we floated in a vast expanse of blue sea and sky. Why do they call it the Great Green? The water was the dark rich lapis blue of my Hathor ring.

I dared glance at Antinous. He stared at the military ship rocking near the surf at the mouth of the river. His face was devoid of emotion, but I knew his mind whirled. I followed his line of sight and saw the small figure of River God in the prow.

We watched him grow smaller as he watched us row away. He never raised his hand. He never moved. Then he was too far away to see.

When I turned back to Antinous, he was staring at me. For a brief second, I wanted to crawl inside his head and read his thoughts, but I didn't honestly want to know.

I met his eyes with complete frankness. He had seen me stripped naked of all pride and then cast aside. I had been exposed. I had nothing left to hide. And then I remembered the General's seed growing inside me.

They lifted us aboard the ship in a kind of sling, like the morning of the hunt, when I was lowered to the ferry—the day everything changed.

I balanced on the listing deck, slippery with salt spray. Twenty rows of oarsmen, three to a bench, lined each side, shackles binding their ankles. The captain barked orders in Phoenician, and the red square sail snapped and then billowed against the azure sky.

Antinous and I leaned against the wood railing with a wide space between us. We still didn't speak. I was grateful for the Grecian wool in the brisk and damp air.

The shoreline slipped further and further away until it disappeared over the horizon. Goodbye Egypt.

Antinous led me aft to where the captain's cabin filled the broad deck. Inside, the salt scent of sea mixed with tangy cedar. Small windows high up let in light and air. An ordinary wooden table and two chairs stood in the middle of the cedar-paneled room; finely-woven carpets covered much of the plank floor. There was one bed built into a narrow box hung with heavy drapes. Large painted chests lined one wall.

"I think it best you restrict yourself to the cabin during the voyage to Cyrene. We want nothing to arouse suspicion. From there we shall book passage on a ship bound for Kos."

I looked around. My new home. I looked at Antinous. My new husband. He avoided eye contact. What kind of honeymoon voyage would this be?

"If you concur, of course," he added, finally looking at me. "It will be only a few days."

At least he considered my opinion.

Antinous placed a clay jar of wine, loaf of brown bread and a hunk of white cheese on the crude table.

"I think we both need food."

His voice had that same flat, detached tone; everything happening had nothing to do with him.

"Do you have the Emerald Tablet?" I asked.

He set the package on the table. It was wrapped in the same antelope skin as in the library. When I folded the corners back, the green faience glowed.

Stroking the finely-etched script, I wondered if the power Hermes believed dwelled there would pass to me now.

"The chest with green markings contains clothing."

Antinous indicated a rectangular cedar box painted with the geometric patterns of Greek vases.

The chest was filled with brightly-colored cloth and several blond wigs in Greek style. A leather pouch lay on top. I opened it—a glint of gold—Greek jewelry.

I turned to Antinous and said, "Thank you."

The corners of his mouth turned up, not a real smile, but still progress. I took hope. The tension in the cabin eased ever so slightly.

"The chest beside it is also for you."

I opened the red lid to dozens of scrolls. For a moment, I forgot the awkwardness between us and gave him a dazzling smile.

He took a swallow of wine and looked back at me over the rim of the cup. The ice in his eyes melted a degree.

"Hermes sent you a gift."

A large rectangle leaned against the cabin wall next to the chests. I lifted the drape of blue cloth with silver stars. The heavy wood frame was painted a deep red, but there were no flowers; they must have come later. The mirror itself was polished bronze.

I stroked the frame and fingered each silver strut. Brand new.

"Hermes made it for you. He said to tell you that it is a 'cosmic mirror.' He said you would understand."

Above and below, past and future, reflecting back on each other. The Red Mirror. Hermes *Trismegistus*, Hermes Thrice-Greatest, my father, had given me the way home.

CHAPTER 27 THRICE-GREATEST

Antinous spent the rest of the day on deck, leaving me alone in the cabin.

Yards of fabric, twisted and wrapped in complicated pleats and ruffles, weighed down my body. Surely Greek women sometimes wear gowns less cumbersome and not wool.

I rummaged through the chest until I found a simple sleeveless caftan of soft, pale yellow linen. The cloth was so finely woven it had to be Egyptian.

A large clay *amphora* contained fresh water, on the cold side, but it would do for a sponge bath. I looked in the chest for cleansing oils and found a new copper razor. I would let the hair grow on my head; Greek women don't usually wear wigs. But what body hair did they shave? I'd have to ask Antinous. My tutors hadn't included Greek hygiene in their curriculum.

The leather pouch held three short necklaces exquisitely crafted in gold, with no beads or precious stones. One had tiny owl charms; one was made of links shaped into oak leaves. The third was a heavy thick chain trimmed with scores of delicate tassels.

But I chose my piece with golden vultures, crocodiles and rabbits. A string of lucky charms, it represented overcoming all obstacles. I wasn't supposed to wear anything Egyptian, but any Greek woman could easily have bought this necklace in the market as a souvenir of her travels.

Finally, I tucked my medicines and Kiya's vial along the side, at the bottom. My fingers caressed the amulet on my wrist; the poison vial was hard, like a small bead. Did I dare take it off? Was I safe now?

I dozed on the bed, and when I woke, it was dark. Antinous sat at the wooden table, concentrating on an open scroll in the light of a single oil lamp.

"What are you reading?" I asked idly from the shadows.

"It is the treatise by Thales that introduced Egyptian geometry to Greece." He sounded enthusiastic; there was a new shine to his eyes.

Thank you, Hermes, for my years with tutors. How long ago had he had made his plans for Antinous and me? Since my birth? Since before?

"What is your opinion of Pythagoras and his postulates on deductive reasoning?" I asked.

"Pythagoras takes Thales to new levels," Antinous answered quite passionately. "He hypothesizes that mathematics is the key to the cosmos."

He looked directly in the direction of my voice, and I felt the first contact.

"Pythagoras sees numbers in everything," he added.

I saw Eben with his magic incantations, calculating feverishly.

"Divine numbers are central to the beliefs of Kabbalah. Do you think there is any evidence, Antinous, that Pythagoras has been influenced by the Hebrew mystics?"

"He studies now at the Mystery School of Neith. All knowledge is contained in the library, including that of the Jews."

Antinous sat in a halo of light in the quiet cabin. The lamp burned evenly. The night was silent except for the sea washing against the hull, carrying us west along the coast of Africa to Greek Libya. Even the seagulls slept.

I enjoyed that we spoke Greek together. It's a lilting tongue that tickles the ears with vowels. No guttural sounds or hiccups, Greek is all music and poetry, easy to modulate—easy to insinuate other meaning.

"I regret I did not meet Pythagoras while in Saïs." My voice resonated like the low notes of a lyre.

His eyelids flickered. The glow of the oil lamp lighted his face, casting delicate shadows on perfect bones.

"Pythagoras would enjoy your intellect, Isidora. He teaches that men and women are equal."

Isidora. My new name. I took his use of it as a sign that we could start anew.

Antinous took a sharp intake of air when I came into the ring of light. His pupils were large and black; only a thin band of blue surrounded them.

The cut of my gown was loose, but designed to fall on the curves of the body, along the rise of my breasts and the slope of my hips. The hormones of early pregnancy were rounding out angles. I was fast becoming a curvaceous Greek.

He sat sideways to the table. His long legs with tight loins and rounded calves were stretched out and crossed at the ankles. The fabric of his *chiton* draped on his muscled thighs. His body was indeed perfect, exactly proportional, every muscle toned. He must have wrestled all his life.

I glided smoothly and silently toward him. When I leaned over him to ease the scroll from his hands, my swollen breasts pulled at the yellow linen.

Ever so slowly, never taking my eyes from his, I raised my gown to my knees and straddled him. My soft loins squeezed his hard thighs.

Antinous was so still, he might have been a statue. He didn't blink; he didn't breathe. I placed my palms on his chest. His muscles were so tense, his skin so smooth, he even felt like marble. But heat rose off him, and the tang of salt mixed with his strong scent of male. I could feel the warmth of the sun in his flesh.

In one day at sea, his skin had turned golden in the way of fair Greeks who reflect the sun. His eyes were transfixed on my face. Would he reject me tonight as he did in the tunnel?

"Husband," I whispered, and leaned to brush my lips against his.

I had no warning. He was on his feet in one movement, his hands on my buttocks, my legs straddling his thighs. The chair crashed to the floor. The table rocked. I expected the lamp to fall and splatter oil and fire on the carpets.

Antinous drove me straight to the wall. It happened so fast, I could only throw my arms around his neck and hang on. His mouth was on mine and his tongue down my throat. My head slammed against the cedar paneling. He held me with one hand and dragged my caftan up past my waist with the other. Then he jerked his loincloth off and flung it across the room.

He plunged into me and pounded me, both hands back on my buttocks. Banging me and banging me against the wall, he must have rocked the whole ship.

When he took his mouth from mine and allowed me to breathe, I used my cheek to force him to turn his head, and then one hand to hold him there. I put my tongue in his ear and blew and sucked gently, enough to torment, but not enough to damage.

He went wild and climaxed with a jolt that wracked his whole body. The rough edges of the wood paneling scraped my back as he collapsed against me, pressing me into the wall, his forehead on the cedar close to my ear, his breath coming in gulps. He never loosened his grip. I was sure the flesh of my buttocks would forever show an imprint of his fingers.

His biceps bulged when he walked us to the bed, my thighs squeezing his thighs. Then he tossed me down and flipped me over in one swift movement, dragging me up on my hands and knees. He ripped the Greek wig away and yanked the linen gown over my head. I heard seams tear.

Not possible, but he was iron-hard again. He thrust into me, holding my hips in both hands and lifting me up and into him. My face buried in the blankets, I reached to grab the back of his thighs and hold on. The two of us rocked with such force, the joint where the bed met the wall creaked with strain.

He rolled me to my back with his tongue deep in my mouth at the moment he entered me again. I wrapped my thighs around his waist, locked my ankles, and lay back, eyes closed, surrendering to pleasure. I let him ravage me, my arms over my head, stretched out on the bed, palms up. We were both drenched in sweat.

Like a master choreographer, he turned us on our sides and pulled my hips into the curve of his belly. I lay limp and helpless as a rag doll.

His hands massaged my engorged breasts tender from new hormones. I cried out in pain, but put his hands back when he stopped. I'd never felt such raw sensitivity. Agony and ecstasy in the same moment.

I gasped when he slid his finger onto my engorged bud. Moans reverberated through my chest and vibrated in my throat. My bud flowered. My womb contracted and contracted.

Antinous cried out and went rigid, shuddering twice, then a third time.

We lay panting, completely spent, sweat glistening on our bare skin in spite of the cool sea night, my full breast filling his warm palm. I nestled my hips against his flat stomach and felt his lips cool on my bare scalp, his breath warm on my skin.

When he turned over to his back, he held me tightly, never letting go. I burrowed into him, my shoulder in his armpit, my cheek on his chest. We didn't speak; the sound of our breathing was louder than the swells of the sea.

I thought only to shower him with affection, but when I eased on top of him and began kissing his lips, just small nibbles that traveled around their fullness, he hardened again.

Three times! Oh, this Greek indeed had many talents!

The flicker of twinkling sparkles flashed in the dark when I pushed myself up on bent knees, straddling him, one leg on each side of his waist. He reached up and touched a tiny rabbit charm reflecting the lamplight.

Fecundity. I knew his character by that choice.

I laughed lightly, a sound like small golden bells, and rocked slowly back and forth, in a steady rhythm. He caught my tender breasts in his hands, gently squeezing their fullness.

There was no doubt in his eyes now.

"O Antinous Thrice-Greatest, my husband! We are going to have a wonderful life."

I didn't need to summon the Power at all.

CHAPTER 28 CLEOPATRA'S BARGE

I heard no ringing bells or pounding this time, but simply opened my eyes in Las Vegas. With Hermes' Red Mirror in the ship's cabin, I decided to go home, and I was there.

I left Isis in her new life with Antinous. Surely she could be happy with him. The decision about the child was hers; she had a choice.

Aisha didn't cuddle in my armpit or purr into my ear, and I remembered she was at Sonny's next door. How many hours had passed? How many days?

"Welcome back."

Hector relaxed in my gray leather chair, the footrest up, a green bottle of Heineken in his hand. He had on straight-legged jeans, a white T-shirt, tight across his broad shoulders, and loafers with no socks. He must have used my shower. His hair was damp, combed back in chestnut waves.

He flashed that brilliant smile.

"Congratulations," he continued in a light tone. "I regret I could not see you all the way, but it was part of the deal with the Commander. I trust he was an *hombre* of his word."

I felt a little disoriented. Last I had seen Hector, he wore a white linen loin cloth and headdress below deck on a warship on the Nile.

"*Cerveza?*" he offered with another smile. "You must be thirsty."

I hopped in the shower, washed my hair, pulled on a pair of jeans and black V-neck sweater and reappeared. Hector still reclined in the chair, but two frosty green bottles now stood on the coffee table.

"How long have you been back?" I asked.

"Long enough to get hungry. I fried some eggs. You could use more food in your kitchen."

"I have to watch my weight."

"You do an excellent job." He smiled while his eyes assessed my sweater and jeans.

Sitting Indian-style on the zebra carpet, I towel-dried my hair and combed it out, taking sips of icy Heineken in between. Hector just watched me, not saying anything.

When I finished, he looked over at the Red Mirror.

"Is this something that you do all the time—these little *aventuras*? Is life not exciting enough for you here?"

I didn't have an answer.

He took a swig from the bottle and looked straight into my eyes. There was only a hint of tease in his.

"So what now, Isis? Or is your name Aphrodite? You were *guapissima* as a Greek."

"What do you mean 'what now?' I just got back."

"Don't play games," he said a little sharply. "What about us?"

If he wanted honesty, then that's what he'd get.

"I don't know, Hector. I wish things were as straightforward as I used to think. I could use some simplicity in my life."

"That usually means there's another man."

Hector put his feet flat on the floor and leaned forward; his jeans stretched tight over his thighs. He was very fit, with long lean muscles, not the kind you get from pumping iron in the gym. He studied me for a long moment. The flecks in his eyes matched exactly the red highlights in his hair. There was no tease in his expression now.

"You could use me in your life, Isis," he said flatly, "but apparently I am not enough."

He didn't sound upset or angry, but more like he stated an unpleasant fact.

I felt terrible, like such a bad person. He had just saved my life.

He was almost out the front door when he turned. I just knew he was going to say something to make me feel even worse. But

Hector was always full of surprises.

"I will not make your life difficult, Isis. I am patient. I will be here when you are ready. You will be one day."

Barb was over the top with relief when I called. I filled her in with some quick details and promised more over drinks later at the Stirling Club.

"Barb, it's okay that you told Hector. He saved the day."

"I had to tell him. He was positive you wouldn't make it without him. I believed him."

"He's very convincing."

"He's very committed," she corrected. There was a trace of envy in her voice. "It doesn't get better than Hector, you know."

"I know. He's perfect." I didn't sound terribly convinced.

"Is it Rasheed? Is that what's going on? What's he ever done to help you? I see only pain."

"He got me to the Phoenician ship," I answered. But I didn't tell Barb how cruel he had been, how he ripped my heart from chest.

"Well, I can't find out anything about him," Barb complained. "I think his last name is phony. Lars says Rasheed likes to fly under the radar—whatever that means."

I didn't want to admit that I knew no more about Rasheed than Barb did. Well, not exactly. I knew about River God—just not about him in *this* life.

"Wait!" Barb said before I could hang up.

I thought she was going to nag me more about Rasheed and braced myself. But that's not what was on her mind.

"What's it like when you're on the other side? I can't imagine having my head in two worlds."

"What's it like? It's...well...hard to explain. I almost never think of Las Vegas. Sometimes I even forget I'm me. But when I'm here, I can't stop thinking about Egypt."

I drove over to the office in the afternoon. Ed's face went beet red when he saw me. Smoke poured out of his ears. He puffed up, eyes bulging, candidate for a stroke.

"Where the hell have you been? What's this shit about a sick friend? What kind of excuse is that? Whoever it is, they better be dead already."

I shut the door to Ed's office, closed my eyes for just a moment and summoned the Power. His eyes followed every movement as I slinked over to his desk and slithered onto the leather armrest of the chair opposite him.

His red color paled to white. His mouth hung slightly open, lips slack. I could almost see his tongue. Smoke still steamed from his ears, but not from anger. I dialed it up a notch and leaned rather far forward, arching my back and twisting my shoulders just enough that the generous cleavage of my red sweater was front and center.

"Ed, I was thinking that I should work more from home," I oozed. "I get a lot more done."

I lowered my voice to a hush and wet my lips with the tip of my tongue.

"You wouldn't have a problem with that, Ed, would you? We could meet a couple of times a week, maybe over drinks? You know, just to touch base."

Easing down into the chair, I crossed one long leg slowly over the other, letting my leather skirt ride up my thighs. Black boots hugged my calves to the knees. From there to the hem was smooth skin—lots of it.

Taking a tip from Isis, I had drawn thick dark lines along my lashes; emerald eyeshadow highlighted the deep jade of my eyes. My brazen gaze was direct and full of promise.

"What do you think, Ed? Do you think we can work something out?"

To celebrate my victory over Ed, I stopped by my favorite vintage shop with racks of gorgeous stuff for dirt cheap. When I came out from behind the curtain in red-hot scarlet satin, a tall bleached blonde with Prada sunglasses and Elke Sommers bangs grinned and gave me a thumbs-up. Her teeth, a little too perfect and white, blazed against her dark coppery tan. She was trying on a wide-brimmed black hat with a giant pink rose in the band.

"That dress is *bad*. Buy it. Don't bother to think."

"Thanks." I pivoted in front of the mirror, standing on my tiptoes to get the effect of high heels. Yes, I'd definitely take it.

"Hey, I've seen you at the Stirling Club. You're the Dancer."

"The dancer?" I asked.

"Yeah, I call you the Dancer. You make all those old guys look good, even the *choros* with club feet."

Did I really dance with so many men? Maybe Barb was right about the party girl stuff.

"Call me. I know a little shop in North Vegas you're gonna love."

She handed me her card. It had a glamour shot of her in color that said "*Esperanza por la manana.*" The other side was in English, "Esperanza in the Morning."

"My TV show. That's why the girl's gotta look good—and I can't afford all those high prices on the Strip."

I put her card in my bag.

"You should come on my show some time. I interview anybody with a good story. I like to mix it up—boxers, politicians, singers—gringos too, especially good-looking ones. Don't worry about the Spanish; I take care of that."

Maybe I'd tell her about the Red Mirror one day. Wonder what she'd think of that story.

I put the $40 on my Starwood Points card and walked out into bright sunshine. I breathed in the scent of desert spring. The sky was cloudless, the sun warm on my back, but not hot. There was not a trace of wind. I felt like I'd lost ten pounds. I felt powerful. I just knew great things were coming.

I had just walked in the front door and poured myself a glass of

Chardonnay when my cell buzzed. I didn't recognize the number but broke my own rule and answered anyway.

"Isis, this is Rasheed."

Just the sound of his voice, exactly like River God's, paralyzed me. The air in the room crushed in and then sucked outward. My brain felt like a down pillow.

"Isis, are you there?"

"Yes, I'm here. I'm just a little stunned."

"Why?"

Could he really be that unaware of the effect he had on me?

"I didn't think I would hear from you again."

"Why would you think that?"

He sounded genuinely surprised. He saw no problem with coming and going in my life as he pleased. He took his *we have known each before, and we will know each other again* a bit too literally.

"You just left," I accused him. "No forwarding address. Remember?"

"I told you how it has to be," he said quietly. "There are things you can't know. It's safer this way."

Safe from what? But I didn't ask. Maybe I didn't want to know.

"Well, I'm here now, Isis. I want to see you."

Of course, I knew from the moment I first heard his voice that I'd do anything to feel his touch again. But I had *some* pride. He'd torn my heart out on that ship.

"Isis?"

"Yes?"

"Meet me. Please."

Please. That was a start. What I really wanted was for him to beg—like I'd begged. I waited. Wherever he was, it was quiet. The silence on the phone was deafening.

"Isis, what's going on? I want you, and I know you want me. Why are you playing games?"

Games again. Well, my game was to see how far I could push,

but I lost my nerve when he turned Commander.

"Are you coming to me," he demanded, "or do I have to come to you?"

I was afraid his next words might be goodbye. Besides, it was ridiculous to blame Rasheed for something River God did 2500 years ago. And Rasheed wasn't going to beg. I gave in just like I knew I would.

"I'll come to you, Rasheed."

I didn't want him to sit in the same leather chair that Hector had sat in this morning. They had morphed into each other once, in a dream.

"Good."

I heard relief in his voice. He'd been worried. A small victory, but I'd take it.

"I've got a business meeting at Caesar's Palace. I'll get a suite and meet you there."

I'd felt powerful before I heard his voice. He didn't get to call all the shots.

"I'm not going to wait in your room like some kind of call girl."

I heard him take a deep breath and slowly exhale, summoning patience. I sensed he found me unreasonable, but that it was part of a package deal he had to put up with.

"Okay, Isis. You tell me. Where do you want to meet? In a restaurant? In a bar?"

"What about Cleopatra's Barge?"

Rasheed laughed, the first time I ever heard him—or River God—laugh.

I thought I was pretty clever myself.

"Cleopatra's Barge. Perfect! About 9?" His tone was light, almost playful before reverting to his normal intensity.

"I may be late," he warned. "You know how these things are.

"Sure, Rasheed, I know how these things are. I'll be at the bar."

"And Isis, I only have tonight."

"It's okay. I'll wait for you."

I'd wait for him forever. I was pretty sure he knew it.

I wore the red dress. I didn't hold anything back. Even my hair cooperated. I might keep the bangs. Flesh-toned, sheer stockings ended in scarlet stilettos with thin ankle straps. I wore the black and red garters from the night of the Wynn.

I topped it all off with a red patent clutch and a white mink that cost me $600 in my favorite vintage shop. Esperanza would approve.

The Red Mirror said I looked good enough to eat. *Bring it on, Rasheed.*

The traffic on the Strip at this hour was a nightmare. I took Koval and turned left on Sands, driving past the Wynn with its bittersweet memories of Rasheed in the penthouse suite with stunning view. I used the back entrance to Caesar's, the one only cab drivers know.

A blond valet, about 30, with nice shoulders, took my keys, and I stepped out—long legs, red satin, white BMW. The look in his eyes was priceless. The dress had already paid for itself.

It was early for Vegas. No one else sat at the bar. I eased onto a padded barstool and ordered a Plymouth martini, up with an olive. I had already finished half of it and no sign of Rasheed. I checked my cell again. The only message was from Barb at the Stirling Club.

"I'm at Caesar's—waiting for Rasheed." I said it very cool, as if meeting him was a common occurrence.

"Rasheed! Why didn't you tell me?" she demanded.

"I was afraid I would jinx it. Besides, I know you don't like him."

"Don't let him jerk you around," she ordered.

Actually Barb, I'm looking forward to him doing whatever he wants.

"And it's not that I can't see he's hot," she said in her schoolmistress tone. "He's just a little too unavailable for my taste."

"I'll call you tomorrow, Barb, and tell you all about it."

I put my phone down beside my martini glass. A man took

the stool next to me, but I didn't look up.

"Looks like you're expecting someone," he said politely. "May I buy you a drink while you wait?"

I nearly knocked over my glass when I heard his voice. Antinous had traded his Greek *chiton* for a powder-blue oxford cloth shirt. He had the clean cut, preppy look of a Brooks Brothers ad. His face was golden tan except for the white around his eyes in the shape of goggles. He must be a skier. His hair was a mass of shiny curls. The deep cleft split his chin. He had the same pouty lips. Gorgeous as ever, he outshone any of the statues at Caesar's.

"My name's Anthony—Tony—Callis." He held out his hand for me to shake.

I looked at his outstretched hand and remembered how it gripped my butt so hard on the Phoenician ship that I bruised. For an awkward moment, his hand hung suspended in the space between us, and then he put it on the bar.

"Excuse me if I was out of line," he apologized, shifting his weight away from me. He didn't recognize me, not even a glimmer.

"I'd love another martini," I said with a warm smile. "I just wanted to make sure you weren't a salesman."

"You can tell I'm not a salesman?"

"Believe me, I can tell." I didn't embarrass him by saying I also could see he wasn't local; he had that out-of-towner expectant look, *This is Vegas. Anything can happen.*

The bartender put two icy Plymouth martinis with plump green olives in front of us.

Anthony was so beautiful, it was criminal he was male. I knew a lot of women who paid a fortune to have blond-streaked curls like his. I almost regretted I was meeting Rasheed. I'd love to see if Anthony was as enthusiastic a lover as Antinous.

"I'm from New Jersey," he offered without my asking.

"New Jersey?" The thought of Antinous ending up in New Jersey saddened me a little.

"Well, from Princeton to be exact."

That was more like it. He had to be the best-looking professor in the Ivy League. His preppy clothes didn't hide his muscles one bit. He had the same wrestler's thighs and powerful arms that had crushed me on the ship.

"What about you?" he asked.

"I live here."

"You *live* in Las Vegas?"

I don't know why people are always so surprised when I say that; there are 2 million others like me.

"Living here is like living anywhere, except there's more to do when you go out. And I get to dress up. I like wearing my high heels."

I probably shouldn't have added the last part; the male in Anthony—Tony—couldn't resist looking the length of my red satin dress all the way to those heels. I had no trouble imagining him rip my clothes off as he drove me to the wall of Cleopatra's Barge.

That's when Rasheed came down the concourse. I could spot him in a crowd of a thousand. Like a lioness in heat, I sniffed his pheromones from afar.

He walked with a group of tough-looking men in pricey business suits. Some scanned the room while the others talked. His two bodyguards, Marcos and Gamel, walked close by him.

"It was great talking to you, Tony, but I see my date."

"Sure, I understand. Here's my card. If you're ever in Princeton, look me up. It's quiet there, but I know a couple of places to get a good martini."

He paused for a second as if waiting for me to say something. "You never told me your name."

I hardly hesitated.

"It's…uh…Isis."

"Isis? Isn't that the name of an Egyptian goddess?" Something sparked in his eyes. "It seems like I knew an Isis once, but I can't remember where."

I put his card in my red patent bag.

Rasheed walked up behind me, put one hand on my shoulder and moved my hair away with the other. He touched his lips to the trigger point on my neck, not a real kiss, just a fleeting brush that burned on. He breathed in my scent like an animal before mating. The heat from his hand seared my skin through the satin.

He took the empty stool on my other side, facing me. His legs were open; his knee pressed into my calf.

"You look good enough to eat," he breathed in my ear.

His chiseled lips wouldn't reject me tonight. I wondered if there existed a Hathor Power for men. I wanted to jump him right there at the bar.

"I approve," he said, touching my new bangs. His jade eyes were warm and full of affection.

"Let's have dinner in the room." He was cheerful for Rasheed, almost buoyant. Maybe we both thought of happy times in Thebes.

But then the angles of his face hardened into those harsh lines that make him ugly. His eyes chilled to green ice. His skin actually darkened. He had seen Antinous. No doubt about him recognizing the Greek. Rasheed's face took on the black rage of the night below deck on River God's ship.

I put my hand on the inside of his thigh. High up—to get his attention.

"Rasheed, he doesn't know. Trust me. He has no idea."

He scared me. I didn't like the way he looked at Tony. I slid down from the stool and took his hands. I leaned into him, between his open legs. My breasts pressed into his chest.

"Let's go up to the suite," I whispered, running my fingers through his thick black hair.

Then Marcos the bodyguard appeared and spoke so low that, close as I was, I couldn't hear what he said. Rasheed nodded, but still glared at Tony, who was walking away.

For one wild crazy instant, I thought that Rasheed might be ordering a hit on him.

Taking me by the arm, he guided me across the empty dance

floor, saying, "Why don't you take a seat in a booth over here? I'll just be a few minutes."

We passed a group of hard-looking men seated around a table, and I flashed on mafia bosses deciding who will live and who will die. They stopped talking. I felt their eyes following us.

Rasheed helped me into a red leather booth and then leaned down and kissed me on the lips in a way that said, *This woman belongs to me.*

Everything with Rasheed has to be mysterious and high drama.

Bodyguards milled around with no attempt to be inconspicuous. This was Caesar's Palace; the mob had been coming here since the days of the Rat Pack.

Tony's card read "Anthony Callis, Ph.D., Director of Cosmological Research, Institute for Advanced Study, Princeton NJ." He was legit. It fit my sense of cosmic order that Antinous the mathematician was reborn as Anthony the astronomer. I wondered if he were married, had kids. I wondered about his life with Isis—Isidora—in Greece. I wondered about the General's child.

A waiter set a glass of champagne in front of me at the same time a large man slid into the booth on the opposite bench. He moved fast and sat there before I looked up.

He had a salon haircut, styled back on the sides with neck hair too long for an American. He was clean-shaven, but I would have known him anywhere. His massive chest and biceps stretched the expensive Italian-looking suit. I visualized the thickness of his thighs pulling at the cashmere of his pants.

My eyes fixed on the green silk tie with arabesque pattern at his throat. Dark red blood began to bubble above the knot as I stared.

"Hello, Ishtar. It has been a long time." He called me by the name he'd given me in his Persian tent in the desert.

I couldn't avoid his eyes any longer. I took a deep breath and then exhaled.

"Hello, General."

CHAPTER 29   FULL CIRCLE

Rasheed arrived at my side in seconds. I didn't need to look at him to know his mood. His energy field was like the strobe of a pulsar.

The General nodded his massive head; he had a smug smile on his face.

"Your lady friend is most charming, Rasheed. I envy you."

They knew each other! The shock of it slammed me. But it was in this life, not the other. River God and the General never met in the desert.

"We should go now." Rasheed took hold of my upper arm.

"Wait. Have a drink with me, Rasheed. You and your lovely friend."

The General's tone sounded friendly, but it was clear he expected us to stay.

"Let us celebrate," he suggested in a somewhat teasing tone.

The muscles in Rasheed's jaw clenched, but he didn't say no.

"Let us celebrate relationships—past, present, and future," the General said, looking directly at me.

Rasheed nudged me, and I slid over. We sat so close our arms and thighs touched. As if by magic, a bottle of *Cristal* champagne arrived.

The hypnotic white noise of slot machines played in the background. A DJ tested his sound equipment. With a sudden rush, the early show at the Coliseum finished and the crowd poured out. Herds of tourists streamed past.

Rasheed fixed his unblinking eyes on the General.

"I sense that your beautiful friend and I have met before." The General sipped his champagne and smiled benignly.

I couldn't help my eyes widening. Surely the General wouldn't bring up what happened between us, not in front of Rasheed. If

Rasheed realized this was the Persian who had tasted me, if he had the slightest hint of my ride on the comet, it would take more than bodyguards to pull him off.

"You have the most stunning eyes," the General continued, nodding his massive head at me in approval. "I have always had a weakness for emerald eyes like yours. They have been my downfall on more than one occasion."

He enjoyed himself, happily watching me squirm, waving a red cape in Rasheed's face. But it was the bull goading the matador.

Electric shocks ran from Rasheed's body into mine.

"Rasheed and I are business partners, did you know that, *ma bella*? You must find that a fascinating turn of events."

The General's tone was far too intimate. Did he want a war right here in Caesar's Palace?

The impact of his words on Rasheed was obvious. He hadn't spoken; he barely breathed. He was like the cobra in the desert, eyes fixed, head almost swaying. I had to do something before he uncoiled and struck at the General's throat.

"What kind of business are you in?" I tried to sound polite and disinterested.

"The world is a dangerous place. Everyone feels he must protect himself. I help people do that. I am—what might you call it?—a broker."

He toyed with me. Did he use that vague, taunting tone just to annoy? He succeeded.

"What is it exactly that you broker? Or is it a secret? Or maybe it's secrets that you broker?"

He threw back his head and laughed. It was the same laugh as in the tent when I accused him of not being a man of his word.

The General leaned over the table, closer to me.

"You've got guts, I like that. But then I've always liked that about you, Ishtar."

Rasheed turned his face to me. His icy eyes narrowed. Suspicion and distrust. *She didn't tell me about her plan with the Greek. What other silent lies has she told?*

The General stood out of the booth and spoke to Rasheed, who still stared at me. I couldn't tear myself away from Rasheed's accusing eyes.

I found myself wishing that he had River God's black eyes, The glint of hard obsidian would be easier to bear than this cold green glass.

"I look forward to doing business with you, Rasheed. I am confident of our mutual success."

"*Á vedeci, bella.* It was my pleasure to see you again. I am sure this is not the last time we shall run into each other."

When I looked up at him, his eyes were not unkind; they twinkled. They told me that we shared a secret, and that he was willing to keep it that way—at least for now.

He walked away, his bodyguards around him, devastation in his wake.

The bubbles in my glass rose in a continuous stream. I hadn't even tasted the champagne. I was afraid to look down at my dress, afraid there would be a lurid stain of bright blood gushing from my slashed throat.

Rasheed's aura had gone black. His left eyelid twitched in a spasm.

His dark side frightened me; his jealousy twisted his mind and shut off his heart. If he learned the truth, he might go after the General. He might not survive. I don't know if anyone could survive a frontal attack on the General.

Rasheed pulled back from me with each heartbeat; the heat of his arm cooled as we sat. His face formed frigid, harsh angles. He always could turn his feelings from hot to cold like a shower faucet.

I was losing him. He retreated as fast as one of Tony's galaxies hurtling through space.

I would gladly have lied, but my mind was a blank. I couldn't explain away the General. He had gotten his revenge without raising a hand.

"I'm going home now." I said it quite simply, without much emotion in my voice.

He slid out of the booth and stood. I slid after him. He didn't help me. I hate a booth when you get out. It's so hard to be graceful, in control.

I folded my white mink coat carefully over my arm. I forced myself to relax the hand gripping my red clutch. Every movement was concentrated not to show my desperation.

But as hard as I tried, I couldn't stop my eyes from filling with tears. My three-inch heels put me on level with his once lush mouth. It seemed impossible that those hard lips had pleasured me and made my soul sing.

I wanted to kiss him, to warm him from stone to man, but his granite mouth was cold. Just like the night below deck, there would be no melting Rasheed. I didn't bother to summon the Power.

"Maybe you'll call me when you can let go of the past."

My voice was soft and tinged with regret, but not particularly weak. I think I sounded more resigned and sad than anything. But I'd decided Rasheed had to bend a little.

I walked away. He didn't try to stop me. He hadn't said one word since he first came to my booth and faced the General. I don't know how long his eyes followed me before I disappeared in the crowd.

I don't remember the drive home. Even the next morning, my mind sped, but went nowhere. I kept seeing faces, as they looked in Egypt, as they looked now, changing back and forth. There seemed to be no rules about who remembered what. I was a stranger to Tony, but Rasheed knew him instantly. Hector had seen me as Isis the moment we met at Carla's party.

I sensed the General knew much more than any of us. His words—without really saying anything—severed Rasheed from me with the precision of a surgeon.

And I recognized everyone. Well, at least as far as I knew.

Barb called twice before I had the courage to answer. But instead of her usual "I told you so," she was sympathetic and caring.

"I'm sorry. I really am. I know this guy has a hold on you that just won't let go."

"Well, I think we can count Rasheed and me as over. At least for a while. Maybe for this lifetime. There's no reaching him when he's like that."

"Want to have lunch? I've got a client at 3:30, but I'm free until then."

"Thanks, but I'm going to call Hector."

"I think that's a great idea."

I was just about to ring off when Barb said, "By the way, I've been thinking about these trips you take."

I waited.

"I mean, if Hector can go through the mirror, then anyone could. Right?"

"I...suppose so...I don't really know," I answered cautiously. Where was Barb going with this?

"Well, I was thinking that if you ever decide to do this again, maybe I could go with you."

I was stunned. Barb? No-nonsense Barb wanted to go through the Red Mirror?

"My love life's not all that great," she said. "And you did come back with three gorgeous men."

Hector picked me up in his white Range Rover. He wore the straight-legged jeans with a pale yellow polo shirt and lizard cowboy boots. A worn bomber jacket lay on the back seat.

"*A donde vamos?*" he asked with his broad, white smile. "Your wish is my command."

He looked so like Hetmus-hor in that moment. The confident Hetmus on the morning of the hunt before he lost me in the sandstorm and everything went wrong.

"You decide. I just needed company."

What I needed was to be with someone who wanted me.

He smiled in a way that said he was pleased, but didn't comment. We didn't talk for a while. I stared out the huge windows of the Range Rover and told myself that Rasheed didn't deserve me.

Hector focused on the traffic. He reached over once and squeezed my hand.

"You look beautiful today. Even more beautiful than Aphrodite."

Of course, that reminded me of the ship and River God. Rasheed filled me for a moment, but I pushed him out.

"You have many beautiful things in your home. *Muy impresionante.* My mother would say you have an excellent eye."

I rarely brought men back to my condo, but when I did, they weren't much interested in the furniture.

"Show me where you find such treasures in Las Vegas."

"Seriously? Most men don't like shopping."

"I am not most men."

He was certainly not. For starters, he had gone through the Red Mirror.

I keyed the address into the GPS. The traffic thinned as we moved along Flamingo away from the Strip.

"You're not married, are you?" I asked.

I'd never asked Rasheed if he were married. I'd never asked Rasheed anything.

Hector laughed and beamed one of his smiles on me.

"No, Isis, I am not married. I have been waiting for you."

"I'm not very good at commitments either," I answered.

He turned his head again, and we locked eyes for an instant.

"We will have to work on that," he said with a direct look that gave me a jolt.

His thighs stretched the tight jeans; his biceps stretched the band around his polo shirt sleeves. I looked at his strong hands on the steering wheel. Why hadn't I noticed those long, powerful fingers?

"What's Argentina like?" I asked, rather suddenly interested in exploring my options.

"Buenos Aires is full of life, like Las Vegas. But I grew up on an *estancia*, a ranch."

"So you're a cowboy. That explains the boots." *And those powerful thighs.* I envisioned his long legs squeezing the horse's sides as he twisted and dipped in the saddle.

My boot comment wasn't funny, but we laughed. So easy between us, no effort at all.

"Where did you meet Carla?"

"Rio. At a polo match."

"You must have liked her a lot to come to Vegas."

"I told you that she means nothing to me. *Nada*, Isis."

I liked the way he mixed in a few words of Spanish when he talked. Charming. Yes, Hector was definitely charming.

"So, what is it that you actually *do*? I mean, besides play polo."

"I used to chase all beautiful women. Now I chase only you."

"Are you telling me that you're a playboy?"

"I prefer to think of myself as a man, not a boy."

We pulled into the parking lot of the antique mall on Eastern, the one where I bought the Red Mirror. Hector followed me down the aisles filled with armor suits, models of sailing ships, neon beer signs and embroidered Spanish shawls.

I should have known Hector would be an expert hunter. He went straight for quality and examined each piece carefully before going on to the next. He had a great eye himself.

"My mother has a wonderful collection of antiques—South American, European, some Asian. You will love it."

He had no doubts about us. Did he have a Red Mirror of his own that looked forward in time, instead of back?

"Here's where I found the Red Mirror. Over there, against the Chinese screen."

No one was in the stall at the end of the maze, just like the first afternoon I saw the Red Mirror, and just like the day I bought it.

Hector pulled me back into him, and lifting me just a few inches off the ground like I weighed nothing, carried me behind the yellow-flowered screen. He kissed my neck and my throat and nibbled at my ear. I whimpered as he stroked my breasts.

"I have wanted to do that since you first got in the car," he breathed into my neck as he turned me around.

"The security camera," I protested.

But his tongue went deep in my throat and then in my ear. All the while his big hand with his strong cowboy fingers was between my legs. I was alive at his touch even through the thick denim.

He leaned me slightly backwards into a bookcase.

"You are so desirable, Isis. I want to touch you forever."

A vase fell first. Hector grabbed it in midair. But the bookcase kept swaying, and when I reached back to steady it, I knocked a shelf loose. A stack of dusty books tumbled to the floor. Then something heavy landed with a thud.

I stared in horror at the mess. Hector grinned.

"Look what you do to me," he said and kissed me lightly on the lips.

I don't think the security camera worked, because no one came running.

"Nothing's broken that I can see, so we're saved," I said.

Then I thought, it probably wouldn't matter to Hector. He'd just write a check. He wouldn't even think of cleaning up.

But Hector bent to the floor and picked up a canvas-wrapped packet. I recognized the shape immediately. Luckily it had landed on a soft pile of books. He turned the crumbling fabric back and a glint of shiny green glass shimmered in the fluorescent light.

"I think this piece is really old," he said.

I could tell by his voice that he was a little awed.

"Is this something for you, Isis? Couldn't you read Greek on the other side?"

The neat rows of hand-etched Greek letters covering the hard, glassy surface formed words so familiar I could have been reading from today's newspaper.

the following to be the truth…

The Emerald Tablet.

The Tablet wasn't actually the size of a laptop, but more like a thick, chunky atlas. I couldn't remember if I'd ever actually held it in my hands before. It was surprisingly heavy.

The Red Mirror and the Emerald Tablet. What were the odds on me finding them both here? Only I didn't believe anymore that I ever found anything, but that fate found me.

I looked around the stall, half expecting Hermes Trismegistus to be there, smiling warmly from behind some screen. I even imagined his calming touch on my hand.

You are the chosen one, my daughter. It is your destiny to protect the Tablet.

Hermes wasn't finished. I wasn't finished. The circle of souls wasn't finished.

Hector slid his hand around my waist and pulled me back into him, not hot with passion, but in a loving and tender embrace. He wrapped me in his arms, holding me close, but not too tight. I could fly away and still come back to rest.

Leaning my head on his chest, letting him carry my weight, I relaxed into the cocoon of his warmth. Safe. Hector always made me feel so safe.

At first I was tempted to tell him everything. I thought of translating the Greek for him, of sharing the secret to cosmic power. He knew about the Red Mirror. Why not the Emerald Tablet?

Hector and I would have no secrets. I would tell him everything. And he would tell me. Not like Rasheed.

"*Go slow,*" warned my small inner voice. "*Hector has not quite proven himself.*"

"*But he'll do anything for me,*" I argued. "*He went through a mirror into a past life he didn't believe in.*"

"*What does Hector believe in?*"

"I'm not sure," I admitted. *"Himself?"*

"What would Hermes say?"

Hermes had already said it. The world wasn't ready. It didn't seem any more ready today than 2500 years ago.

So I didn't tell Hector and had my first secret from him. The first lie is the hardest. The next is easier. The third is no effort at all.

"This tablet is something quite special," I said cautiously. "More special than you could ever imagine."

"Then you must have it."

He grinned with the confidence of a man who has never known struggle. Life to Hector is like polo—a fast sport, based on swift maneuvers and quick response. Obstacles are simply shifts in the line of ball. He didn't fear losing one game. He looked forward eagerly to the next.

Happy Hector. Being with him was like watching Re rise on a clear morning.

When he saw how serious I was, he took my chin in his fingers and looked me deep in the eyes. His eyes were the warmest of browns freckled with those iridescent red specks that match the highlights in his hair.

"It's yours, Isis. *Qualquier cosa.* All you have to do is be you. I don't want anyone but you. And I want you just the way you are."

He leaned down and kissed me gently.

"Anything. And everything. It's yours if you just let me give it to you."

Trouble is, now that I had the Emerald Tablet, couldn't I manifest everything myself? I had the Power. Did I have to choose? Couldn't I have River God, too?

☞ The End ☞
except

EPILOGUE

You might be wondering what happens after I sail for Greece with Antinous, but I have no further memories of that lifetime. As real as the events are when I experience them, it's a bit like starting a play in the second act and leaving before the final curtain.

I don't know how the story ends, but I imagine that I have the courage to tell Antinous the truth.

We are close enough to the rocky coastline of Kos to see a red-roofed white village crawling up the hillside. The sea is calm and a deep shade of blue—almost the color of the Hathor ring I left behind.

"I am with child, Antinous. But not your child."

"Am I to be a father so soon? You are, indeed, a remarkable woman, Isidora. Life will never be boring with you."

"Are you not going to ask who the father is?"

"You can tell me, but I cannot see the relevance. A child grows within you. It is a matter of biology. You are my wife. All that you are is now part of me."

He smiled, kissed me briefly and then pulled me into his side.

"Everything comes from the One. We are all one."

I try not to think about River God and the fate his gods ordained. The Persians invade and the Egyptians lose. I prefer to fantasize that River God escapes to Kush. But knowing his devotion to duty, I suspect he fights to the end. A noble death is the most I can hope for.

Hetmus-hor and his family had the kind of wealth that survives even conquerors. His father undoubtedly marries him off to a Persian princess to secure the family's position.

The Isis incarnation is finished for now. But I will go back, just not to her. I'm a different person because of Isis and she was a different woman because of me. My future changed my past just as my past changed the present.

Three hundred years will go by in Egypt before I cross through the Red Mirror into the life of Athena of Korinth. My next incarnation is a tale of Alexandria, perhaps the greatest city in all ancient times. At the heart is the Library, a center of learning and repository of every book written.

The Egyptians welcomed Alexander the Great as the slayer of Persians and their savior. Little did they know the price. Egypt would become Greek.

I won't tell you who I meet in Alexandria, but you can probably guess. Hermes Trismegistus isn't finished; my role as protector of the Emerald Tablet isn't finished. The circle of souls continues.

🦉 The Emerald Tablet 🦉

One life is not enough...

Book Two of the Red Mirror Series

available in eVersion and print

Author's Comments

The ancient story is *historically plausible*. Another term might be *faction*. Everything that happened in the book could have happened during this era of Egyptian history classified as 26th Dynasty of the Late Period. The date is 526 BCE. The introduction of camels to Egypt, coins to commerce, the influence of the Greeks, and the invasion of the Persians are facts.

The Egyptian characters in the book with a pronunciation guide are listed just after these comments.

I have fictionalized the personality of the real Psamtik III (*Psammetichus III*) who lost the battle of Pelusium and the siege of Memphis to Cambyses, King of Persia, within months of becoming Pharaoh.

Hermes Trismegistus or Hermes Thrice-Greatest is a legendary figure like Merlin. His life is shrouded in mystery and steeped in the myths of the Emerald Tablet popularized in the film and book "The Secret." The *Hermetica* (named after *Hermes Trismegistus*) is the foundation for alchemy. If you are interested in more information about the Emerald Tablet and Hermes, you can read my research at: www.SandraOfftheStrip.com/The Emerald Tablet

Names in Egyptian history can be very confusing as both Egyptian and Greek versions are used interchangeably. The Greek names for cities are often more familiar to the general audience, so I have used *Thebes* over *Waset* and *Saïs* over *Sa*, among others.

I have included paraphrased translations of Egyptian poems, songs, sayings and proverbs from papyri, stelae and shards. I thank Miriam

Lechtheim for her compilation of translations in "Ancient Egyptian Literature, Volume III: The Late Period" and R.B. Parkinson for his compilation of translations in "Voices from Ancient Egypt." The toast by Hetmus to Isis on the day of the hunt is borrowed from an inscription on Tutankhamun's wishing cup.

The Red Mirror, red sofa and bust of Antinous, can be seen in my book "Sex and the Zen of Shopping," or at my author website www.SLGore.com.

If the story of Isis intrigues you, and you would fancy a more intricate, steamier version with richer sub-plots and a couple more characters, you should check out "The Red Mirror." The longer "author's edition" version also contains a glossary of Egyptian terms with a mini-encyclopedia of Egyptology, as well as a sample chapter from "The Emerald Table," the second book of the Red Mirror Series ~ *One life is not enough...*

Then there is "Isis Erotica," the 'X-rated' version of the story boiled down to action and passion.

Cast of Characters

Isis [Eye sis] - Isenkhebe Nefrusobek [EE sin ke bay Ne fru sew beck]; Ishtar [Ish tar]; Isidora [EE sa doe ra]

Her four lovers (in order of appearance)
River God - Egyptian Commander = Rasheed [Ra sheed]
Hetmus-hor [Het-moose hoar] - Egyptian Hunter = Hector
General Sher [Cher] - Persian general = The General
Antinous [An te no os]- Greek = Tony

Rest of cast (in alphabetical order)
Aisha [Eye sha] - Las Vegas cat
Araxa [A ra xa] - Persian Officer
Barb - Las Vegas VBF
Ankh-hor [Onk hoar]- Nobleman and father of Hetmus-hor
Carla - Las Vegas friend
Crown Prince - Psamtik, son of Pharaoh Amasis
Ed - Isis' boss in Las Vegas
Eben [EE den] - Hebrew Kabbalist
Elaine - College friend
Esperanza - Latina TV hostess
Gamel [Ga mel]- Rasheed's bodyguard
Goliath the Nubian - Slave in service to Isis
Hermes Trismegistus [Err mees Tris me gis tus] - Isis' father
Maia [My ah]- Initiate to Isis
Marcos - Rasheed's bodyguard
Pehtes [Pay tes] - Egyptian cat
Qeb-ha [Keb ha] - Eunuch priest
Scribe - Consort of Crown Prince
Sit-hathor [Sit ha thor] - High Priestess & mother of Isis
Zavan [Za van]- Persian Officer

ABOUT THE AUTHOR

Born with wanderlust, forever living in a fantasy world, Sandra Gore escaped the prairies of Kansas to follow the yellow brick road on an odyssey that took her to Europe, Africa, Latin America and the Middle East.

Starting with a one way ticket to Iceland, Sandra returned with a Viking husband, an art degree and speaking five languages.

A love of travel, classical history, languages, mysticism, food, shopping and romance led Sandra to create the novels of the *Red Mirror Series*: **The Red Mirror** and **The Emerald Tablet**. She is near completion of the **The Black Scroll**.

As a self-challenge to test her range, Gore re-cast the story of Isis of The Red Mirror in two other versions: **Isis Erotica** and a sanitized PG-rated version, **Isis BeachRead**.

Her non-fiction publications include the self-help manual **Sex and the Zen of Shopping:** *How to Live Rich by Shopping Smart* and memoir contributions to three **Life Choices** anthologies.

Expect a cookbook of Sandra's own recipes plus those of talented, food-loving friends from around the globe. You can find samples from time to time on her blog.

The happily married Nielsens have a grown daughter and a son and divide their time between a California beach house and a Las Vegas condo.

SANDRA'S BOOKS

Red Mirror Series by S.L. Gore ~ *One life is not enough*
Published by Tajine Publishing in print and eVersion

The Red Mirror 🐍 (Book One)
 - Pharaonic Egypt, 525 BC
The Emerald Tablet 🦎 (Book Two)
 - Greek Egypt, 215 BC
The Black Scroll 🐍 (Book Three)
 - Roman North Africa 130 AD

Isis *Erotica* 🦢
Published by Tajine Publishing in print and eVersion

Isis Beach Read 🕮
Published by Tajine Publishing in print and eVersion

Sex and the Zen of Shopping: Live Rich by Shopping Smart
Published by Tajine Publishing

Life Choices Anthologies
Published by Turning Point International
Navigating Difficult Paths: "A True Love Story"
Pursuing Your Passion: "The Muses Whisper"
It's Never Too Late: "Road to Vegas"

Tajine Publishing
2550 E Desert Inn Rd, #443
Las Vegas, NV 89121

tajinepublishing@gmail.com
702-279-6556

Author website: **www.SLGore.com**